October Nights

Thirty One Tales For The Halloween Season

By Kevin E. Lake

Copyright Kevin E Lake 2020

Edited by Truman Jackson

*This work, in part or in its entirety, may NOT be reproduced or distributed, for sale or for free, without the express written permission of the author or the author's representative(s).

*This is a work of fiction. All places, events and characters appearing in this work are products of the author's imagination. Anyone who feels as if they are being represented by any of the characters, events, or locations in this work is merely suffering from a guilty conscience.

To be read with all lights on...

...one of which should be kept on while sleeping.

Just in case!

October 1

No Vacancy

It's been nearly twenty years to the month, if not to the day.

I remember, explicitly, that it was October. The leaves were majestic, in their full autumn color, the air was crisp- not cold, mind you- just crisp, perhaps a feeling that must be felt in order to be understood, and it simply felt like a great day to be alive. It all brought about a certain feeling of nostalgia that comes around this time each year, and I found myself trying to figure out just where in the heck all the time between back when I'd be racing home from school to put on my costume, no doubt just one of many plastic cheep-o's from the local department store that you worn over your clothes that I'd donned throughout the years of my childhood, and now had gone.

Here I was, walking down the streets again, door to door. But it was a different town, different streets, with a different costume, and all for a different purpose. No, I wasn't looking for candy. I was looking for money. And the more the better, because the more I found the more I'd get paid.

No, I wasn't a door to door thief, I was a door to door salesman, pitching stocks, bonds and mutual funds for a sizable Wall Street firm where I'd spend the next six years of my life before going into private practice for two years, after which, I'd finally accept the fact that the gig just wasn't for me. Sure, I was okay at it, and I got the bills paid, but I simply had absolutely no passion for what I did the whole time I was doing it. I wish I'd left the business sooner, but hey, at least I finally got out.

I'd driven out into the country, the next county over, actually, from the city in which I had my office to go prospecting. Door to door, twenty five contacts a day. I had grown up in the country, and I just seemed to do better with my fellow country people. I lived and worked in a University town, and there were quite a few intellectual elitist types who loved to pounce at my Appalachian American accent, and ask, "Are you from Kentucky?" with a look on their face similar to one you might wear if you realize you've just stepped in dog shit.

"No," I'd say, wondering what where I was from had to do with what I was doing. "I'm from West Virginia."

"Oh," they'd then say. "Same thing." They'd take quite a dramatic pause at this juncture while they were looking down, as if in deep thought, trying to recall something they'd forgotten. "I can't be bothered," they'd say, and then shut the door in my face.

I never experienced this out in the country, and people seemed to give me a little more time to say who I was and what I was doing, and more than just a few of them would actually invest their money with me. It took me a while to realize, but most of the country folks I'd deal with actually appreciated seeing a hard working young man, out there beating the bushes, trying to drum up business, and they'd give me ten or twenty thousand dollars to invest in a safe, tax free bond, to reward my efforts, and because they liked me, and in time, many of these folks would end up investing hundreds of thousands if not millions of dollars with me.

Most of these folks, out in the country, lived in tiny little brick ranchers, like I'd grown up in, and drove twenty year old vehicles that still looked like they'd just been driven right off the lot, like my family had always driven, and they never allowed the results of the efforts of their labors lead them to think they were any better than anyone else. They were not materialistic, and by making sure to spend less than they earned, over time, many of them became millionaires even though their incomes had never really been that high. By the time I was up and running with a successful business, I realized all those highfalutin yuppie types who were too hung up on where I was from, because of my accent, didn't have any damn money to invest anyway, and they wanted to simply strike first with some sort of demeaning insult, as a way to hide that fact.

On this beautiful October day I'd parked in the lot of what appeared to be an old, abandoned motel. The kind that was probably booming with business back in the 1940's through the 1950's, but then started dying and eventually went by the wayside due to the interstate highway system that was built on the other side of the mountain. This place might have made it to the early eighties, but I'm sure by then it was done for, as was the rest of this little village of a town, due to all the box stores that started going in up and down the interstate by then.

The only thing left around here now was a dusty old grocery story, one overpriced gas station, this abandoned motel, and a bunch of self made millionaires with blue hair and gray hair, the very people I'd come out to meet, face to face, one door to door adventure at a time.

But I would have rather been a kid again trick-or-treating.

I got out of my car and locked it, and as I pulled up on the handle on the door to make sure it was locked (not that it really needed to be in this area) I noticed that the old sign for the motel was on. It was flickering. The "no" portion of the "no vacancy." The "vacancy" part was completely out, as was every other thing of electrical integrity around me, but the "no" just kept flickering. Very much like one of those neon bug catcher light thing-a-muh-doodles you see on people's porches in the summer.

This intrigued me, and I half thought I was seeing things. Maybe just the sun glaring off the old curved, blown glass, as it *was* getting to be about noon. Curious, I walked over and stood under the sign, and sure enough, the damned thing was blinking in and out, not at a consistent, but at a rather random cadence.

I looked through the windows of the door, barely able to see through all the dust that was probably nearly as old as I was, and I saw an old man sitting behind the counter reading a newspaper.

Oh, how I'm dating myself with this story. Okay, kids, newspapers were where people used to be told what to think by the media back in the days before the internet. They were these huge pieces of paper, with stories that may or may not have been true printed in them, and the back pages were mostly filled with advertisements from the companies who paid sponsorship fees so the newspapers could be printed. All this media stuff is printed online now, heck, you're probably reading this book in e-format, so that doesn't need to be explained, but way back in the old days, at the turn of the current century, things were different.

Instinctively, I reached down and grabbed the door knob and twisted it. It was unlocked, so I opened it up and walked right in. It was always my goal to make twenty five contacts a day while out cold calling, and if nothing else, at least I'd be getting the first one out of the way, right here at the parking lot where I was leaving my car.

"Morning," I said as I walked in. "How you doing today?"

"Morning was hours ago," the apparently grumpy old man said. He looked like he was ninety if he was a day old. "What do you want?"

"I just wanted to come by and introduce myself," I said. I told him my name, and that I'd recently opened up a new investment office in the next town over, and that I had some really good paying tax free, insured municipal bonds and yada yada yada.

"Just stop," he said, as I was about halfway through my spiel of explaining why muni-bonds were so much better for high net worth retirees than bank certificates of deposit (CD), and every part of it was true. Still is. I'll never understand why anyone would ever put money into a bank CD other than for a short term goal. Like, if you know you want to take a vacation next year, and you have the money now, put it in a one year CD. But I was always meeting so many retirees who had money they knew they never needed to use, and they'd roll it over in one year bank CD's at next to nothing percent, over and over and over. For the life of me, I never understood why they just couldn't comprehend putting it in longer term, insured, tax free bonds that paid literally five times as much interest.

But hey, their lack of knowledge was job security for me, and it *was* my job to make them aware.

"You're not getting any of my money," he said. Very gruff. And I'll point out here, that not even for an instant the entire time I was in his office, did he ever look up from that paper. Not once.

"Sir," I said, my canned response for rejection already on the way out of my mouth. "I understand that you feel safe with the bank, because you can walk in any time. But our firm's been around for more than a hundred years, yada yada yada," I continued.

"Go on, now," he said, flipping to the next page. "Get on down the road. We ain't got no vacancies."

"I bet," I said, a light chuckle following. "How long's it been since you've let a room in this place?"

"You take care, now," he said, completely refusing to dignify my question with an answer. "Get 'ta gettin'."

I saw that I was getting nowhere, and I wasn't about to waste my time. Something a guy who trained me a little when I'd just started selling investment told me, and it was something that I'd learned to be true, was that once they're over eighty, don't spin your wheels trying to get their money. "These people don't even buy green bananas at the grocery story," he'd said. "It'll just break your heart. Knowing they've got more than a million sitting in the bank doing nothing for them. But they don't make changes at that age."

I left the man to his paper and I made sure to pull the door shut on my way out. I looked up at the no-vacancy sign on my way out and it had stopped glitching. Strange, I thought to myself, how the old thing had even glitched in the first place. I guarantee you that sign was older than me. And it didn't even seem like the place was still wired for electricity. It wasn't warm enough for a fan or air conditioning to be on inside, and there hadn't been, and it was a pretty bright day, without a cloud in the sky, so there was no need for the man to have any lights on inside, but it just seemed strange. No humming from a refrigerator that might be back in the office. No clickety clacking from the ice machine. Not even a lamp turned on in the corner for ambiance.

"You got outta there just in time!" a voice came from the house across the road from the motel. I looked over and there was a man in his early fifties standing on his front porch. "I was just about to call the law on 'ya, and if you come over here a trespassin', I still will!"

Geesh, I thought. Maybe I would have been better off in the college town today. Two jerks in a row?

I kept going and started knocking on more doors. There was more walking out here in the country than back in town, as the houses were farther apart, but at least the people were friendlier.

Usually!

I eventually knocked on the door of a little old lady who appeared to be about eighty, so I was very polite with her, and not pushy, because of that whole 'we don't even buy green bananas' deal, and then I went on my way. She had been my twenty fifth contact for the day, so my day was now done.

The next morning I was sitting in my office when the little old lady I'd met the day before, and who *was* in her eighties I would indeed find out when I opened her account, pulled up, riding shotgun with her husband who was driving their beast of an old ponderosa red Cadillac that looked brand new, though I knew it was probably more than twenty years old.

"Can we come in?" she asked when she walked in the door.

"Absolutely," I said, shocked that she'd stopped by.

"Now write him a check, dear," she said to her husband as soon as they walked into my office and sat. I hadn't even pitched them a product.

The old man took out his checkbook and wrote a check for fifty thousand dollars. "Put that in something tax free, goddamn it," he said, nearly as gruff as the old man I'd met the day before. "I don't care, as long as it's triple B rated or higher." The man knew about bond ratings, which was done to measure their safety, but it was no big surprise. Anyone who can simply pull a checkbook out of their pocket and write a check for fifty grand usually knows quite a bit about money.

I spent time with the couple, and I found out that the man, again to no surprise, knew far more about money than me. Sure, I'd been college educated and trained by arguably the best investment firm in the world, but I still barely met my monthly obligations, and it seemed, far too often, that I had to buy groceries on credit cards. It would take another twenty years before I'd realize, hey, welcome to life in your twenties. Too bad I was in my forties before I finally started cutting myself some slack for so many ways in which I lived during my twenties.

As I continued talking with the couple I learned that the old man had been born the youngest of eleven children, quit school just in time to be drafted and sent off to fight in the second world war, came home injured and half crazy, and then went on to amass millions by buying a ton of real estate in the right place at the right time.

"So do you guys know that old guy at that old rundown motel down the road from you guys?" I asked them when our business was done. I was hoping to get a referral. Hey, if these octogenarians were willing to toss me some of their green banana money, maybe they could convince the other old codger to do the same, if they knew him.

"You mean old Harvey?" the old man said. "That owned the old motel there at the crossroads?"

"Yeah," I said. "I didn't get his name when I stopped in yesterday. But I assume that's him."

"Oh, dear," the old lady said. "You didn't meet Harvey if you were by there yesterday."

"Sure I did," I said. "I noticed he was in his office, so I popped in. He ran me out about as quick as I entered."

"That old bastard's been dead for three years," the old man said. "That damn motel's been an eyesore for thirty years. Ever since it shut down."

"You're kidding," I said, incredulous. I knew what I'd seen the day before. I knew who I'd talked to.

"We'da had the damn interstate if it weren't for him," the old man said. "They came through there, 'ol Eisenhower's boys, back in the fifties, trying to buy everyone out. He wouldn't sell. Lost two of his baby brothers in the war, and he said the goddamn Government had got enough from him, and they weren't getting his land."

"What about eminent domain?" I asked, the Government's power play by where they take holder-outers' land for a fraction of its fair market value when they refuse to sell.

"Oh, they threatened him with it," the old man said. "But he dug in deeper and said they weren't gettin' nothing of his. No one was. Hell, he had offers to sell the motel even after business all but died completely, and he just held out. Sat in there with all the rooms empty reading the papers and the huntin' magazines."

"Wow," I said. I could think of no other words more appropriate for this new information, so I said it again. "Wow."

"Didn't think the old bastard was ever gonna die," the old man said. "You know the saying, only the good die young. They oughta add to it, that curmudgeonly old pricks live forever."

"Now dear," his wife said, slapping him on the arm. "Stop saying all those bad words."

"Hey," he said, starting to rise. "I'm glad of it. That just means I'll live forever, too."

I laughed at that (he didn't) and rose with them and walked them to the door.

The old man would later tell me, when he stopped by once, alone, a couple years later, after his wife had passed, that the reason he came in that day and brought me fifty thousand dollars was because his wife had approached him crying the day I'd met her at the door. She'd told him that a young man had stopped by the house that looked so much like their son it was uncanny.

"She looked like she'd seen a ghost," he said. Those exact words, and it sent chills down my spine, because obviously, I'd seen one only an hour before meeting his wife (in case you haven't figured that out yet). "So I wanted to come meet you, and, well, she was right. You look just like him."

The couple had had only one child; a son. He would have been old enough to be my father if he were still alive, as he had been part of the baby boomer generation. He had gone off to college in the southern part of the state, a different college than the one in the neighboring town where I worked, and while on the way home one weekend during his second semester at school he'd driven his car off of a bridge during a rainstorm and he had been killed.

The old man would die within months of the passing of his wife, and this couple and the experience I had with them has never left me. Not just because, in time, they'd invest more than half a million of their green banana money with me, but because of the other experiences. Old Harvey, and my uncanny resemblance to their son.

I've heard it said we've walked this world before, and we'll walk it many more times. I just can't help but wonder how much that might be true.

The End

October 2

You'd Better Not Take More Than One!

No one knew where he'd gotten it from. This sense of entitlement combined with greed.

And it's not like he was materialistic or showy. He was neither. Despite all the 'stuff' he'd acquired at other people's expenses, through sheer trickery, deceit, dishonesty, and down right criminal fraud at times, you could drive past David's house or see him on the street and you'd think the man didn't have a pot to piss in.

His parents had been hard workers. Farmers. And this was back when farmers in America were actually the ones out there doing the farming. Getting their hands dirty. Not using fancy machinery or sneaking immigrants who may or may not be legal into the fields under the cover of darkness of predawn to do the planting and the harvesting for them for half the price as what they'd pay someone they had to hire through legal means, as long as it was cash.

So David had had good examples, through both his mother and father, set for him. And he had three siblings, a sister and two brothers, who all worked for everything they'd ever had, and who never thought that the system, or anyone in it, owed them anything.

Oh, but David.

What a piece of work *he* was.

Back in school, he'd always cheat. He'd bully people into doing any of his projects, and if they didn't take their tests with their papers positioned just so at the extreme sides of their desks so he could copy their answers, they'd be likely to walk into school the next day with a shiner (that means 'black eye' for any millennials reading this). And as he aged, it was more of the same, just to greater degrees.

David had managed to get a labor job with the grounds workers at the college in the next town over right after high school. He'd kept it damn near a year before he was able to convince the Department of Social Security that he'd torn up his lower back doing something or other while on the job. They hadn't known to ask him about his pre-existing condition- the result of a sudden fall he'd taken one Halloween night half a dozen years before, while in middle school- from which he'd never fully recovered.

The fall had hurt him badly, but not to the degree of making him permanently disabled as far as earning a living goes. He could have worked plenty of office jobs and never had a problem, but what's the fun in that? Not the office part. The whole working in general part. So he pulled his best Charlton Heston (that was a famous actor a long time ago, in case you're a millennial), and got SSID approval, which, of course, got him a tax free monthly check for life! And now that he had income, for life, he had the time he no longer wasted going to work. Time he now used to scheme, and that's what he did, and he started with his own relatives.

David had an aged aunt and uncle who lived up the road from him, both in their eighties, and both of them barely able to get around outside of their home. Neither of them could drive, safely, anymore, and everyone else in the family bitched and moaned and came up with a million different places they had to be on the days they needed to head into town to get groceries or go to the doctor. Insert David; appearing to be their knight in shining armour, but who was really just the devil in disguise.

David volunteered to be their chauffeur, their lawn care guy (as long as no one was looking- that goddamn sister of his had turned him in for social security fraud already by this time, and he couldn't risk that mess happening again by being seen doing manual labor without pain or difficulty), and of course, he would put himself in charge of the old couple's finances.

Their adult children, living three states away, were somewhat happy that mom and pop were being looked after, but since it was David, and they knew his ways, they were a bit worrisome. Not enough to move three states over and do the job themselves, mind you. They had their own lives. So they hoped for the best, but prepared themselves for the worst, and it was really to no surprise to them when mom and pop passed and David, who'd conveniently written himself in as their power of attorney, was awarded their house and property, and the few hundred thousand dollars they had in the bank. Oh, they made a half feeble attempt to fight it, but the judge said that David's name was on the P.O.A. so there was nothing they could do. Having been the recipients of a few shineers (remember kids, that's a black eye), courtesy of cousin Dave, back in the day, they chose to let it go.

This windfall of sorts, the money and assets David was able to steal from his cousins, having had the time to do so by stealing a steady paycheck from the taxpayers, allowed him to up his game. Now he could walk into any bank, and with plenty of cash and a new house, which he was using as a rental property, he could start getting personal loans and mortgages to buy more rental properties, and he'd devised a scheme to do so and never make any payments on the mortgages, or at least not very many and with no regularity. Yes, David had now figured out how to commit mortgage fraud.

After acquiring another rental property, David made the first three payments, but then he contacted his lender and told them that due to financial hardship he would not be able to pay the mortgage of the property in question. The millenial on the other end of the line asked no probing questions. He simply took David's info down, while watching a compilation of memes videos on YouTube on his smartphone at the same time (those millennials are really good at multitasking), and thus David had to make no payments on that mortgage for the next six months.

After six months of making no mortgage payments, the lender called and let David know that they were going to do a mortgage readjustment, by where they would allow him to start making his mortgage payments all over, from the beginning, and that they'd lower his payment, somehow, so he'd have no difficulties making them. It was a Hail Mary of sorts, instituted by Congress after the mortgage crisis of 2008, thus allowing customers to pretty much rob mortgage companies the way the mortgage companies had been stealing real estate from customers before the crises, by knowingly approving mortgages for people they knew would never be able to make the payments, and then foreclosing on them and then selling their properties. The real estate market had been booming back then, so the mortgage companies saw it as easy pickings. And when it didn't work out for them, that was okay, because the Government bailed them out, and that was great.

Until this new law was passed.

And the conniving, cheating, lying and scamming Davids of the world have been robbing *them* of free houses ever since.

"Send y'all's appraisers," he said, defiance in his voice, already contemplating his diabolical plan to hold the process up even longer as he still hadn't rented the property. "Sons-a-bitches!" he said, making his way out the back door and to his outbuilding. He knew exactly what he was going to do, and he was headed out to grab the industrial grade Stihl chainsaw, valued at about a thousand bucks, that he'd stolen from the department of transportation people when they'd come through last time clearing the powerline right of way in front of his house. *Hey*, he'd told himself as he picked it up, making sure that snitch bitch of a sister of his wasn't anywhere around. *If they're dumb enough to leave their shit laying around while they head to their trucks for lunch, they deserve it.* He'd made sure to conveniently *not* be home when they came by after lunch to ask if he'd seen it, and, hell, since it was Government property, they never came back to question him again. He was sure 'ol Uncle Sugar was more than happy to buy them a new one.

Chalk another one right up the ass of the taxpayer by way of good 'ol boy Dave.

He'd never admit it aloud to anyone, but David had to admit to himself on his way up to his rental property that wouldn't rent, that this part of his plan hadn't worked. Sure, he'd planned on scamming the mortgage company out of quite a few payments, but he had wanted to make the payments every other year or so, for the sake of keeping his credit score high enough to be able to go out and get *more* loans to not make payments on quickly soon after.

The house wouldn't rent, because too many people knew too much about it. Like the fact that the last three families who'd lived in it had had at least one family member die in it. Not a good track record for a house. There was a name for houses like that. People referred to such houses as haunted houses, and it was bad for business if you owned one and was trying to rent it.

What was even creepier, if you were to ask David, was its history before the multiple family deaths. Specifically, who'd lived in it before it had been bought by someone who lost a child in it, and then rented it out after that to two more families, both of whom would lose a child in it, before being sold, with good riddance, to David.

The witch!

"Stay away from the witch's house," his parents would bark at him on his way out the door every Halloween when he'd been a child, way back in the 1950's. They didn't need to tell him, because he and every other kid in the small farming community already knew to stay away from the witch's house.

They'd all seen her at one point or another. She was bent over, walked with a cane, and she wore a tall black hat and everything. She looked just like a witch should, down to the hairy mole on the side of her face. And the strangest thing about her was, that even though she was every bit of eighty years old, back when David was a kid, was that everyone's parents remembered her as being every bit of eighty years old when *they'd* been kids, as well.

It was the last year that David had gone trick-or-treating. He'd been in sixth grade, and since he'd been big for his age and already a bully, most of the kids assumed he wasn't afraid of anything. This, of course, back during the time in life when no one really realizes that bullies are afraid of everything. It's why they're bullies.

But when the other kids dared David to go to the witch's house for candy (cowering over in fear of the upcoming shiner, which never came, and I don't need to remind you millennials what that is again, do I?), he wasn't about to reveal to them at their young age, and his, that he really *was* terrified of everything, and that was why he spent so much time beating people up, so they wouldn't notice, so he put on his best Heston face (uh 'hem), and marched right up to that old bitch's door, as he always referred to her, and knocked, knocked, knocked.

There were at least half a dozen kids hiding behind the privet hedges thirty yards from the witch's front door, all excited and curious, and not a single one of them made a single sound. As soon as David had finished knocking, it was as if God was up there in the sky and he'd pressed the mute button on planet earth. There were no sounds. Though it was a warm October night, and they were in the south, there were no frogs, no crickets, no owls, no nothing!

And then the floorboards on the other side of the door creaked.

David felt sweat drip from his hairline. It ran down across his forehead and burned when it went into his left eye. He'd been too frozen in fear to wipe it away before it went into his eye. But now that his eye was burning, David reached up to wipe it just as the witch opened the door holding a dish of individually wrapped candies.

"Aren't you supposed to say something?" the witch said, as David simply stood and stared at her. He was in complete disbelief that he was face to face with and only two feet away from the old witch. The only people who were in near equal shock were all the kids hiding behind the privet bushes.

"Trick-or-treat," David said, barely able to get it out.

"Let's go with treat," the old witch said, raising the bowl a bit so the movement of her doing so would grab David's attention and remind him where he was and of what he was doing.

David looked down, into the candy dish, and he reached in. Being that David was David, greedy little prick, even as a child, the thought of taking one and only one candy never occurred to him. Taking one of anything edible would never occur to him, and it's why in adulthood he'd push the scales to three hundred, even though he was three inches shy of six feet tall. He'd never seemed to care about the fact that gluttony and obesity went hand in hand.

"Ah, ah, ah," the old witch said, teasing, but serious. "Take only one."

David looked up at her, and his hand instinctively let loose of all the candy he'd grabbed.

But then something happened.

David felt fear. Real fear. And he knew it. And the way the old witch smiled at the exact moment he'd felt it let him know that she knew it to.

And man, did that piss him off!

"Fuck you, you old rotten ass whore!" he said as he grabbed the whole dish of candy from her, jerked it hard, and then turned and ran off her porch. He'd made it halfway down her walk, at the end of which the other kids were now coming from behind the privet bush, in complete awe of what David had done, when it happened.

David would swear for years later that one of the stones of the walk actually raised up out of the ground, and not to toe level, but to half way up the shin level, and it caused him to fall. The next day he'd have a bruise on the front of his right shin, where he'd claimed the stone had hit him, and a few of the kids, when threatened with a good 'ol shiner (see four pages previous, paragraph two for meaning if you've forgotten, you whippersnappers) would claim that they'd seen something, too.

Though in constant fear of being attacked, as if by a wounded bear, at any time, the kids rallied together and helped heft David home. He'd miss the whole next week of school, and the doctor would say he might never recover completely. It was those very words from the doctor that hatched David's plan of a SSID disability check even at such an early age.

"Ah, bullshit!" David said to himself, aloud, as he turned up the short dirt road, or the long dirt drive, whichever you preferred to call it, that led to his unrented and seemingly unrentable rental house. "No one's scared of it. It's just in a bad spot. Location, location, location."

David parked his car, the one he'd not made a payment on in two months, despite having all that money in the bank, because the repo man only came after ninety days, at which time he'd hand him a check and call him off, just like last time, and walked up the porch steps, trying not to think of that Halloween night all those years ago. His plan to keep the appraisers away didn't require him to come all the way up to the house- he'd be using that old poplar tree about two hundred yards back on the road for that- but he'd been so caught up in his thoughts of that night, despite his best efforts of trying not to think about it, that he'd driven right past the tree without even consciously seeing it, so he figured he'd take a peek through the windows to make sure everything was okay.

When he reached the porch at the top of the steps, he felt his heart skip a beat, and then he felt a sudden rage at the sight of a dish of candy sitting on an old stool, with a handwritten sign in the middle of the candy which read 'take only one.'

"You sons of whores!" David wailed, and he already knew who'd done it. That little bitch of a man named Joshua who he'd gone to school with all those years ago was an appraiser, and David was convinced he'd been out ahead of him to play this little prank. "You've got an ass whoopin' comin'," he said, thinking of Joshua, as he bent over and collected the dish of candy. No need to waste it. It *was* food, afterall. So he turned and took it back to the car with him and turned around and drove down to the old poplar tree a couple hundred yards away.

When he reached the tree, David got out of the car and opened the back hatch of the Subaru Forester and pulled out the chainsaw, all while gnawing on his already third piece of candy. He cranked the chord and the saw started right up on the first pull, and he was thankful that the Government never spared *any* expense when it came to spending the taxpayers dollars on equipment.

David looked up at the top of the tree before making his first cut. Most people, seeing the tree with it's beautiful leaves of fall gold- leaves shaped like t-shirts some people would say- and all those beautiful leaves blowing in the breeze wouldn't cut a tree of this size, age, and splendor down if you paid them. It had weathered more than two hundred years of drought and winter and flood and social discord from the antish people who lived beneath it to become the towering giant that it was, but all David viewed it as being good for was to block the road so the appraiser couldn't make his way to the house to do his job. At least until they subcontracted someone to come out and remove the tree, because David sure as hell wasn't going to come out and move it, why, because he had a bad back and all. He figured he could easily miss another six months of mortgage payments by doing this.

David had cut down plenty of trees in his life (even though they could never prove he'd cut down the one that fell on his sister's double wide shortly after she'd reported him for disability fraud), so he knew exactly how to do it. Pick the direction you want the tree to fall and make your fist cut. A straight line going almost to the center of the tree. Then, you simply walk around to the opposite side from there and start cutting out your wedge, about a foot above the original cut on the other side. A freaking moron could do it.

And David was proof.

Just as David was finishing cutting his wedge, the huge, monstrosity of a tree began falling across the road, David safely standing on the opposite side of its fall.

But then it happened.

Had anyone been around to witness it, and had they been under direct threat of one of David's shiners (okay, we all know what those are by now, right?), they might have said that they'd seen something, too.

What David saw, and it was the last thing, by the way, that he would ever see, was the freaking tree stop falling and simply be held by some unseen force, suspended, in midair. And then he saw the adjustment. It all happened so fast, yet it seemed like it was in slow motion. Despite however fast it was happening in real time, David didn't have time to move out of the way as the trunk of the tree came flying straight back at him, knocking his head off upon contact, and then continuing it's fall, burying the fat bastard with more than two hundred years old and twenty tons worth of yellow tulip poplar.

The End

October 3

You Ain't Hackin' Up My Punkin!

"What is this *crazy* obsession you have with pumpkins?" his wife always asked him in June when he'd go out into the backyard and till up a space of land with a shovel and bury a pack of pumpkin seeds he'd bought down at the local Walmart. They'd always come up in past years, but they'd never amounted to anything. The soil was too hard, he never thinned out the sprouts, and he'd never given them nearly enough water.

But this year was different, and she made sure of it. This year, she encouraged him to get out there and thin out the pumpkins, and she even got out there with him and helped him till the soil properly, at various places around the entire property, because pumpkins need space. They needed to vine out at least fifteen feet in all directions, and that was per plant, so by the time you property spaced a couple dozen pumpkin plants around the yard, well, do the math.

Not much yard left.

But she didn't mind, and she was happy to help him and sacrifice her lawn for one year so the man she loved could have the pumpkin patch that might produce at least one pumpkin of his dreams.

Because this year, he'd finally answered her question.

About his crazy obsession with pumpkins.

And it had broken her heart.

And it made her cry.

***

He was nine years old and still hell bent on making his father proud.

It wasn't an issue of being noticed. He was noticed plenty. Noticed by the swift end of a fast moving leather belt anytime one of his father's tools went missing (later discovered to have been misplaced by his father), or any time his father had had a bad day and he, the boy, had not, and was happy. Or anytime his sociopath sister wanted to be entertained by a good whipping and would make up some shit her little brother had done or said, but that he really hadn't.

But if he could just make his father proud, the whippings would stop, and he'd realize he wasn't a worthless little piece of tripe who'd made his life more miserable by having been brought into it. Another dependent. He hadn't asked to be born, anyway, but now that he was here, he was certainly made to feel as if it had all been his fault. Like he'd directed his father's sperm into his mother's egg by remote control.

But this would be how he would do it. It would take several months, which may as well have been eons for a nine year old little boy, but this nine year old little boy had learned to think quickly, think long term, and think out of the box, well ahead of his years.

He had to.

Because the whippings hurt.

"Now get the hell out'a my way, I said," his father said, knocking him in the head with the end of the gardening hoe. He was working the soil to plant the corn. The boy was trying to help, as he always did, but once again, he was simply getting in the way. He'd heard his mother forcing his father to take him to the garden with him so they could finally have some 'father and son time' that didn't require a whipping, but it was obvious the father, once again, didn't want the son around.

"Take these seeds over there in the corner and plant 'em," the father said, handing the boy a packet of seeds at random.

The nine year old little boy looked down, reading the packet as he walked to the far corner of the garden where all the clumps of sod and roots had been piled up and discarded.

"Punkins!" he said, excited, as he read the label on the package aloud.

He toiled the soil as best he could with his hands and his little trowel, but all he seemed to do was tear up the bits of grass. He decided he needed more dirt, so he filled a five gallon bucket to the rim, realized it was too heavy for him to carry, then dumped half of it out and made two trips of it. But once he'd gotten the fresh soil on top of the pile of sod and roots, and planted his pumpkin seeds an inch and a half deep and three inches apart- three seeds in each hole- just as the back of the package had instructed, and he covered them up and he looked out across his job well done and gleamed with pride...

Whop!

A big open hand slap to the back of the head.

"I told you to bring back the bucket when you were done!" his father said, obviously aware that the boy's work was complete.

***

Throughout the summer, the boy went to the garden daily to check his pumpkins. He'd thinned them out as he was supposed to do, all according to what it'd said on the back of the seed packet, and since the refuse pile had been so far from the main crops of corn and peas and string beans and tomatoes, the twenty feet long vines had gotten in the way of nothing else. He watered them every other day, unless it rained, and he couldn't wait to tell his father of the progress each evening over dinner.

"They're really growing, Daddy," he'd say between bites.

"Shut up and eat," his father would say, without even looking in his direction.

"The boy called me fat today," his sister would say, glaring at him through hateful eyes. Eyes that would indeed sit deep within the face of a morbidly obese and miserable woman some day in the future.

"I'll whoop him after dinner," the father would say.

His mother, like always, said nothing.

***

But Daddy noticed the pumpkins come September. At least the two biggest. They got so big by the end of the month that Daddy started bringing people home with him from work to show them the pumpkins *he* had grown. "Check out these two over here," he'd say, leading his collegue, usually an underling who felt obligated to go home with him to see his garden, because Daddy *was* a foreman.

"*Damn*," the men would always say. No women worked in the mill, so Daddy always brought home men. "Those are big punkins!"

"'Bought the biggest you've ever seen, ain't they?" Daddy would say.

"Sure as shit are," the men would always say in agreement. No matter who Daddy brought home- and there were at least a dozen different men brought home in October alone- they all said the exact same things. "Damn!" and "sure as sit are!"

"We're gonna have the biggest jack-o-lanterns in town this year!" the boy said a week before Halloween, just as the guy who drove the fork lift had finished saying, 'sure as shit are.'

"We're gonna *what*?" Daddy said, instantly and very incredulity.

"Jack-o-lanterns," the boy said. "It's why I grew 'em."

"You grew 'em?" the forklift driver said.

Whop!

"You ain't hacking up my punkin!" Daddy screamed at him, and then gave him another whop on the back of the head for good measure. "Get your ass back to the house and wait in your room. I'm gonna give you a whoopin' when I get there!"

The forklift driver tried not to let the sadness on his face show as he watched the boy heading home, head down and snivelling, and he couldn't help but think that the boy would either grow up to be a drunk or a serial killer, but definitely someone prison bound.

Or successful beyond measure.

***

Two days before Halloween, one of the two pumpkins went missing. Fortunately, it was the smaller of the two, and though it would have tipped the scales at just over one hundred pounds had it been weighed before it had been stolen, outweighing the boy by at least forty pounds- and there would have been no way the boy could have even lifted it alone- the boy got the blame and the whipping that went with it.

"They ain't gettin' this one," Daddy said, cutting the stem of the larger pumpkin with his hacksaw. The stem was too thick for a pocket knife. He'd called that one sissy man over at the mill that worked in the office and made him bring over a dolly. They rolled the pumpkin onto the dolly and wheeled it back to the house and weighed it on the bathroom scales that would send big sister into her fist clinical depression a few years down the road, and it came in at one hundred and thirty five pounds.

"Damn!" Daddy said. "That's the biggest punkin I've ever heard tell of!"

"Sure as shit is," the sissy man who worked in the office over at the mill agreed.

***

"Carve up my punkin!" Daddy said, glaring at the boy with eyes glazing and red like he was still drunk from the night before. That was one of the things about Daddy, though. Daddy didn't even drink. It would be nearly another thirty years before the boy would learn the term "dry drunk" and be able to look back and realize his daddy had been one. The boy would go on to learn lots of psychological terms in adulthood by way of a long line of shrinks, his lasting gift, if there was one, from Daddy, and the one term that served to define Daddy most aptly was plain and simple.

Narcissistic bully.

"This is going to be bread," Daddy said, hacking the pumpkin apart. He'd already taken the top off and the seeds out, and he wouldn't let the boy fry them in butter and douse them with salt, because these seeds needed to be dried and used next year to grow even more pumpkins of this size. Sadly, they'd all be eaten by mice while stored inappropriately out in the woodshed during the upcoming winter.

"And this is going to be pie!" Daddy said, forcing the top onto the tupperware container he'd crammed the last batch of slices into.

By the time Daddy was done hacking up the pumpkin so that the boy couldn't turn it into a jack-o-lantern, the refrigerator was more than half full with tupperware containers stuffed with pumpkin and the rest was filled with aluminum foil wrapped pumpkin pieces, because they'd run out of tupperware containers. Over the next ten days the pumpkin slices would all rot and go to waste, as Daddy never made anything out of the pumpkin. No bread. No pie. No nothing.

"Hey," Daddy told the boy when he spoke of how they could have had the largest jack-o-lantern in town on Halloween, "Halloween is over, anyway."

And then he gave him a whipping.

***

She'd been in the crowd at one of his book signings. She could tell by the way he gave more of a motivational speech than he did actually talk about writing, that he had a tough veneer he was using to cover up something underneath. Not in a *I've got a deep dark secret* kind of way, but in a *I know I'm worth something 'cause God don't make no junk* kind of way. Like someone somewhere at some point had told him he was no good and he'd spent the rest of his life trying to prove to anyone who would take note that he was.

As she got to know him in time, after that first time they'd met, when he'd attempted to autograph the book for her, but signed his name on the tablecloth, because he didn't look down to mind what he was doing, because he couldn't quit staring at her, she'd learn he was pretty damn good at pretty much everything he'd ever done. He'd been a star athlete and a top ranked salesman at a couple different firms in a couple different industries before realizing it was time (not too ironically after Mommy and Daddy had both died) to stop trying to prove things to others and pursue his passion and to his own self be true, which involved leaving the city in which they'd first met during the book signing, continuing to write from the heart, and loving her to his last day.

But those last days, hopefully, were far into the future, and for now, there were ghosts from the past to dispel.

It had taken a long time for him to open up about his past- his childhood, specifically- and when he did so, it was usually by accident. Something would slip. Something that started out like a pleasant memory, but then quickly turned into a story of abuse which he didn't want to talk about. He'd stop himself short everytime the bad parts would start to come up, but the longer she was with him the more she was able to get out of him, and this led him down the road of healing.

"We're going to do it next year," she'd told him last October, when she'd finally heard the pumpkin story. They were out for a stroll through their neighborhood, and they'd stopped to admire the largest jack-o-lantern in town.

"Do what?" he'd asked.

"Grow the biggest pumpkins in town so we can have the largest jack-o-lantern in town!"

And she'd stayed true to her word. She'd not only forced him to go buy the seeds and get to planting, but she'd gotten out there with him and had helped him with all the work. From the thinning out of the mounds to the watering and the pruning of the vines to exactly fifteen feet long each, she was with him every step of the way!

And the best part? That was when, two weeks before Halloween, they harvested, with the help of a couple of friends and over a few bottles of October Ale, a nearly three hundred pound Atlantic Dill pumpkin which would indeed end up becoming the largest jack-o-lantern in town on Halloween night!

***

Trick-or-treat came and went, and they'd enjoyed handing out the candy and watching as all the kids and their parents alike ooed and awed over the biggest jack-o-lantern in town. Oh, how she wanted kids of their own, but he was terrified he'd end up being the kind of father that Daddy had been, and she didn't force him, but she felt that in time he might change his mind, but she would never try to force him to do so. For now, she simply enjoyed their togetherness.

As they lay in bed two hours after the last little goblin had taken a fun sized Snickers bar, and they'd at least practiced making a baby, she asked him if he really thought the sawed off shotgun under his pillow, the one loaded with rock salt, was necessary.

"Let's just call it a precaution," he said, smiling.

The shotgun had worked its way into the scenario back in August, when they'd accepted the fact that they'd somehow managed to grow the most successful pumpkin patch in the county right in their backyard, and they weren't even farmers. Thoughts of The Ghost Of Daddy Past started filling, not just his head, but his dreams at night. Visions and dreams of Daddy coming back from the other side to carve up his pumpkins, all so that he could not accomplish that which he'd set out to accomplish. Having the biggest jack-o-lantern in town on Halloween night.

He'd talked to his best good buddy about the dreams, and his best good buddy happened to be a shrink down at Region 10, and he'd told him to get the shotgun and the salt shells, and that if The Ghost Of Daddy Past came back, blast his ass away with rock salt, because that's how they did it in that show his wife loved to watch on Netflix so much. The show about the two brothers who spent their time running around chasing ghosts and demons. He said his wife claimed to love the ongoing storylines, but he knew the truth of it was that she had an almost alarming celebrity crush on the guy that played the older brother.

He took the advice from his shrink buddy, feeling as if he'd done the counselling that day, giving his friend a sounding board for his near alarming jealousy of an actor his wife would never meet, and he'd gone to the local Walmart, waiting the three days for the background check to clear, and then he bought and brought home the only firearm he'd ever owned in his life. His wife had taken care of obtaining the salt shells, and a simple hacksaw had done the trick on the barrel, and now, on Halloween night, after having achieved his near lifelong objective of having grown the largest pumpkin in town, which had become the largest jack-o-lantern in town, he lie in wait.

Sure, Daddy had been dead these past ten years, and there was no such thing as ghosts, and Halloween was already over…

…but no one knew that mean old son-of-a-bitchin man of a father he called Daddy all those years ago like he did.

So still.

He waited.

***

He heard the back screen door creak the way it always did when opened from the outside. After that, he heard the hard door creak on the hinge the way it did whether opened from the inside or the outside.

Why would a ghost use a door, he thought? Immediately after, he thought, *because that's the kind of prick the man was in life, and I'm sure it's the same in death. Anything to disturb someone else, especially me!*

He looked over and saw that she was deeply asleep. She'd never taken issue with him sleeping with the sawed off shotgun under the pillow this Indian Summer. Their buddy at Region 10 helped set her at ease, assuring her it was just one final push toward 'letting go.' And he'd asked her if she thought that one actor on that one show was hot, and she'd said he was, and it hadn't made him feel a bit better about his own situation at all.

He grabbed the gun and silently slid open the drawer of the nightstand on his side of the bed and took out the two salt shells. He'd never shot the weapon, but hell, he figured if Daddy actually came back to be a prick from beyond the grave, it would be done up close and personal enough to where he couldn't miss, weapons training or no weapons training. It was hard to give a whipping from a distance.

He krept down the stairs, and he swore he heard a racket in the kitchen. Drawers opening and closing. He reached the foot of the stairs and got around the corner just in time to see that Daddy had found the butcher's knife in its proper place; in its slot on the right side of the knife holder. His wife was anal about putting it away after she'd done the dishes, whether she put the other dishes away or not, because she didn't want to take the risk of one of them slicing their wrists open while reaching into the strainer to grab a glass for a drink of water. The thing was razor sharp.

"Look at you," The Ghost Of Daddy Past said as he entered the kitchen. He was holding the knife out in front of him, testing the tip with translucent fingertips. "All high and mighty. Got'cha the biggest jack-o-lantern in town, and now you think you're something you're not."

"You're not real, Daddy," he said, raising the shotgun up and leveling the barrel at face level with Daddy's ghost, just in case he was. He'd loaded both barrels on his way down the stairs. "You've been dead a decade."

"Ha!" Daddy said. "And you didn't even come to the funeral, you ungrateful little prick!"

"How'd you…" he said, trailing off, amazed that he knew.

"I was there you dumb shit!"

"This is just a dream," he said, blinking his eyes, knowing it wasn't.

"Boy, look at you," Daddy said, stepping toward him. "All uptown now, ain't ya? Wrote ya a couple books a few people's read, and now you're thinking you're all debonair. Boy, you ain't nothing different now than what you've always been. Pure white trash!"

By this time, Daddy was right in his face, leaning forward, eyes bulging and red, just as they'd always been in life and when he'd be leveling his insults to the boy to make sure, even back before the boy had started grade school, to keep him in his place. Let him know he was nothing but lower than whale shit shit, and he'd only ever be nothing but lower than whale shit shit.

"Let's take you down a notch or two," Daddy said. "I'm gonna give you a whoopin', but I'm gonna get out there and take care of that punkin first, you ungrateful little shit!"

The Ghost Of Daddy Past turned and walked toward the living room, well on his way to the front door, just off of and in the lawn which he had a mission; a mission to carve up the largest, by far, jack-o-lantern in town.

"Daddy?" the boy said, hearing his own voice as that of a nine year old boy, not a thirty nine year old man. When Daddy turned around, he pulled the trigger and both barrels gave Daddy a hard blast of rock salt, and Daddy disappeared back into thin air as strangely as he'd appeared in the first place. "You ain't hackin' up my punkin!"

She came downstairs and found him with the gun. She was certain he'd thought about his father and the pumpkins he'd grown as a little boy so much these past few months that he'd had a dream so vivid there was no way he could have not thought it to be real. She was only happy he'd not been hurt.

And as she hugged him, she couldn't help but notice that the knife she knew she'd put away, like always, was lying on the threshold between the kitchen and the living room.

"Let's go make a baby," he said to her, pulling his head back from her shoulder.

"For real?" she said. "Not just practice?"

"For real," he said, and they went back upstairs, and they did.

The End

October 4

Time To Pay The Devil His Due

Kurt was not a bad guy. He was a good guy. He'd just been misguided in his youth. Heck, even that's not a fair description. Kurt had simply had no sense of direction. His father had been a drunken bastard, and his mother, the perfect enabler for his father, never cared. About him or anything. Apathetic is the best term to describe her.

And Kurt really had planned on going to college. He'd always wanted a better life for himself and his own family if he were to have one someday. He did *not* go off to college to avoid the draft, despite what his father told him. He'd used the term *unpatriotic coward*, but it's what he'd meant.

Kurt couldn't help getting caught up in all the protests while he'd been in college. And he wasn't really pissed off at the establishment as much as it was that the protests provided an outlet for his overall general state of rage. He wouldn't realize it until midway through life, but he'd really been mad at his father. And hell, his mother for never caring enough about anything, for that matter, as well. And the protests, (hell, he'd gone to Berkeley, so there was always one going on somewhere on campus about something going on in the world) gave him the perfect outlet to blow off his steam and distill his rage.

So, Kurt kinda sorta *did* go to grad school to avoid the draft, but by this time, he'd had relationships with his friends and fellow protesters and he couldn't just head off the some shithole in Southeast Asia and leave them over here fighting the good fight without him. Besides, he reasoned at the time, the world needed a few more folks with master's degrees in history, anyway.

But this had all been a very long time ago, and even that midlife crisis stage, when he'd finally seen for the first time that all his angst and anger had been rooted in his inner child's feelings toward Daddy Dearest was a generation ago. Kurt was old now. Wearing face masks to the grocery store, frightened to death he'd get COVID-19, because, hell, he was seventy five years old, so contracting the virus would really translate into a death sentence.

But even more than COVID-19 and the Republican party, Kurt was scared much more of something more powerful than both.

The devil!

***

They'd been protesting abortion. Well, not actually abortion, but the Government's idea to keep it outlawed, during the Roe V. Wade days when it happened. That's when Kurt signed a pact with the devil. He never really meant anything by it, other than to piss off all those right winger Christian types that kept showing up at the rallies, over there on the other side of the street, with their signs depicting Kurt et. al. as baby killers and murders and hell bound heathens.

"Ya'll goin' ta hell!" the folks on the other side of the street would shout. "For killin' ya'll's babies."

"We're never going to have babies, you ignorant fucks!" some of the girls protesting alongside Kurt would yell back. "We're lesbians, you fucking idiots!"

"Then ya'all's goin' ta hell for fornication!" the people on the other side of the street would yell. "The Bible says a man ought not lay with another man!"

"We're women, you ignorant fucks!" the lesbians would yell back.

And so it went, until some preacher dude came across the street and got in Kurt's face, seemingly at random, and told him to turn his life over to the Lord and Savior Jesus H. Christ. Kurt told him he'd been born okay the first time, and he'd rather sell his soul to the devil.

At this point, the preacher man smiled in such a way that Kurt's gut instinct told him that the man might not really be a preacher man, but the devil himself. Or one of his agents. *Nah*, Kurt would think to himself and sometimes say aloud, at least a million times since that day. *Couldn't have been.*

"Why," the man said with a southern drawl, which was strange, since they were in California, "you don't have to sell your soul to the devil. He'd be more than happy to take it for free."

"Fuck you, hillbilly!" Kurt said, shoving the man. He'd realize only years later, when looking back on it, that he'd shoved the man as much out of fear as he had out of any sort of anger. There had been something about the guy. His eyes. How Kurt could have sworn they'd shimmered red for just an instant. "I'll pledge my soul to Satan and get all my friends to do it, too," Kurt continued when he saw the guy smirk, just after his eyes may or may not have twinkled red. Kurt viewed the smirk as a challenge, and it was a challenge he was willing to accept.

"Oh?" the man said, never raising his voice. He then looked around at Kurt's friends. The little spat had gotten their attention, and they were watching, waiting, perhaps, to see who might throw the first punch. "Any takers?" the man asked, when he noticed he had an audience.

"I'm with you, Kirk!" one of the lesbians who'd been trying to explain the unlikeleness of a lesbian ever giving birth to one of her counter protesters said.

"Um," Kurt said, low. "It's Kurt."

"What about you guys," the lesbian said, directing her challenge to the rest of the group. Two of the men took two steps over to join their allegiance, but the others just kept staring, for just a moment, and then started not so casually making their way into different parts of the mob to continue their protests.

"Jessica?" the lesbian said to what had appeared to be her partner.

"Hey," Jessica said. "I'm not really, um," she was looking for words. "I'm just bi-curious, really," she said, and then of all things, she walked over to start discussing something which couldn't be heard with the man she'd been explaining the birds and the bees to and then the two of them walked off, arm in arm, and just like that, Jessica's days of bicuriousity had come to an end.

"There's four of us," Kurt said, his tone letting the man know his challenge had been accepted.

"Do you now and forevermore pledge your souls to Satan?" the man asked, drawing close enough to be heard clearly by the three men and one woman that was Kurt's circle of support, Kurt, of course, included.

"Yes!" the group said in unison, having perfected the ability to do so with all their 'hell no, we won't go,' lunch counter experiences in recent months.

The man stepped even closer, and said, "say it one at a time. 'I pledge my soul to Satan.'"

All four of them said it individually, as if making a pact, one by one, though none of them felt good about it. But none of them were about to back down from this dumb redneck with a southern accent and a nose that sloped down from between his beady little eyes to a sharp point below. Beady little eyes, by the way, that they would all say years later seemed to twinkle red as soon as they'd said those words they'd all later come to regret.

"Good day to you, then," the man said after Kurt had said the words, rounding out the pledge of all members in the group, and then he simply slipped into the mob on the other side of the street, and they never saw him again.

Until the next time they each saw him again...

***

Sheila, the only woman of the group who'd taken the pledge, would see the man again first. And she didn't have to wait long to see him. She would see him again the following weekend when she got behind the wheel of her little Volkswagen Beetle after consuming way too much alcohol, marijuana, LSD and something in pill form she'd never tried. She'd been having problems with the transmission, but the brakes had always seemed to work just fine.

Until that night.

That was the night she flipped the Beetle in a sharp turn and was thrown halfway out the window, the car crushing her ribcage and the lungs they were supposed to protect. Most people saw bright lights or butterflies they'd been chasing as toddlers at moments like this, but Sheila saw the blood she was spewing out of her mouth, and a passerby, a man who appeared to be out for a walk. He walked over to her, bent over her, and smiled. He had a sharp, pointy nose and two beady little eyes that twinkled red for just a minute before everything went dark.

And then Sheila saw an eternity's worth of hell's burning flames. She's still there, as you read this, now, actually. Seeing the flames and feeling the heat of those flames.

***

It would be a few years after that before Dan, one of the two men who'd joined Kurt and Sheila to make that pact back at Berkeley would see the man again, but sure enough he saw him. After hearing about Sheila's accident years before, Dan had automatically remembered the pledge they'd made to the strange man, all out of anger and spite, and thought that it was just too coincidental to be a coincidence. Out of remorse, regret, but mostly fear and guilt, he'd done a complete one eighty in regard to his views, belief system, and lifestyle, and he'd completely turned his life around, all in an attempt to live an amends for the pledge he'd taken.

Dan had gone on to graduate from Berkeley, but instead of shacking up with some good looking guy in San Francisco and spending the rest of his life protesting whatever cause he could find to protest and opening a small restro that specialised in shitty sandwiches and overpriced coffee, he'd gone back south, to Alabama, where he was originally from, and of all things, joined the clergy.

Dan had hidden his sexuality really well by marrying a somewhat decent looking girl who'd been working down at the Quickmart, nights, and they'd even procreated and created a couple of offspring. Dan had to admit that the experience wasn't half bad, and that with a few more years of practice, he could even get around to almost liking it.

He'd gotten himself a pastorship at one of the many local Baptist churches who were always raising money to build a bigger building, and he'd gotten really good at getting folks to fork over their rent and utility money, convincing them that if their faith in God was strong enough, they'd still figure out how to meet their bills for the month, even after giving their bill money to God. "Give 'til it hurts!" he'd proclaim twice on Sundays and every Wednesday evening.

Dan had been in the church the night he saw the man again. He'd just finished 'counselling' a man, like himself, married with kids, but completely and totally gay, in the church office. And on one of the pews. And once in the church's kitchen. The man came by a couple times a week for 'counselling' and Dan really wrestled with it, because though he enjoyed helping the man with his wicked ways, and I mean *really* helping him-

and boy, did they get wicked- he could tell that it was keeping him from really getting into that whole wife with two kids thing in such a way that he'd at least look convincing. Even to any of his old buddies from back in Berkeley.

Dan had made the mistake of being in the church and staying after his gay lover had left on the very night that a group of racists had decided to firebomb the church with Molatov cocktails, because they didn't like the fact that the number of blacks in the congregation had recently surpassed the number of whites. By the time Dan figured out what was going on (it took all of about ten seconds, but the bottles filled with flaming gas had come in from all the windows on all four sides of the church), it was too late. The smoke filled his lungs and he had dropped to the floor and did his best to crawl to safety, but no safety existed in any direction. Just before he took his last breath and entered a flaming pit much hotter than that of the church which was burning, he had a glimpse of hope as he saw a man walking through the smoke toward him. His hopes of it being either a fireman or a good samaritan were dashed when he saw the pointed nose and caught the red twinkle in the beady little eyes.

***

Brain was next to see the man. He might have known that he was on the devil's short list, had he stayed in touch with the others that he'd made his deadly pact with, but hell, he'd just been at Berkeley that day for the protest. He hadn't even been a student. He jumped over with Kurt and the gang to challenge the Bible beater, because it had simply seemed like the thing to do in the heat of the moment. Besides, even if he'd thought there might have been something to selling, rather, *giving* your soul to the devil after Sheila and Dan's death, he no doubt would have forgotten all about it, or considered it folly, looking back on it, because so much time had passed since they'd died.

Thirty years!

Good ol' Brian had actually gone off to the war he'd protested so much around Berkeley and found that military life, other than the part of trying not to get your ass shot off in third world shitholes not worth fighting for, as he saw it, wasn't half bad. He'd gotten used to the three hots and a cot and the steady paycheck, so he'd stayed on once his drafted duty was up. He'd actually go on to use the G.I. Bill to get his ass into college after the war (though not Berkeley, and he kept all his activities from back in those days as secret as he could), and ended up getting a master's degree, a commission, and he eventually made his way to Lieutenant Colonel before retiring from the U.S. Army and landing himself a way overpaying civilian job at the Pentagon in D.C. He couldn't tell anyone what he did, but what he did was help run up the profit margin on conventional warfare weapons and munitions, and because of this, helped make sure wars were no longer fought to be won, but sustained, in order to keep those hyperinflated profits rolling in for the long haul.

Brain had been standing in the hall of the western side of the Pentagon just a few minutes after 9:30 a.m. on the morning of September 11, 2001, staring out the window, wondering how in the hell the news he'd just heard about what was going on up in New York City could really be happening when the plane came smashing through the window out of which he'd been staring. Despite having seen the plane in time to have at least made a short run for it before getting killed, he stood frozen in fear, unable to move, and the next to the last thing he remembered was how the pilot's eyes were small, beady, and how they flashed red for just a second, and then the last thing he remembered was Berkeley during the Row V. Wade demonstrations.

And then things for Brian got really, really hot!

***

Kurt had heard of Sheila's car wreck shortly after the pact, but that was old news a long time ago. He wasn't surprised about how Dan had gone. Hell, everyone knows how those rednecks are down south. Of course he'd heard about the Pentagon, but had he known Brian had been one of the nearly three thousand to parish in the attacks that day, it would have made no difference, because he'd not even gotten his name back at Berkeley.

But Kurt never forgot about the pact, and he knew that in time, it would be time to pay the devil his due. His final due, that was, as Kurt knew he'd been paying them most days of his life ever since dealing with the devil when he came to call that day.

Kurt's first wife had left him for a good looking shyster. The man hadn't had beady little eyes or a sharp pointed nose. He had sea green eyes and a perfect nose, but Kurt could swear he saw the red twinge in the man's eyes the first time he'd met him. His wife had been with them. Neither of them knew him at the time they'd met him- doing so through a friend of a friend at some sort of block party or other informal gathering most yuppies hate going to but wouldn't imagine not being seen at. A month later, Kurt walked in and found the man flat on his back on his marriage bed, with his wife flat on her back on top of him- lying down reverse cowgirl. The oddest thing of what he saw when he walked in was not the position that Kurt and his old lady had perfected themselves, but that red glint in the man's eyes, and the smirk on his face, and not a hint of fear. Kurt had simply shut the door, left the house, and only went back once to pick up his belongings. No kids meant a simple and quick divorce.

The second divorce had not been so simple and quick. With his next wife, he'd fathered two children, and before that whole mess was done and over with, both kids, two daughters, would be turned against him, and he'd not spoken to either of them in more than thirty years come the time of his death. He'd been the one to do the screwing around that time, so there was no good looking lover with sea green eyes that happened to twinkle red when doing the devil's work, but his ex-wife's lawyer had those twinkling eyes, and when Kurt's lawyer and himself had his wife ready to settle for fifty percent of all the assets (few they were), and the house, plus alimony in lieu of child support so Kurt could at least take the tax writeoff, her lawyer talked her out of it, his eyes flashing red as he did, Kurt was sure, and she took it all.

He'd seen the red eyes twinkling in the doctor who'd told him a few years after that that his mother's brain tumor was inoperable, and the best they could do was keep her comfortable as she passed, and he saw it in his old man's eyes every time he got drunk and bitched about his coward, draft dodging son who never got anything right. He often wondered if the red had been in the old drunk bastard's eyes before he'd made his deal with the devil, and he'd just never noticed. Some people, Kurt thought, were possessed by the devil or his minions, deal or no deal.

It was thoughts of his mother and where his adult daughters might be that were filling Kurt's head as he walked out of the local Whole Foods, taking his face mask off as he did. His thoughts kept him from making out any details among the screaming going on outside the story. If he had been paying attention, and hearing those details, he'd have noticed that there was a protest about the Governor's recent order to wear a protective face mask in order to enter any place of business, statewide, until further notice, because of the pandemic.

"Fuck tyranny, boomer!" a young man of the younger, millennial generation said, running up to Kurt, smashing a pumpkin he'd stolen from the Halloween display in front of the store at Kurt's feet, just as Kurt pocketed his facemask. "America! Fuck Yeah!" He then coughed in Kurt's face, and just as Kurt's brain registered what was going on (as well as flashing back to the time in 1972 when he'd thrown an egg in the face of a veteran stepping off a plane, coming home from the war in Vietnam that Kurt, himself, had avoided by going to graduate school), he noticed the young man had beady little eyes and a sharp pointy nose, and as he turned his focus from the man's nose back to his eyes, he could have sworn he saw them flash, ever so slightly, red.

The man smirked at Kurt as the police dragged him away, threatening to arrest him. They quickly released him to pull another protester off of another baby boomer coming out of Whole Foods, and the man slipped back into the crowd of protestors, but not before glancing back at Kurt and giving him an all too familiar smirk.

"Oh shit," Kurt thought, thinking again of the egg tossing incident from all those years ago. And there had been more than one. "It all comes home to roost, and the devil will have his due."

Kurt didn't go to the hospital immediately, though he did assume his number was up. The devil had made his life a hell on earth, but it looked like it was time to visit Hades in real time, and really soon.

A few days later he was in the hospital getting the news. He was placed in quarantine where he spent more than twenty days, cut off from everyone else except the men and women in hazmat suits. The whole time he lay on his back, he felt as if a crushing weight was continually gaining weight on his chest.

And then it happened.

A new man in a hazmat suit came to see him. A man in a hazmat suit who had beady little eyes and a long, sharp nose. His beady little eyes went from black to red and black to red.

"I didn't mean it," Kurt said, barely audible. The virus had progressed to the point where Kurt could barely breathe. "I was in the wrong place. Wrong time."

"Yes," the man said. "Just like when you came out of Whole Foods. Wrong place. Wrong time."

Kurt found that he couldn't draw a breath after the last words he'd spoken. His body froze and his eyes widened as he called on any bit of strength he had left in his lungs to pull air.

The man in the hazmat suit smiled. His eyes glistened red.

And Kurt slept.

Until he woke up shortly thereafter…

…in Hell.

The End

October 5

This House Ain't Haunted (But It Is)

You would have thought he'd have a name like Claudius Snickenbacher, or something like that, because he was such an odd little man with an odd little job, but he didn't.

His name was Jim Brown.

And you would have thought, with a name like that, that he'd be black, as Jim Brown is a pretty traditional African American man's name, like the great fullback that played for Cleveland and was already retired years before I was born, but he wasn't.

He was white.

Actually, he was whiter than white and paler than pale. Hell, I'd almost go far enough out on a limb to say he was damn near translucent.

He wasn't sickly. The god of your choosing *knows* he put in plenty of miles on that bicycle of his. The one without gears. The one that made him look like that creepy kid from the movie Children of the Corn, especially since he wore a near identical Quaker style hat as that creepy kid in the movie.

He was paler than pale, because he didn't sleep most nights. He wrestled with the guilt of all the lying he did. But lying was part of his job, so he had to do it, or he'd be out of business.

What kind of business was he in, you ask? Well, he was in the business of convincing people who lived in haunted houses that their houses weren't really haunted.

Why in the name of the god of my choosing would someone do that?

We'll, I asked him the same damn thing when he approached me and tried to get me to pay him to do what he does for us, but we didn't need his services. He just didn't know it at the time, but he meant well.

It was around this time last year, October, when I first saw him, peddling that old, black, gearless bicycle for all he was worth coming up the hill on the main road down in front of our house. I was down there working on some trees we'd planted when we first moved in in order to create a sound and privacy barrier from the road. Well, that's how it had started, anyway. Seven rows and four hundred trees later we realized we'd basically planted an entire forest.

"What can I do you for, Sir?" I said, as he pulled off the burm into the state's right of way. I could tell he was a local- from the south, that is- because he knew not to come onto my property without permission. That's a pretty easy way of getting shot around here. It's like the sign on the driveway of one of our neighbors a little farther up the road says, "Prayer is a good way to meet with Jesus, but trespassing on this property is quicker."

And I called him 'Sir' out of respect. That's another southern thing. To this day I wouldn't dare guess his age. I'd assume he was my age, but hell, sometimes when I think someone's my age they turn out being as much as fifteen years older, and they've just really taken good care of themselves, or have good genes, or something. And other times, when I see people who I find out really are my age, I ask my wife to please, please pretty please tell me I don't look anywhere near as old as they do, because I'd like to think that I take pretty good care of myself, or I have good genes, or something. The answer I get from her has very little to do with how old the other person, or hell, me myself looks. It mostly has to do with what kind of mood she's in.

"I'd like to offer you my wares," he said, sounding hopeful yet winded at the same time.

"I don't know what you're selling, but we ain't buying," I told him. Another southern thing.

"You don't care about all those things you got going bump in the night?" he said, refusing to take rejection quickly. "And all those things, sounds like someone's walking around in your fields and woods at night?"

I have to admit, he got me there, and I had no way of knowing how. Had he been here before? Maybe before we bought the place?

I walked over and shook his hand and gave him my name, and that's when I found out what his was. "Come on up in the yard and rest a while, Jim Brown," I told him. "Looks like you've been putting in the paces. I'll give you some Gatorade and hear ya out."

I keep a cooler with me when I'm out working. Not a big one. Just big enough to keep a few bottles of water or Gatorade in so I don't have to go back to the house to get a drink if it's hot or I'm just thirsty. I don't mind the extra time it takes so much as I do the fact that the Mrs. usually has half a dozen of things put together on a honey-do list for me when I go in and I never seem to make it back out and finish up what I'd been working on outside.

So me and Jim Brown sat a spell, and drank Gatorade, and damned if I didn't hear one of the strangest stories I believe I've ever heard told.

As it turns out, Jim Brown is a medium of sorts. And an empath. And a devout Christian, which really tears him up because of what he does, and it's one of the reasons he looks so pale and pasty. The man simply doesn't get a good night's rest, not because he wrestles with what he does, and what he knows, but because of what he'd been taught to believe since he was in diapers. You see, Jim Brown has always been a faithful member of the First Baptist Church of whatever town he's lived in- and he moves around a lot, because of work and all- but the work he does has not confirmed what he's supposed to believe about the afterlife.

"You see," he said, once he really got into his spiel. "It's not as cut and dry as Heaven and Hell. Shoot, I still don't even know if either of those places exist, because no one, or no spirit I've ever dealt with has ever come back from either places to tell me about it."

"So where do they come back from?" I asked him. I'd been raised Catholic on Saturday evenings as a child, because my mother was a Catholic, so I knew all about that Purgatory place where spirits were supposed to go and wait in line, or something or other, and I'd been raised Bible beating Baptist on Sunday mornings during my childhood, because that's what my father was. Hell, if anything, as a grown man, I'm confused about all of it and bipolar as hell, because of the experience, if you ask me.

"Most of 'em don't go anywhere," Jim Brown said, taking another long draw from his Gatorade. He'd grabbed the grape when I'd offered him his pick, and that had upset me a bit, because I'd wanted it, and now here I was stuck with original lime flavor. But I'd acted like I didn't mind. That's a southern thing, too. A lot of folks complain that people from the north are too pushy and rude, but I always appreciated the fact that at least you know where you stood with those people. Hell, you can have people down here in the south that you think love you like their own kinfolk, but they cuss your mother's maiden name everytime you leave their place from seeing them, even though they were sweet as sugar to you while you were there. "Most of 'em just stay where they are," he continued. "They don't go anywhere."

"Now, why in the name of the god of your choosing's green earth would they just stay where they are?" I asked him, confused as ever.

"Because home is home," he said.

He went further into detail about what he did. Whereas most people would hire mediums to exercise their homes, Jim Brown was hired to convince people who thought their homes were haunted, but didn't want to believe in such things, that their homes weren't really haunted.

"How do you do that?" I asked.

"Well," he said, picking a piece of straw grass and putting it in his mouth to chew on the end of it while he pondered my question. And yup, in case you hadn't guessed, this is a southern thing, too. "I do it by letting the spirits haunting the place know that they'd better get in line and stop making their presence so obvious, or the home owners were gonna bring in one of them Catholic guys and douse the place up with holy water and burn sage and throw salt and all kinds of stuff. I put some oil on the squeaky wheel, so to say. Get 'em to walk the line so they can live happily ever after, well, without being alive anymore, of course, in the place they want to be."

"And it works?" I asked.

"Most times, yes," he said, very definitively.

He went on to tell me some stories about some of his past cases. The hardest time he ever had was when he was dealing with the ghost of a deaf man. He said he'd lost his hearing during trench warfare of the first world war. Came home and lived a good life after, working as a small engines repair guy in the shop behind his house. Problem was, he had a tendency to work well into the night in life, after which time he'd come in, not caring if the creaky back screen door slammed behind him, and having no knowledge that the third step on the stairs up to his bedroom creaked. He said the reason he had the hardest time with that spirit was because he didn't know sign language. Said he was afraid to bring in someone who did, because then the people living in the house would know something was up. That they had a deaf ghost on their hands.

"What'd ya do?" I asked, fascinated.

"Well," he said. "I went around and did a few small repairs to the home. I oiled the back screen door, and I put a pad on the upper corner where it met the frame, so when 'ol boy came in at midnight, and slammed it, you couldn't hear it. And I nailed down the third step on the stairs."

"But didn't all that convince the people living there that their house really was haunted?"

"Not at all," he said. "I took a few classes in psychology at the Bible college I attended for a couple years before dropping out to pursue my calling, and I remembered a few words like psychosomatic and such, so I convinced 'em it was that. Said if we didn't get these things fixed, they wouldn't have to worry about ghosts, which weren't real, at least that's what I told them. I told them they'd lose their minds and probably have to be institutionalized."

"And it worked?" I said.

"They paid me my hundred dollars, and I haven't heard from 'em since," he said.

We sat in silence for a while, then I finally said, after thinking it through, "Why, Jim Brown. I don't mean no offense, but I think you're a shyster!"

Jim Brown turned toward me with a look on his face that I'd have sworn twenty years before would have said he wanted to fight. And twenty years before, I'd have given him one. But I'm too old to take an ass whooping these days, so I apologized, because like I said, he might have looked about my age, but he could have been quite a bit younger than me and he might could put a whoopin' on me.

"I'll prove it to you, then," he said. "Free of charge."

"Well," I said. "I don't work for free, and I wouldn't ask another man to work for free. Look," I said, trying to figure out a win win. "I'll give you a little something to prove it, but I ain't giving you no hundred dollars. And we don't need anyone or anything that might be still hanging on around here to go into hiding, or silent mode. We've always been live and let live kinda people. Or, well, live and let..." I didn't know how to finish.

"Feed me dinner and we'll call it even," Jim Brown said.

"Deal!" I said, and we shook on it, and that's still, by the god of your choosing, a southern thing.

We didn't even have to get inside the house before Jim Brown was showing me his wares. "Now, I guess you know about them graves over there," he said, pointing to an overgrown bramble thicket just at the edge of the field, where it meets the woods.

"Sure do," I said. "They've been there purt near a hundred years."

"Them's three little girls died in the Spanish Flu of 1918," he said.

"That's what I heard," I said, somewhat impressed but also somewhat skeptical. Just because I'd never met Jim Brown before didn't mean he'd never been around here. My wife and I had just moved here from pretty far away not too long ago, and I was just beginning to get the feeling 'ol Jim Brown might be a local boy messing about with me.

"And hell," Jim Brown said, as we got within the yard proper, the part that's not part of the field. "They's plenty of Civil War and Indian spirits running around out here in the yard with us right now."

I stopped abruptly and looked over at Jim Brown and was about to ask him what kind of a fool he took me for, but that's when I noticed he'd stopped just as abruptly as I had, and he was looking in the kitchen window. My eyes followed his, and I could see my wife in there moving around, cooking dinner.

"Who's that?" Jim Brown asked.

"Why, that's the Mrs.," I said.

"I thought you were here alone." Jim Brown said.

"Now I've figured you out, Jim Brown!" I said, and I had. "You was gonna get me alone in the house and knock me a good one over the head then ransack my stuff and take what you wanted."

He looked at me like he wanted to fight again, and by the god of your choosing, I was ready to go this time. Whether he was ten years younger than me, or ten years older, didn't matter, I was ready to give 'ol Jim Brown a whoopin'!

"You hear the scratching at night," he said, his face relaxing a bit. I'm sure the look on mine put the fear of his chosen god in him. "Sounds like it's coming from the other side of the wall."

"I do," I said, and all of a sudden I forgot I'd been mad.

"That's 'ol Pup," he said. "He knows there's been a new doorway cut into your bedroom from around the other side, and he uses it, as I know that you know, but sometimes he forgets. See, that's where the original door used to be. Your house is really old."

And Jim Brown was right. Our master bedroom was downstairs, off from the living room, and you could still see the outline in the wall from where they'd boarded up the original doorway into the room, long before I was born. Maybe back around the time that other Jim Brown was still playing for Clemson, before he'd even entered the NFL. Our house is more than a hundred years old. A lot of these old farm houses down here in the south are. I shit you not, there's a couple restored log homes out our way that date back to the late 1600's.

And the idea of the ghost of a dog immediately shot into my mind. You see, I have a cat, and she sleeps on top of the dresser in our bedroom. I put a fleece blanket up there for her so she'd be more comfortable back when she'd just started forming the habit shortly after we'd gotten her. My wife hates that cat, mostly because she's jealous of her. I'm the only one she'll let pet her. She loves to lay down on my lap around bedtime, when I'm already under the covers. She lets me pet her for about five minutes, then she bites the living shit out of my hand, and growls and hisses at me, and then goes and gets on her dresser and sleeps. She was a rescue cat, so the god of your choosing only knows what she'd been through before we got her.

Anyway, there's been more than one night, quite a few more, when I'd thought the cat had gotten off the dresser and was walking around on the bed, because I could feel something pounce on the bed and then start moving around. Every time I feel it, I wake up, I look down at the foot of the bed and I see nothing. I look over on the dresser, and the cat's either up there sleeping, or bent in half all fierce, standing up with her hair up, and hissing like the crazy bitch she is. I never thought much more of it than just being a little odd in general until now. Now that Jim Brown was telling me that my house and the surrounding property isn't just haunted by people ghosts, but obviously a dog ghost, too.

"He's gotten old and forgetful," Jim Brown was saying again. "Just don't kick him off the bed when it takes him a while to remember and he scratches half the night before going around and using the new door."

I was looking at Jim Brown in disbelief as he was saying this, and right about that time I heard the back door creaking open.

"Come eat!" my wife called. I told her to set another place, 'cause Jim Brown was joining us.

She said, "who?" and I said, "Jim Brown. My new friend."

"Who the hell is Jim Brown?" the Mrs. said.

"Why," I looked over to my side, ready to introduce him, but he wasn't there. I turned to face the road, and there was 'ol Jim Brown picking up his bike and readjusting that old Quaker hat he had on, just like that creepy kid from that creepy movie. "Jim Brown," I said, as my wife pulled up beside me. "Said he was gonna stay for dinner. I guess he changed his mind."

I could sense my wife looking down at the road, then back at me. Down at the road, then back at me.

Now, I'll admit, I used to have a drinking problem, but I ain't had a sip in many a year. And I know my wife's moody. I told you that when I was explaining about people's ages, and how I sure as shit hope I don't look as old as some of the people my age. And the way she answers depending on the mood she's in. But when she leaned into my face and took a big old whiff, just like she used to when I'd come home soused- again, that's been years ago, now- it was a pretty low blow. She didn't have to go and do that.

"Come in and eat before it gets cold," she said and then she turned and went inside.

I watched 'ol Jim Brown head on down the road, no doubt on his way to try to drum up some business. I'm sure he had bills to pay, too. It was awful nice for him to stop by and try to drum up some business here, and lie to me, and tell me my house ain't haunted.

But it is.

The End

October 6

Moving To The Country

(Originally Titled: The Sheriff Of State Route 601)

I've got nothing against subdivisions or the people that live in them. They're just not for me.

Neither of them.

I'm allowed this view, because I lived in a subdivision for nearly twenty years before moving out into the country. It was a beautiful, well kept community, but it just felt so tightly spaced, and you never seemed to get any privacy. I mean, if you stepped out into the yard to get a break from the family for a few minutes- a little fresh air to clear your mind- you were just as likely to get pounced on by whatever neighbor happened to be outside *their* house and saw you step outside as you were one of the kids or the wife if you'd have just stayed inside.

Don't get me wrong. They were good people, my old neighbors. It just dumbfounded me how they never stopped to think that when a man went outside, it might actually be to simply get some air and be left alone, not be pounced on by someone else. "Oh," they must think you say to yourself before stepping out, "I'm bored. I think I'll go outside and see which self-important neighbor wants to tell me how important they are down at the office, and how that big 'ol Fortune 500 company couldn't operate without their expertise at whatever boring little spoke in the cog of a job that it is that they do."

For the record, I never said that before going outside for some air.

By the time the kids were grown and gone (well, off to college, texting home most days asking me to wire more money), I'd gotten to the point where I would rarely go outside, because I simply didn't want to get pounced on. It occurred to me, however, that since I had kids relatively early in life, I still had far too much life left in me to become agoraphobic.

"Honey!" I said when I'd arrived at that 'ah-ha' moment. "Let's sell the house and move out into the country!"

"Okay," she said, because she'd reached the same damn point, too!

***

We stayed in the county we'd lived in since we'd gotten married right out of college, because we love it here. We just moved about twenty miles out into the county. We'd found a small rancher on six acres, and it was mostly cleared fields, so it felt like we were living on a golf course. The closest neighbor was within sight, but still about a quarter of a mile away. We actually saw him, a seventy-ish year old man, when we'd gone by the house both times to look at it before putting a contract on it. He had been out in his yard, just across our property line and just on the other side of his, gardening. I looked over and saw him staring at us, both times we were out there, and I waved, and he waved back just as friendly and then turned his back to us and kept on gardening.

"That's a good sign," I said to my wife the first time, and "another good sign," the second. She agreed. She said something about hoping he was a widower, and not to be a mean bitch, but because it would mean one less woman around to pounce on her if she took a notion to go outside and stroll through our fields.

We've all heard the nightmares, about how much of a pain in the ass it can be, buying a home, even if you've been through it before, but the transaction went smoothly for us. The house had actually been on the market for a couple of years, and we were able to put down a sizable down payment after quickly selling our old home, because unlike so many of our wonderful neighbors back in the subdivision, we didn't run down to the bank to pull out however much equity we'd built up in our home each year. Whereas our neighbors did so to live a very materialistic lifestyle, we tried to show our children economic responsibility by living one ourselves. With the sale of the old home and what we kept in cash, we could have bought the place outright, but we decided to carry a mortgage on it so as not to be running on fumes, financially, so to say, since we did have two kids in college, and all.

I'll be damned if it wasn't the first day after we'd moved in (the kids were off in school, so they were no help, but we didn't mind), and here came the welcome wagon. Well, he was alone, but still, the very reason we'd moved out into the country- to get away from 'friendly neighbors'- seemed to be rearing itself out here, too.

"Don't worry," my wife told me. "He's alone, and he's just coming by once, I'm sure. Just be nice, and not too personal, and he'll be on his way."

It wasn't the seventy-ish year old man who lived next to us, though I glanced over his way and saw that he was outside. He'd been gardening, but he was now resting on his rake or hoe or whatever gardening tool he'd been using, watching the car that was coming up our driveway. It was a newer model Subaru wagon of sorts, and it had handicap license plates on it. The man driving was alone, as my wife had pointed out, and he looked like he was in need of a shave, a shower, a gym membership and a new diet.

He stepped out of the car and said, "How, do," and just started making his way up to us like we'd known him forever. As he drew close, we could smell him. He honest to God smelled like he never bathed. He wore a full beard, and it was peppery, making it hard to guess his age, but I'd say he was close to the same age as me, perhaps a little older, though his physical appearance made him look a lot older.

"What can we help you with?" I asked. Not in a rude tone, but in one that would let anyone with any degree of basic social skills know that we didn't want to be bothered.

"Well, now," he said, stopping in his tracks and reaching out to grab the rail going up along the steps on the porch. We were standing at the top, blocking the porch, giving no indication that we wanted him to come up and 'sit for a spell,' as many people down here in the south like to say before basically moving in for a month. "Ain't no reason to go greeting people like that. Especially when you're new and they ain't."

"What is it that you need?" I said, ignoring his passive aggressiveness. I'd dealt with people enough in life to know that most of them view any sort of kindness as a weakness. I wasn't trying to have a dick measuring contest with this guy, but I wanted to make it clear to any curiosity seekers that we expected would drop by on the new people, like this guy, that we weren't here to satisfy curiosities. We were here because we wanted to live in peace and be left the hell alone.

"I can see you're not in a good mood," he said, letting go of the rail and turning back toward his car. Once he reached it, he opened the door, and just before getting in said, "I'll just stop back another time when you're not so upset."

And then he drove away.

***

About a month passed after we'd moved in, and spring was starting to turn to summer, and we'd decided to start a garden ourselves. We used to garden, way back when we were new in our old subdivision, but gardening was one of our passions we'd given up, because we'd gotten sick and tired of going outside, full intentions being to spend an hour in the garden, only to never even reach the garden because one or more of our friendly subdivision neighbors would see us out and come and tell us how important they were down at their jobs, or whatever.

We'd rented a tiller from one of those powertool rental places, because we wanted to make sure we were going to stick with gardening before going out and spending a grand on something like that, and we were tilling up a nice, flat plot of land when we heard a voice behind us say, "that ain't where you're supposed to have your garden."

We turned around, and we saw the fat, dirty, stinky man who'd driven up on us the day after we'd moved in. "The people that lived here before always had their garden over on the other side of the house. Now, they had special soil hauled in for it and everything. You need to stop tearing up this perfectly good patch of grass and get on around the other side of the house and garden."

"Who the hell are you?" I said, walking up to him, almost right into his face, but after getting within five feet of him, I could smell that moldy old never takes a bath smell, and I chose not to get any closer.

"Boy, you keep on," he said, "and you're gonna find out who I am. I'm just trying to help you."

"What makes you think anything we're doing here is any business of yours?" I asked.

He smiled as big as he could- ear to ear- and he looked like a coal miner who took December jobs as Santa, and he said, "I'll stop by and check on you folks regularly. Because I'm friendly. When I see you out, I'll make sure to always stop by and say hi, and eventually I'll catch you in a good mood." And then he began walking back to his car, which was back in our drive about one hundred yards away. It's why we'd never heard him pulling in.

"It's okay if you just wave and keep on going," my wife said. "You don't need to stop." She was trying to be friendly about telling him to fuck off, but he was at ninja level when it came to passive aggressiveness, so her efforts were futile.

"Oh, I'll stop," he said, stopping and turning to face us as he did. "Because I'm friendly." And then he turned and walked away.

***

The next day, I happened to notice the old man that lived beside us out in his garden. As long as we'd lived there, he'd never come over to meet us, nor had we gone over to introduce ourselves to him. I had the suspicion that he appreciated it as much as we did, and when I got to talking to him, that day, I'd find out I was right. He was a live and let live kind of guy, and it's why he'd left the city and moved into the country himself, a long time ago.

"Sorry to bother you," I said, walking up to the edge of our properties' border. "But I wanted to finally introduce myself to you. My wife and I just moved in about a month ago."

He put down his rake and walked over to the property line and extended his hand for a shake. "Name's Burt," he said. I told him my name, and we exchanged a few simple pleasantries, but I didn't want to waste any more of my time, or his, than I had to, so I cut right to the chase.

"I'm not a gossip," I said, "but I have *got* to ask you about someone that I think lives out here."

"Dirty fat bastard in the Subaru?" Burt said, instinctively.

"*Yes!*" I said. "How did you know?"

Burt threw his head back and laughed loudly.

***

I learned from Burt that the dirty fat bastard in the Subaru was named Roy Jinkens, but everyone called him the sheriff of state route 601. "Because he's always up in everybody's business, telling them what they can and can't do," Burt had said when I asked why they called him that, this dirty fat bastard in the subaru.

Burt said the guy was just a few years older than me, and he can remember him back when he was a kid. He said the guy actually lived up the road about two miles, but back when he was a kid, he'd actually get up early and walk to the various school bus stops scattered along the old country road in order to pick fights with other children.

"That's how I saw him first," Burt said. "I was out early, getting the paper, and I saw him get up in another boy's face just down by the road over there," he said, pointing toward a widespot on the other side of the road. "He told the boy he'd heard he'd called him a queer. The other boy said he never called him a queer, so then Roy told him he didn't take kindly to him calling him a liar. The other boy told him he'd better back off, because his daddy had told him that if he ever felt like he was gonna get into a fight to hit first and to hit hard, and he was getting the feeling old Roy wanted to fight."

I was listening to this story, this bus stop tale, with deep interest, as knowing how this dirty fat bastard in the Subaru had been as a child could lay a somewhat decent foundation for understanding him as an adult.

"Then 'ol Roy told the boy he was gonna be in a fight, so he'd better hit first and he'd better hit hard, so that other boy drew way back and clocked him a good one! I could hear the pop from over here. Thought it was gonna take 'ol Roy's head off."

"What happened?" I asked.

"Oh, Roy turned and smiled at that other boy then lit into him like a lightning storm in summer time. That poor boy had to have his jaw wired shut and he ate through a straw for three months after that."

"Jesus," I said. "Did Roy get expelled?"

"Hell, no!" Burt said. "He's local. And let me tell you. I moved here in 1972, and I'm still considered an outsider. If your great, great grandparents weren't from here, and everyone between them and you, you're an outsider, and the few households of locals who remain view you as free entertainment, as far as any harassing they want to do goes."

"I had no idea," I said, and I was truly amazed. "We've lived downtown for a quarter of a century. We met in college, and we stuck around after we graduated, because we like it so much here. I had no idea people were like that around here."

"Welcome to country living," Burt said, laughing as he did. "So many people leave town life to come out here thinking they're gonna be left alone, then they find out about the busybody locals who don't want to let 'em. Most of 'em are on some form of welfare, mostly disability for injuries or conditions they don't really have. And all they do is run up and down the road all day harassing people."

Burt went on to inform me that the dirty fat bastard in the Subaru lived on a forty acre tract of land he shared with his two brothers and a sister. Their parents had been long dead, and half the siblings wanted to sell the land, the other half wanted to keep it, and they all had white mobile homes with black trim sitting twenty feet apart from each other right in the center of the property.

"With that much land," I said, "why didn't they spread out? Give themselves some room?"

"It'd be harder to fight all day and night with each other," Burt said. "Oh, they're dysfunctional as hell. Always calling the real sheriff on each other. And this is family we're talking about."

Burt told me more stories about the harassment this man, this dirty fat bastard in the Subaru, this sheriff of state route 601, had carried out on others who'd been new to the area in years past. He said there was a couple just up the road who had a dog, a little terrier, that stayed in the house, and every time they'd take it out for a walk, or to use the bathroom, on their property, which was about five acres, the sheriff of state route 601 would pull up their drive and get out and lecture them about leash laws. Burt said the couple had tried to be polite at first, like my wife and I had been, but he kept on harassing them until they finally told him to go fuck himself.

"What happened after that?" I asked. "Did he finally leave them alone?"

"Seemed to," Burt said. "But that couple's dog went missing two days later. And he'd gone missing from inside the house."

"No way," I said.

"Yes way," Burt said.

"Did they call the cops on the guy?" I asked.

"Sure," he said. "They didn't do anything. Cops told them to be more polite to the locals."

"Jesus Christ," I said. "Is it like 1950 around here?"

"Nope," Burt said. "Just life out in the country. And everyone out here who's a local is kin to each other to some degree, so be careful."

"How do you know if they're local?" I asked.

"They look like white trash hoarders," Burt said. "Don't bath much, and if you look around their properties, they're all hoarding something. Either hay, firewood or old vehicles."

Already, in my mind's eye, I was seeing some of the houses up and down the road that must have belonged to generational locals. Our area is actually quite affluent, and known for it, so when you drive out these old country roads, you'll see these vast, beautiful estates. The owners must literally spend ten thousand dollars a month having their lawns maintained. Because we're talking about twenty acre lawns that all look like golf courses, and they all have plenty of shrubbery and ornamental bushes and flowers to trim around.

But then, after about every fifth beautiful estate, you'll have an old shitty farm with an old shitty dilapidated house on the front of the property, with a bunch of old shitty stuff piled up on the porch, and around the side, and out back. Hell, it looks like the back portions of the properties, at least as much of them as you can see from the road when you pass, are freaking landfills.

"Why do they live like that?" I asked Burt.

"To spite the new people with money that's come in here, mostly from the northeast, and bought up all the land that used to be theirs. The land they had to sell off to settle estate taxes as each generation before them died."

"You're kidding me," I said. "Like sour grapes?"

"Pretty much," Burt said.

The locals in the area were all worth millions on paper, because the real estate values had skyrocketed in the past half century, but they had no cash flow, other than what they got in social security disability each month for being some sort of disabled but really not. Burt explained to me how they got on that gravy train. Basically, they all have a cousin who's a cousin of someone's cousin down at the SSI office who has a cousin who knows somebody's cousin who can get their cousin to tell their cousin to approve these people's claims, because, well, they're their cousin's cousin.

Yes, I'm serious!

Anyway, the next day, after learning all of this and much, much more about the sheriff of state route 601, my wife and I decided we'd put up a gate down at the end of the driveway. We were almost done digging the last of the four post holes we needed to lay the posts for the small fence that would bookend the gate when none other than the sheriff himself drove by. We heard his car slowing to a stop, and I remember thinking, oh, no, and then he stopped right there in our drive and got out and began his lecture about how we better had called the utility company before we started digging to make sure we didn't hit any lines. As he was talking, I couldn't help but notice a young black man sitting in the front passenger seat of his Subaru.

"Who's that?" I asked, cutting the sheriff off in mid-sentence, my head nodding toward his companion.

"Ain't none of your goddamn business who that boy is," the sheriff said, and then he began his tirade again.

I'd had enough. As Popey would say, I'd had all's I could stands and I couldn't's stands no more, so I told him to go fuck himself.

"Really," he said, and he said it with a smile. I remembered the fight story Burt had told me, and I immediately began thinking my mouth might have just signed my death warrant. The dirty fat bastard didn't look like he could fight his way out of a paper bag these days, the shitty shape he was in, but when it came to pure, down and out meanness, I'm sure he could fight his way through a rattlesnake den.

After smiling at me, sinister like, he got back in his car and he drove away.

That night, while lying in bed, talking to my wife about how it was going to be a hot summer, because we were already using the air conditioning, the air conditioning went off, and the light we keep on in the hall went out, and the next day we'd find the main line going out to our electrical box on the side of the house cut in two.

***

"You know who did it, don't you?"

It was Burt. He'd walked up behind me while I was checking the electrical box on the side of the house the next morning.

"Yup," I said.

"And you know calling the law's of no use," he said.

"Yup," he said.

I turned and asked, my voice sounding pitiful, "what in the hell do I do?"

Burt looked at the ground and huffed through his nose. "Ignore him," he said. "It's the only way. He'll continue to harass you relentlessly, even if you completely ignore him and don't even acknowledge him, for probably two or three years, but in time, someone else will be the new guy out here on state route 601, and the good sheriff will move on."

Just as I was internalizing Burt's advice, which I could see as being, sadly, the only way I could deal with this passive aggressive asshole, I remembered the young man I'd seen in the dirty fat bastard's Subaru with him the day before. I asked Burt about it.

"God knows who that one is," Burt said, rolling his eyes.

"What do you mean, that one?" I said, completely lost.

"The sheriff and his brothers raise chickens," Burt said. "Their other brother and their sister take care of selling the eggs. They make sure not to claim any of the income, not just because they don't want to pay taxes, but because they don't want to lose their disability. You know, that whole *too injured to work thing* doesn't go over so well when you're working."

"Yeah," I said, following along.

"Well," they go down into town and get young men a lot of times, mostly black men, and bring 'em out when it's time to clean the hen houses. God," Burt said, looking down as if in thought," they probably have five thousand chickens up there on the back part of their property."

"Really," I said, finally understanding a little more about why the sheriff of state route 601 was so stinky and dirty. "Do they go get kids from the University? Students interested in earning some drinking money?"

"No," Burt said. "He gets 'em from the bus stop."

"Where?" I said.

"The Greyhound station. Down on West Main. He gets transients. Young men on their way to nowhere just coming from nowhere else."

"How often?" I asked.

"Not sure," Burt said. "I see him with a couple a year, but it could be more regularly than that. Like everyone else out here, I've learned to look the other way if I even *think* he's coming. No one out here ever goes by their place to visit him or his siblings, who, frankly, are as fucked up as he is, they just leave everyone alone is the only way their different. And there's a lot of people you'll actually see run around to the back or side of their houses out here if they see his car coming up the road."

Burt stopped, and I could tell he was thinking of something else, perhaps another story of the sheriff of state route 601 harassing someone else. A story worth sharing. So I didn't rush Burt, or his thoughts.

"You know," he said, when he finally spoke again. "This sounds nuts. But I've always had the crazy idea that one of these days they're gonna be up there digging up scores of bodies."

"What?" I said. "I don't think I'm following you," I said.

Burt looked up at me, and the look on his face was one a person wore when they realized they'd said something they probably shouldn't have, so he said, "Oh, nothing. Hey. I gotta go."

And he did.

***

My wife and I bought this house out here in the country a long time ago. We finally got our kids through college (and graduate school), and those kids made us grandparents about ten years ago. Our neighbor Burt passed away about five years ago, and we've had no more problems with the sheriff of state route 601.

Burt had been spot on with his advice on how to get rid of the sheriff. By ignoring him. It was hard at first, because the man would drive back and forth in front of our house if he saw us out and just stare us down, and sometimes, if I were out jogging, he'd trail me and refuse to pass, but even then, I was able to completely ignore him. And like everyone else out this way, I made sure to *never* get close to *his* property.

And everyone out this way now understands that that had been his strategy all along. The best way to keep people away- to keep prying eyes off of you and your place- was to be such an annoying neighbor that no one would ever think of just dropping by to say hello.

And possibly find the bodies.

It turns out, about six months ago, that one of the transients the sheriff of state route 601 had hired to help him shovel chicken shit was not a transient, but the runaway son of a state senator from out in California. He'd run away to experience "real urban life," as he'd stated in a letter he'd left behind, having felt that growing up rich and privileged kept him from knowing the true young black experience in America.

As you can imagine, since the young man came from wealth and privilege, his father being a senator and all, when the young man never came home and was not heard from again, despite his skin color, people gave a shit, because what everyone really knows and what everyone's really too afraid to state publicly, lives with money matter. Black *or* white. Period.

They've found forty two skeletons scattered across the forty acres that belong to the sheriff and his siblings so far, and they're not done digging yet. Not even close! And the damndest thing of it is, is that some of the skeletons they've found belonged to people who went missing back in the mid 1960's. Apparently, the sheriff and his siblings were just carrying on a family tradition.

But more creepy than that? Some of the other locals? These folks who are cousins of someone's cousin who is a cousin to the sheriff of state route 601's cousin's cousin? They've all been putting up "no trespassing" signs on their properties, as if, all of a sudden, they're afraid that the authorities might come digging up their back forties next.

My wife and I have found a cute little cape cod in a nice little subdivision right in the center of town, and we've ratified the contract on it. If all goes well, we close next Friday, and we'll be moving over the following weekend. Just in time for Halloween. I guess we'll miss our space, but it'll be nice having trick-or-treaters again.

And we'll feel much safer, and we probably won't view all those annoying subdivision neighbors as quite so annoying, anymore.

The End

October 7

Careful What You Wish For

(This story is true... potentially)

I'm sure you've heard it said, what goes up, must come down. If it seems too good to be true, it probably isn't true. When the wind's at your back, prepare to duck.

Well, unfortunately, these expressions are true.

And I didn't listen.

Here we were, after we'd made bank- and I mean some *really* mad cash, as in a midsize truck load of it- working the most recent, very heated Presidential elections. I mean, let me tell you, if you can get yourself the right job working on a Presidential campaign, there's a lot of money to be made. But when you can get yourself working on *both* campaigns- yes, that's right, the campaigns of both parties- the amount of money you can make seems as if it should be illegal!

So am I a campaign manager? A publicisist?

Neither.

A journalist?

Not even.

A blogger!

Yup, that's right. A blogger.

Ever seen any of those old movies, like "It's A Wonderful Life," where there's that one scene where everyone's getting in on the ground floor in plastics? Or cement? Or the stuff they now use to plumb houses with? I think it's called PEC? It's supposedly way better than the copper pipes they used to use, and if you got in on the ground floor in PEC you're probably richer than the generation who got in on the ground floor in copper piping?

Everyone thought that the days of getting in on the ground floor of something and making a killing from it were gone after the dot com bubble, something that really turned out to be the dot nots.

Not true!

Social media was the next big thing in America, and it made the world smaller, figuratively speaking, so it was also the next big thing around the world, and if you were able to get in on the ground floor in social media, to any degree, man, was there bank to be made!

And we did it with blogging.

You see, people are more skeptical about what they see on the internet these days, but just a few years ago they believed every single thing they saw on the internet, because up until the advent of social media, when anyone and everyone could now be a know it all and a qualified source, much of what you did see on the internet was true, or, in the case of mainstream media, at least somewhat true, just twisted and turned to fit an agenda.

Not anymore. Not with social media and largely because of all the online blogs, the owners of which 'spread their wares' so to say by harnessing large social media pages and channels in order to distribute to a large following.

For the first few years, well, up until the 2016 President election, really, Facebook was the wild wild west of information. Anyone could write anything they wanted to write and publish it to a blog and then post it on their Facebook page, and people bought it hook, line and sinker. It was all good if you went to these sources to get advice on how to cook a better casserole, or which baits worked best for bass in the summer, but if you were getting your news from these sources? May God have pity on you and what you think is really going on out there, because it's not.

Don't think for a minute that the people writing that crap you read on the internet even believe any of it themselves. I know, because I was one of those guys. I'm a writer, first and foremost, and I can write about anything and make it sound true. Hell, I've written instruction manuels for Chinese manufacturing companies before, because they needed someone to write instructions, in English, on how to put their stupid plastic pieces of shit things they make together, and they paid me handsomely to do it.

Going into the elections, I'd write a story about how the Replican candidate would be best to lead our nation, especially due to whatever issue of the day that was going on at the time, etc. etc. And then, I'd turn around and write the same damn piece, stating the Democratic candidate would be best for the same reason, etc. etc., and then I'd publish one story on our blog that catered to conservatives, and I'd post the other on our blog that catered to liberals. I'd then write a piece about how much the Republican candidate sucked, and then one on how much the Democratic candidate sucked, so on and so forth. And then we'd distribute this garbage all over Facebook and make bank.

Okay, so by we, I mean my wife and me. I did the writing, she did all the spamming to the various Facebook pages we either owned ourselves or that we had partnered with others on, allowing our partners, of course, to post on our pages. At one time, our collection of pages totalled more than five million fans and our monthly blog views were over ten million. What did that translate into as far as money goes?

Between $20,000 and $35,000 a month!

And we did that for two years!

Do the math!

And then it all came tumbling down!

What went up, came crashing down. We'd known it seemed too good to be true, and it turned out it was. Unfortunately, we forgot to duck.

Mark Zuckerberg realized, finally, that there were tons of us out there making tons of money on Facebook and he was getting no cut from any of it. And it wasn't just bloggers. Anyone who had anything to sell was reaching a worldwide audience on his platform, and up until the end of the 2016 elections, they were doing so for free.

Zuckerberg has never hidden his preference in politics. He is extremely libereal, and he detests President Trump. He thought, like many Democrats, the idea of Donald Trump, until that time a real estate mogul and television celebrity, becoming President of the United States was downright laughable.

Until Trump won the election.

Zuckerberg lost his mind, and he made his bias in politics clear by swinging the axe against all conservative Facebook pages. That translates, roughly, into him shutting the pages down, completely eliminating them from Facebook, and permanently suspending the accounts of the pages' owners. His given reason? "Violation of Facebook terms and policies."

As you can imagine, when you go from making $30k a month to practically nothing, you get concerned. We contacted Facebook headquarters, and it was never explained to us what policies we'd violated.

But hey, we still had our liberal pages, because we were playing both sides from the middle, right?

Wrong! As our new President would say.

The double whammy was that Zuckerberg decided he'd start charging a toll fee, so to say, to post on your own Facebook pages. At least, as far as allowing your followers to see your posts. Basically, you now had to pay $60 for up to one thousand of your followers to be able to see your post if it had an external link. And there was no guarantee that your subscribers or followers would even click on the link if they saw the post. And in the world of blogging, if they don't click, you don't earn the advertising revenues (hence those clickbait titles that make you click). This meant we had to spend $60 in the hopes of making $3 (which is how much we'd make if all one thousand people our blog post was served to actually clicked on the link), which meant we were automatically losing $57.

That math made no sense.

Hence, we were now out of business.

We've always paid our taxes. However, we paid them when we filed our taxes. One year, after having made hundreds of thousands of dollars, and owing over sixty thousand dollars in Federal and State income taxes, we laughed, knowing we had more than a hundred grand in cash in the bank, and we were amazed to be able to pay the taxes in one fell swoop by way of electronic debit and still have loads of cash leftover.

The next year, after having made hundred of thousands of dollars and owing about the same as the year before in taxes, we weren't laughing, because the blogging bubble had burst, thanks to Zuckerberg's political bias and greed, right after the election, and we'd gone from making the numbers I've already bragged about to making less than two thousand dollars a month, and that is *not* an exaggeration. When the bubble burst, it did so like a nuclear explosion. When the taxes were due, we were broke and didn't have the money to pay them.

"How in the hell are we going to pay the taxes?" my wife would ask, sitting in our backyard, which was larger than the neighborhoods we'd both grown up in.

"How are we going to pay the mortgage and keep this place?" I'd say in answer to her question, which I knew wasn't an answer, but it's what was on my mind. We'd managed to buy our dream home during the good times, and I didn't want to lose it during the bad times.

At some point, we'd started a YouTube channel, but we'd never really focused on it, so we decided now might be the time to make it our saving grace. We began making videos about the things we do around our property, like gardening, and raising chickens and rabbits, and planting fruit trees, and we garnered a small audience, but we weren't putting up the numbers we needed to pay the bills.

Until I got an idea.

"I've got it!" I told her one day.

"What?" she said.

"People love paranormal crap. Let's make videos, claiming our place is haunted, and we'll get a larger audience, and the day is saved!"

"That's stupid," she said. "That stuff's not real."

"I know that, and you know that," I said, "but there's tons of people out there who believe it. Let's give it a go."

"Whatever," she said. "We've missed our first mortgage payment. We've got two months to figure it out before they start foreclosure."

We knew a bit about the history of our property, having been told it by the near ninety year old lady we bought it from. Our house is roughly one hundred and twenty years old, and it's had at least four deaths in it. Our driveway, for centuries, used to be the main road through our small, rural farming community. At one point, it would have had enslaved people marching along it, on the way to auction down in the city, twenty miles away. There were civil war battles fought in our fields. Three of the people who died in the house, little girls during the Spanish Flu Pandemic of 1918 were buried in the woods out back. There was more fodder here to work with than anyone could imagine.

Our first haunted video idea was simple. I was going to take the camera out and start talking as I walked up and down our long driveway in the dark. And we're out in the middle of nowhere, so when I say dark, I mean pitch black dark. My wife was going to hide about halfway up the driveway, and when I talked about the enslaved people on the way to auction, she was going to rattle some chains we'd lain out in the bushes. When I spoke of how Confederate soldiers marched up and down the road during the civil war, she was going to light a lantern we had and trail me, about twenty yards back. And when I got to the part of the road that was closest to the graves, she was going to cry like a little girl.

The plan was foolproof. Or should I say, foolworthy.

"Honey," I said, the night we were to shoot the video. "It's dark. Let's get out there and get this done before it gets too late. I want to watch a movie on Netflix."

"Just wait," she said. "I'm talking to my mother." My wife never looked up from her smartphone as she continued her conversation with my mother in law.

"Tell her you'll call her back," I said. "Let's get this done."

My wife usually loved the opportunity of using me as her excuse to get off of the phone with her mother, so I had no doubt she was going to do so this time. Our driveway is long, close to a quarter of a mile, so I decided to take the camera, head out into the dark, and start walking down to the end of the drive and begin shooting the video. My wife, certainly, would get off the phone and head out and get in place. Her first spot of action was about two thirds of the way down the driveway, so the logistics of it all seemed like good time management to me.

Looking back on it now, I should have known something was different about the night air. Sure, it was October, and temperatures dropped quicker once darkness fell than they did in the summer, but when I went out and started walking down the drive, the temperature felt as if it had dropped a full twenty degrees in the three or four minutes it had taken me to head inside and tell my wife we were ready. *You're just scaring yourself*, I remember thinking, then I thought nothing more of it.

I got to the gate at the end of the drive, and I waited a full five minutes to allow my wife time to get in place. The moon was half full, and my eyes had adjusted to the light, and the gray of the gravel on the driveway stood out, so it would be easy enough to see as I strolled up the drive, telling my story. I'd practiced my pacing during the day. The time in which I was trying to do it was seven minutes. Long enough to tell the story, but not so long that I'd lose the audience's attention.

"Ready or not, here I come," I said, hoping my wife could hear me. I heard the chains rattle, so I knew she was in place and we were good to go. I clicked "record" on the camera and started heading up the driveway, telling my tale.

"Human beings were paraded down this road, on their way to be sold once reaching the city, twenty miles away, a humiliating scar on our nation's history," I said as I passed the point in the drive where my wife and the chains lay a few yards away in the bushes. Right on cue, the chains rattled, but instead of following me up the drive, they ended up heading in the opposite direction, quickly!

Ah shit! I remember thinking. *My wife is totally fucking this up! Stay in character. Stay in character. Maybe she's ad libbing.*

If she had a plan, it was one I couldn't begin to figure out, because it sounded to me like the chains were heading for the next county, as if she were acting as if an enslaved person had escaped from bondage and was heading for Canada.

I kept going, and when I was another third of the way up the long, dark driveway, I started talking about the Confederate soldiers who used to march along this very route. My wife must have dropped the chains and come running back, without them, as quickly as she'd run away with them, because exactly on cue, I saw a lantern light up behind me, in the camera, about twenty yards back.

And then I saw another.

And then I heard horse hooves.

Stay in character, I remember thinking. *Stay in character. Man, she is really ad libbing! But how's she making those sounds? Is she using an app on her cellphone?*

The lanterns dimmed, and the sounds of horse hooves dissipated as quickly as they'd both appeared once I was another one hundred yards up the driveway. I passed our house and headed to the edge of the woods and told the sad tale of how three sisters, all under the age of twelve, had died in our house and were buried in these very woods.

"You know we're here?" I heard a voice call, softly, from the woods. My wife was doing an excellent job of changing her voice. She was only supposed to fake the sounds of crying, but she'd been ad libbing everything else so far, so this was dynamite!

"Can you see us?" the voice came again. "Can you hear us?"

These last two questions, however, came from different voices. Alas, my wife was making it sound as if all the voices were different. Three different voices, as if they were truly coming from three different girls. My wife was really going above and beyond. I was feeling guilty now for having doubted her.

I stopped filming after finishing up with something about what it's like living on a haunted property, and then I told my wife I'd stopped recording and to come on out. I heard nothing. I figured she must have quietly made her way back into the house while I was rapping things up.

I headed back into the house, and there, in the living room, sat my wife, still on the call with her mother. "Shit, Mom," she said. "I've got to go! Mr. Man is pissed!"

She got off the phone and then she stood and walked to the backdoor, where I was still standing, and grabbed a light jacket, pulling it on as she slipped out the backdoor. "Come on," she said.

"You're kidding, right?" I said, following her outside.

"What?" she said. "There's still time for a movie. Come on. Let's get this done and find out if it works."

"Stop yanking my chain," I said, and my gut was telling me that she wasn't.

"What are you talking about?" she said. She could tell I was scared, so she immediately became the same; scared. She knew I was not yanking *her* chain any more than she was yanking mine, so she ran back inside the house and I followed.

Once inside, we played the video I'd recorded, and the stuff we saw and heard on that video- the same stuff I'd seen and heard while filming it- had us locking all the doors and all the windows.

We've come to realize this is not our house and property. It belongs to them. And both are extremely haunted. And we've discovered many, many more types of "them" since that night that this house and land belong to. More stories for later, but hey, isn't that what this book is all about?

But we've turned it into a win/win. Because we're back in business!

But we've also learned to be very careful about what we wish for.

Because this time, we got it.

The End

October 8

Secret Admirer

Some of the most terrifying stories you'll ever hear are not the stories that have ghosts and ghouls and creepy crawlies, but stories that have real, living, breathing, flesh and blood human beings. We, as a species, have got to be about the most terrifying creatures to walk the earth.

Comes now such a story.

We have to go way back to 1995 or so for this story. I was a third year college student (I'd say "junior" but since it took me six years to graduate, I don't know if that would be the right term to use), and I was working my way through college by waiting tables or cooking in various restaurants. I'd had other jobs off and on throughout college, but waiting tables was the one I liked best, because if you had even a halfway decent personality and if you were halfway decent looking, you could make bank, and I did!

I lived off campus while in college, at least after my first year, and I usually moved to a different apartment each new year, like most college students, so I used a P.O. box down at the local post office for my mail. Yes, this proves that we have to go way back to the old days for this story. No social media yet, hell, no internet, really, unless you were a Government or business bigwig, and we certainly did have cell phones.

One day, as was my typical daily routine back then, I walked to the post office, which was right down the road from my apartment, and checked my mail, and then I got in my crappy old beater car (a brandy colored 1988 Chevy Celebrity) that I got somewhere for $600 the year before and headed for work. I usually didn't receive mail, which I always viewed as a good thing- no mail equaled no bills- but on this day, I had. I'd received a greeting card.

The card had no return address, so of course this made me curious, and it wasn't anywhere near my birthday or any holiday. I ripped the envelope open, read the card, and discovered that I had a secret admirer. It was a quite lengthy note, written in a woman's hand, in which the author stated that they loved coming to the restaurant where I worked just so she could see me. She went on and on about how handsome I was, and how she liked the way I moved, yada yada yada.

I was twenty two years old at the time, so number one, I was flattered, and number two, I envisioned, in my mind's eye, that my secret admirer was my age, or thereabouts, and that she was smoking hot, of course. I was excited and couldn't wait to find out who she was.

That evening at work, I made sure to give an extra smile to every pretty girl in my age group that came in. I guess I pissed off a lot of husbands and boyfriends, but I was so excited about finding out who my secret admirer was that I didn't really care.

A week went by, during which my secret admirer did not reveal herself, and then another greeting card came. This one wasn't so flattering. As it turned out, my secret admirer revealed a little more about herself. She claimed, in her letter, that she was in her late sixties, and that she was a very wealthy widow. Her husband had been rich, and he'd left her a fortune, and she needed a good looking young buck to carry her bags around Europe for her when she went on holiday.

Okay, I was creeped out this time. Remember, I was twenty two, so sixty something was ancient! Here I am, in this story, going back to the days before the internet and cell phones. Back then, at my age, I viewed someone of her age as having been born during the time of the dinosaurs. Just as I'm sure millennials view me today, at forty six, as of this writing.

That night at work, I sure was looking around at the female customers again, but no longer with excitement, hoping to see the smoking hot twenty something year old girl who I'd hoped admired me, but fearful of seeing the sixty something year old grandmother who actually did. As I looked around it seemed like all of the old ladies in the place were staring at me. As I went from table to table, making eye contact with all of the older women as I passed, they all returned my gaze and they all smiled politely. Looking back on it now, I know they were just being friendly. But when it was going on, I was convinced that each one of them was my secret admirer.

I was so freaked out, my anxiety level so high, I felt like I had to talk to someone about it. My floor manager, Tina, approached me, and she said she could tell I was anxious, or worried about something, and so I decided she would be the one I'd talk with about my secret admirer.

I filled Tina in on the cards I'd received in the mail, and she told me she understood why I seemed so nervous. She said she'd help me try to figure out who my secret admirer was, but she didn't use that term. She used the term stalker. She told me the old bat was probably crazy, and that I wasn't safe. We needed to figure this thing out, and I could trust her to help me.

The following week I received another card, and this time, the tone was taunting. "Ha, ha, ha," it began. "I can see that you have enlisted help in trying to figure out who I am. Good luck! I am not going to reveal myself to you now. I wanted our relationship to be between us. Now it will be only known to me. I am still going to come into the restaurant every night and watch you while you work. Because you are so good looking.

And I like the way you move. But you will never know who I am!"

Okay, this took creepy to a whole new level. Knowing what I know now, I should have gone to the police. But at the time, I was a young, bravado man, and the double standard with this kind of thing weighed too heavily on me to do so at the time. If this were happening to a woman, everyone would expect her to report it, and her creepy stalker man would go to jail. But when this type of thing happens to a man, sadly, it's considered by too many in our society to be humorous. And if the victim seeks help, he's to be made fun of; viewed as weak. Let me tell you, nothing about being stalked by a sixty something year old woman was funny at all!

I showed Tina my newest card, and she read it, and then she said, "Oh, my God. I know who it is."

"Who?" I said.

"You mean you haven't figured it out?"

"No," I said. "Enlighten me."

"Wow," she said. "I can't believe you haven't figured it out."

And then she walked off and got back to work. Just like that. She never enlightened me at all, and at the end of the night, I was called into the office by the manager and fired!

Okay, so you're probably wondering why I was called into the office and fired, right? Had it been the boss's wife who'd really been stalking me?

No.

Nothing of the sort.

"What the hell kinda business do you think I'm running here?" the boss, Mr. Wilson said, when he got me alone in his office. "A whore house? Are you some sort of gigolo?"

"What?" I asked, completely confused.

"Are you whoring yourself out to these old ladies that come in here to eat?" Mr Wilson asked. He was a short man, about five feet six, and he was in his seventies, but he was rough and tough and full of grit. He was a retired Marine, and he'd fought in the Korean war. When he spoke, everyone around him stood at attention.

"I don't know what you're talking about, Mr. Wilson," I said.

"You're fired!" he said.

"Why?" I asked.

"For coming in here and trying to pick up these old ladies with money. I know all about it."

"You've got it backwards," I told him. "I'm not trying to pick them up. They're trying to pick me up."

"Ah, bullshit!" he said. "Get out and don't come back."

At that point, he grabbed me by the elbow and literally threw me out of his office. I went home, dejected. Not only had I never been fired before, but he'd gotten it all backward, and I really needed that job.

I couldn't sleep that night, at least, until I devised a plan on how to get my job back. I'd take all of the cards I'd received from my secret admirer to the restaurant the next day, before it opened, and I'd show Mr. Wilson that I was telling the truth.

And it worked!

And I found out who my 'secret admirer' had been all along.

Tina!

"Tina!" Mr. Wilson yelled, storming out of his office after having read the cards. Tina was filling up the ketchup bottles on the tables. "Get in my office!"

Tina and Mr. Wilson went into his office and he slammed the door shut behind them. I heard screaming. Lots and lots of screaming, coming from the office, but I couldn't make out what was being said.

About a minute later, Tina came out of the office, crying. She marched over to the server's station and grabbed her personal effects, and then she marched right out the door, never to return.

Tina had sent me the cards. It never occurred to me to even think of how some random old lady had gotten my mailing address. Tina had been able to access it through the personnel files in Mr. Wilson's office.

To this day, I do not know why Tina did what she did. Did she have a crush on me? Did she feel as if she were in love with me?

Or was it the opposite? Did she feel like she hated me? Did she view me as an arrogant college kid? Did she view me as a threat to her position as floor manager? So she was trying to scare me into quitting? I was a pretty damn good waiter.

Or, was Tina, as I feared was the sixty something year old woman she portrayed herself as being, simply and completely, definitely and totally, bat shit crazy?

Again, I still don't know, even a quarter of a century later, as of this writing, but I think I'll put my money on the bat shit crazy part.

The End

October 9

Killing The Competition

Fall was usually as festive in the small town of Horton, Illinois as Christmas was in most big cities' town squares. Though the population was less than three thousand, Horton prided itself on being the pumpkin producing capital of the world, as the sprawling midwestern farm community grew more tonnage of pumpkins each year than in any other town in America.

But this fall, there was a dark shadow hanging over the small burgh of Horton. Small as the community was, there had been several accidents that had resulted in as many deaths. Deaths that left women widowed and children fatherless. In one case, one man became a widower, and his two children motherless.

That had been the first accident. It had actually happened back in the summer. It was the oddest of accidents, and most folks didn't think it was an accident, but people didn't like the idea of saying that someone actually committed suicide. But when they found Mrs. Hampton, hanging from a water hose in her garage, with a note written in crayon which read, "I can't take it anymore," everyone had come to the same conclusion. Her death was not ruled a suicide, however, because a handwriting expert (the folks in Hampton were amazed there were such people as handwriting experts) had concluded that the note had been written in the hand of a child. After sampling her children's handwriting, it was determined that the note had not been written by either her son, who was in middle school, or her daughter, who was going into fourth grade this year down at Horton Elementary School. And the fact that the note had been written by a child ruled out any ideas of foul play as far as Mr. Hampton was concerned.

The local police department's chief decided he did not want whispers of a murder in his town, especially an unsolved murder, because he sure as shit wasn't going to take time away from his bowling league to get out there and solve it, so the word murder would not be used in this case. So, since both suicide *and* murder was out, it was determined that Mrs.

Hampton had somehow slipped while attempting to hook her water hose up to the beam on the ceiling of her garage which held the garage door opener's motor. She had to have been confused, somehow thinking the water spigot was up there, and when she slipped and fell, she did so just right, so that the hose wrapped around her neck as she fell. It must have been a kink in it, is what the police chief said, which made it tie up in a perfect knot like that.

The explanation of Mrs. Hampton's death, that it was an accident, didn't make a whole lot of sense, but it kept vicious rumors from circulating and embarrassing the family, and besides, everyone knew that Mrs. Hampton was a morning drinker (wink, wink), anyway.

People found it odd when, a month later, Mr. Hicks died in his sleep at the ripe old age of thirty eight. He'd gone to bed the night before, perfectly healthy and in good spirits, and he simply never woke up again.

The end.

Just kidding.

It was only the end for Mr. Hicks.

Mrs. Hicks was questioned when the autopsy came back, because it was found that Mr. Hicks had died of suffocation. It was almost as if someone had held a pillow over his face so that he couldn't breathe, but the thing of it was, was that when he was found by his children the next day, a son in middle school and a daughter in the fourth grade, after their mother had told them to go wake their father for breakfast, there was no pillow on his face.

Mrs. Hicks' questioning didn't last long, because the police chief believed her, that she had nothing to do with it, because she had alibis. Her children and her daughter's best friend, Lexy. Lexy had been spending the night with the Hicks' Daughter, as the two had been friends and classmates since kindergarten, and Lexy, nine years old, had trouble getting to sleep if she spent the night at a friend's house, because she was scared. Mrs. Hicks had gone into the family room, where the girls and her son were camping out for the night, planning only to stay long enough for Lexy to fall asleep, but she ended up falling asleep herself and sleeping with them all night. All three of the children who'd been in the house that night confirmed her story. She was there, asleep before them, actually, when they went to sleep, and she was there sleeping when they woke up.

The police chief attributed Mr. Hicks' death to an accident. He accidentally rolled over on his face while sleeping, and he was in such a deep sleep that when he started suffocating, he simply couldn't wake up.

And then the police chief went bowling.

School had started by the time the third accident took another of the small community's members. And this time, it rocked more than just the children that the deceased left behind, because he *did* leave behind a daughter in middle school and a son in fourth grade, but a full one fourth of the small community's children knew the man well, because he'd been their bus driver.

There were only four buses for the small elementary school in Horton, because only four were needed. Logistically, the community's layout was a public school transportation system's dream. Horton was basically two huge figure eights which connected in the center, making the need for bus routes simple. It was like a clover leaf. Four buses to make four loops.

Mr. Tim, as the kids called him, had just finished dropping off the kids at the elementary school when he'd had his accident. His bus had gotten up to speed, just like normal, but when he came to a small series of turns in the road, turns that dangerously weaved around the side of a considerable hill (we'd say *mountain*, but come on, it's the midwest), he could not slow down. As he began descending the hill on the other side, the centrifugal force of the mass of the bus took over, and the bus tumbled over the hill, all fifty feet of the hill, and Mr. Tim got crushed by the weight of the bus as it rolled.

It was later determined that a child's thermos from their lunch box had somehow rolled up from some point back of the bus and had gotten lodged under the brake pedal of the bus. When Mr. Tim tried to hit the brakes, he couldn't, because of the thermos.

The chief of police didn't even have to question anyone about this death, though the community was beginning to ask a lot of questions among themselves, and he was able to get to bowling night a little early.

Mr. Bozeman was the next to go. He went in early October. His death, in an eerie way, was very similar to that of Mrs. Hampton's. He'd not died in his garage, and there had been no note written in crayon, and in the hand of a child, but he was found hanged to death in the school.

Mr. Bozeman was one of the fourth grade's homeroom parents. He'd stayed after with some of the other homeroom parents to help decorate the school for Halloween, the town's biggest holiday, what with all those pumpkins, and whatnot. When all of the other parents had finished their divvied out decorating responsibilities and were gathering to leave, and they could not find Mr. Bozemen, the small cluster of *always wanting to be seen doing something for the school* group began looking for him.

And they found him.

Hanging by a string of orange Halloween lights, right in the middle of the foyar, just inside the front doors of the school's main entrance.

"Jesus," the chief of police said when he arrived on the scene, trying to figure out how to attribute this to an accident. "I need a beer," he said to no one inparticular. "I'll be at the bowling alley."

The small community of Horton felt fortunate that there were no more accidental deaths leading up to the town's massive Halloween celebration. Some people who spoke in hushed tones about foul play amidst in the community were afraid to go to the big celebrations, which were always kicked off with the jack-o-lantern carving contest down at the grade school, and there was even some talk in the community about cancelling the festivities just in case, but when the town's council came together for a special meeting of the minds to discuss the issue, it was determined that Halloween must go on.

"We are starting off by honoring the memories of our lost friends and neighbors," Mr. Heart, the elementary school's principal said at the beginning of the ceremony. The jack-o-lanterns, carved by nearly every kid in the small school had been placed on display, and the judges had made their rounds. The results were tallied and the residents of the small town, a good many of them, anyway, -the ones who'd not been scared to go out for the festivities- stood by, awaiting the announcement of the winner. This was a really big deal for the small town of Horton.

"We send our thoughts, prayers and well wishes to the friends and family members of Mrs. Hampton," Mr. Heart said. "Let's have a moment of silence."

Everyone in attendance bowed their heads. Some of them cried. But Lexy, who was in fourth grade, mumbled something, barely audible, but something which the chief of police, standing just a few feet away from her, believed he'd heard. Something about *no more cheating from the Hamptons.*

"We also send our thoughts, prayers and well wishes to the friends and family members of the Hicks family," Mr. Heart said, just before asking for another moment of silence. As he was speaking, the chief of police silently and, unnoticed, made his way closer to Lexy, who he clearly heard say, "no more carving your kids' pumpkins, you cheater."

Thinking quickly, the chief made his way over to Mrs. Hannah, the head judge of the jack-o-lantern carving contest. She'd held that honorable position for the entire twenty years she'd taught at the school. "Who won this contest last year?" he asked her when he eased up beside her.

"Why, Sally Bozeman," Mrs. Hannah said. "Such a shame about what happened to her father."

Sally's father was the recently deceased Mr. Bozeman, who'd gone peacefully in his sleep.

"Who won the year before that?" The police chief asked Mrs. Hannah.

"Why, that would have been Misty Eddins," Mrs. Hannah said. "What a shame about…" and then she trailed off, suddenly realizing that Misty Eddins' father had been the recently deceased Mr. Tim, the childrens' favorite bus driver.

The chief of police looked over and saw little Lexy mumbling something else as Mr. Heart was asking for another moment of silence, remembering that it had been her thermos, Lexy's thermos, that had gotten stuck under Mr. Tim's brake pedal. Little Lexy had been spending the night with the Bozemans on the night of Mr. Bozeman's mysterious death.

"Who's winning this year?" the chief of police asked Mrs. Hannah, quickly turning to face her again as he spoke.

"You don't think," she trailed off again.

"Who's winning?" he asked again.

Mrs. Hannah looked at her clipboard, and said, "Pete Stevens."

"Change it," the chief said. "Make it Lexy Strohm.

"It's the Stevens family's turn," Mrs. Hannah said, incredulously. "Both Pete's mother *and* father are homeroom parents. They do so much for this school. And they did such a good job carving Pete's pumpkin for him. It looks just like Shrek!"

"Make it Lexy Strohm," the chief said again. "This is a matter of police business. And potentially, life and death."

"But her pumpkin looks like shit," Mrs. Hannah said, trying to say the last word as quietly as she could, because there were children and a few pruedes in attendance. "She carved her *own* pumpkin and looks like a crushed bag of assholes!"

"Aren't all these kids supposed to carve their own pumpkins?" the chief asked.

"Of course," Mrs. Hannah said. "But everyone knows that if they want to even stand a chance of winning, they have to let their parents do it for them.

"That changes tonight," the chief said. "Or I have reason to believe we might have another accidental death between now and *next* Halloween."

"You seriously don't think…" Mrs. Hannah said, proving her prowess at trailing off.

"Let's call it a hunch," the chief said. "And let's play it safe."

"Mrs. Hannah. Mrs. Hannah."

It was Mr. Heart. He'd been calling for her as she'd been debating with the chief of police.

"We'd like you to come up and announce this year's winner."

Mrs. Hannah worked her way through the anxious, if not fearful crowd. "This year's winner," she said when she got to the front of the room, and before she could change her mind, "Is Lexy Strohm, from our fourth grade."

The crowd, large as it was, was silent. They'd seen the jack-o-lanterns on display, and it wasn't that they could remember how terrible Lexy's looked, it was simply that they couldn't remember it at all. It had left no impression on them.

"We did things a little different this year," Mrs. Hannah said. "In the past," she went on to explain, "we've always encouraged our parents to help their children with this contest, due to safety reasons, with the use of knives and all. But we have to admit, that sometimes we've overlooked the parents helping perhaps a little *too* much when doing our judging."

The members of the crowd looked around at each other. They began nodding in understanding. Everyone knew that a kindergarten child could not make those perfect looking Star Wars fighter crafts, or those Marvel Avengers characters on their own.

"This year," Mrs. Hannah continued, feeling more confident now that she could tell people were getting on board with her ad libbing, "we judged predominantly on the merit of whose pumpkin had been done exclusively by the student and its originality, and without a doubt, Lexy's stood out among all the really, really wonderful pumpkins in the competition, so please help me in congratulating this year's winner."

The crowd finally responded the way it should have with the announcement of the winner, and Lexy walked to the front of the room to take her prize, a gift card redeemable for one pumpkin pie per visit at one of the local delis (and it was redeemable for life!) before the entire group. She swelled with pride, and she shed a few tears that only come from those who know what it's like to put forth great effort in order to succeed.

And there were no more accidental deaths in the town of Horton after that.

And the chief of police was never late for bowling again.

The End.

October 10

The Tale Of 'Ol Red Eyes

*For P.J.
The Greatest Story Teller I've Ever Known

"Now boys, this is the last ghost story I'mma gonna tell ya."

P.J. was old by now, by our standards. He was fifty. We were fifteen. And it was our greatest aspirations to achieve his age and his aged wisdom on our own some day, but Christ, how many people actually lived for half a century?

"Because last time I came up and told ya'll fellers ghost stories, I was kinda wondering if I was even gonna make it home or not. I'm gettin' too old to outrun the devil, or his helpers, so I gotta stop this storytellin' business if I ain't too late, already."

P.J. had grown up on the mountaintop where we were camping. It was his cabin. It had been his home for many years, before he'd decided a few years before the time in which our story is set to build another one at the foot of the hill, about half a mile away. And it was a half mile straight up and down, so it might not have made much sense, from just reading this, to go through the efforts of building another house only half a mile away, but I'd challenge anyone reading this to try to drive that half mile in winter time. This was West "by God" Virginia, and these were the Appalachian mother loving mountains!

"And the only reason I'm gonna finally tell ya'll fellers this story," he continued, "is because I feel like I've gotta get it off my chest."

P.J. was a Vietnam War veteran. He'd served twenty years in the Navy, and after he retired, he went back to live up the hollow where he'd grown up in the middle of the Appalachian mountains in West "By God" Virginia.

"Now the first time I saw him," P.J. said, "had to have been, oh, thirty years or so ago now."

"First time you saw who?" I asked.

"'Ol Red Eyes," he said, as if *I* were crazy. "So the first time I saw him, me and three of my best good buddies had been out a huntin'. Turns out, it was actually Halloween. So after we was done a huntin', we decided we'd build us a little campfire right there in the woods where we'd regrouped, and we'd tell us some ghost stories."

He had us pulled in already, even though it was just the beginning of his tale. He was good like that.

"Of course," he said, with a look on his face that said he was re-remembering something, "I was the one ended up telling all the stories."

Even in his youth P.J. had been the greatest storyteller for miles around. It's as if he'd been born with the gift. You either have it, or you don't, and P.J. had it. It's the kind of thing that you can't just get good at, I believe, and I also believe that had P.J. ever pursued a career in writing, people today would be saying, "who the hell is Stephen King?" And for the record, King is my favorite author, so that's meant as a compliment.

"So, boys, did I tell a good one *that* night! I mean it was a whopper! One of the stories that you just make up as you go along, and that's so good there's no way you could ever remember it and tell it again. It was one of those, you had to be there to hear it while it was told, kinda stories."

"You mean," I said, "it wasn't true?"

"Hell no," P.J. said. "The best ones never are. Like that one guy said. Fiction has to make sense. The true stories don't make no sense, so they're not that good."

"Then how do we know that the story you're telling us tonight is true?" one of my buddies asked.

"'Cause it don't make no sense," P.J. said without hesitation. "And it ain't that good. It's just what happened, and I'm just trying to get it off my chest."

The master was at work. By saying this, he knew exactly what he was doing. It made us want his story even more. True or not.

"So after I tell these boys this story," P.J. continued, "we all head off the hill for home. We all lived up this holler, but our houses were all spread out quite a ways, see."

I dared to look around the room, and I saw that my buddies were all staring at P.J., wide eyed, completely enthralled, just as I had been before looking away from him, so I looked back at our speaker.

"So we all head off the hill in three different directions. I get about a hundred yards down the hill, andI hear what sounds like footsteps coming up behind me. So I stop, and I look back, and about fifty yards back, I see these two red eyes just a glowin'. Why, I ain't seen nothing like that in my life."

"What was it?" one of my buddies asked. We tried to never interrupt P.J. when he told us his stories, but man, they were so enthralling, so it made it hard.

"Why, it was 'Ol Red Eyes," P.J. said, again, without hesitation.

"Who is 'Ol Red Eyes," I asked.

"Don't reckon I know," he said. "But I think I have an idear, and if'n you boys'll just stop interruptin' an old man, I'll get to it."

We all mumbled, "okay," and he continued.

"So I looked back only once more that night, because I was too scared to look back more than that, and I didn't even look back that other time until I saw the lights on in the house and I knew I could make a run for it and be inside in just a few seconds, and by God, just like in West "by God" Virginia, there were them two red eyes, just a glowin' in the dark."

P.J. took a pause before speaking again. We couldn't tell if it was due to him remembering what happened next, or if he was scared just reliving the memory.

"About twenty five years later," he said when he finally spoke again, which was only a few years back now, my nieces and nephews were up here a campin', just like ya'll fellers are tonight, and I came up and told 'em some ghost stories. And boys, on that night, I told *another* whopper. I mean it was one good enough to be put in a book. Of course, I can't remember it to retell it, because I made it up as I was goin' along. You know the kind. One of those, 'you had to be there to hear it' to really enjoy it kinda stories.

"Well, anyway, on the way back down off the hill, cause I wasn't campin' with them, see, I heard footsteps coming up behind me, just like all those years before. I could tell it wasn't a deer, or a beer, or a coon. I know the difference between a critter that walks on two legs and one that walks on all fours.

"So just as ya'll fellers would'a probably done, I hightailed it to the house and locked the door behind me."

"What was it?" I asked, though I already knew.

"Why, it was 'Ol Red Eyes," P.J. said.

"So what in the hell is this 'Ol Red Eyes thing?" one of my buddies asked.

"Well, if you'll let an old man finish his story, you'll know," P.J. said. We let him.

"So when I was up here last night, telling ya'll fellers stories," P.J. began.

"That Bigfoot Sasquatch story you told us was awesome!" one of my buddies said, and we all elbowed him for interrupting.

"Yeah," P.J. said, giggling. "That was a good one. What a whopper.

"Anyway," he continued, "when I went home last night, after telling ya'll fellers those stories, I kid you not, guess who followed me home?"

"'Ol Red Eyes," my three friends and I said in unison.

"That's right," P.J. said. "'Ol Red Eyes."

"Whad'ya do?" I asked.

"Ran like hell," P.J. said. "And it was hard goin'. I'm purt near half a century old. I'm too old to be outrunnin' demons, and that's exactly what I think 'Ol Red Eyes is, a demon, and that's why I can't tell ya'll fellers any more of these here stories.``

"What's it want?" I asked. "This demon?"

"Purt near as far as I can figure," P.J. said, which is Appalachian American for *the best that I can guess*, "is that 'Ol Red eyes just loves a good story, well told."

And that was it. No further explanation.

"You're kidding," one of my buddies said. He was the analytical type, The one to whom everything had to make sense. He went on to be an accountant for the Government.

"And that's what I was trying to tell ya'll fellers earlier," P.J. said. "The best stories ain't true, cause they make sense. Like that Twain feller said. The real life stories? They ain't as good, cause they don't make no sense."

I would end up losing touch with P.J. for many, many years. I grew up, and I left that little mountain town. I got a college education and moved to a city and became a stockbroker. Years later, when the twin towers fell, I joined the military and got to see the beautiful landscapes and war zones of Iraq behind the sites of a fifty caliber machine gun after having gone down and enlisted in the Army National Guard to get my payback.

One night, while driving across the Arabian desert, near the end of our deployment, during which I'd seen shit that I wish wasn't real, and that definitely made no sense, just like P.J. and that Twain guy said, I made myself a promise. I promised myself that if I made it home alive and not in a pine box, that I was no longer going to do the things that I didn't enjoy doing, like being a stockbroker, and that I was only going to do the things that I enjoyed doing. What I enjoyed most was telling stories. I purt near decided that night, while riding across the desert, hoping not to get my ass shot off, that I was going to go home and become a writer, and I by God did, just like the "by God" in West Virginia.

I went back and visited my old friend P.J. for the first time in twenty years after making it home from the war. I missed him, I missed his stories, but as a combat veteran now, myself, I think I understood some things about him that I hadn't before. His desire to live alone with his family on a mountain top and be left the ever loving hell alone by the rest of the world. Its people, filled with their opinions, all based on shit they saw on t.v., like the news, and from shit they heard from other people, or even things they read in a book, but not based on any actual experience. Hell, it took me no time at all to find out that if I talked about what was really going on in Iraq, and what I saw, I could get my accounts canceled on social media, and everyone would call me a liar, due to that, "my grandfather was a veteran, and he never talked about it, so if you're talking about it, you're lying, and you're probably not even a veteran" bullshit. Veteran's envy, I've come to call it, because it always comes from beta-males who never served and who feel like less of a man in the presence of anyone who *has* served.

But I stopped talking about it purt quick, nonetheless, as P.J. might have said.

But I talked about it with P.J., and he helped me. He helped me immensely. He helped me so much more than those social workers they call counselors at the V.A. and all those goddamn pills they gave me ever did. At one point, I had eight different prescriptions, and son of a bitch if I could even tell you my birthdate when I was on all of them.

But P.J.? P.J. told me stories. He told me stories of his war experiences. He told me what worked for him, as far as coping goes, and he told me that he thought the promise I'd made to myself that night in the Arabian desert would be the best promise I could make to myself and it would be a great thing if I kept it.

And I have.

I wrote a novel very tightly based on my years growing up on P.J.'s mountain. It's a novel called "From the Graves of Babes" and you can get it on Amazon, just like you did this collection of stories you're reading now. P.J. was one of the main characters in that story- well, one of the main characters in that story were tightly based on P.J., even the character's name- and it is one of my greatest honors, to this day, that P.J. got to read that book before he died, an accomplished old man and a hero, just a couple of years later.

The last time I saw P.J., I asked him if he remembered the tale of 'Ol Red Eyes. He said he did. I asked him if it was true or not, and he said, "I read that book you wrote. The one with me in it."

"Yeah?" I said.

"Be careful with your storytellin' going forward," he said, and he said it like a warning.

"Why?" I asked.

"You're gettin' pretty good at it," he said, pausing. "Your storytellin'." After appearing to think for a moment he said, "I fear you're gonna end up gettin' the answer to your own question if you keep at it."

The End

October 11

She Done Went And Threw Me Out Of The House

I'm gonna go ahead and tell you now. Right here, up front. This story doesn't have a thing to do with Halloween. Other than the fact that you may or may not be reading it in October, because it's in a short story collection called October Nights. But if it bothers you that there's nothing paranormal associated with this story, then go on ahead and skip to the next one.

Come back and read this one next summer.

'Cause ya see? That's when this all happened. In the summer.

This past summer.

My wife has a never ending 'honey do' list always waiting on me. She never writes these chores on paper, or on an ink board on the refrigerator. She just tells me what to do when our paths cross around the house, or if I yell in to tell her that I'm going to split up some firewood or go for a mountain bike ride, or a run, or hell, anything. You think I'd learn to just go and do what I want to do, but I don't mind doing what she wants. I just wish her list would come to an end. Or at least give me a day off.

So anyway, I'd come back one morning from one of those mountain bike rides I was telling you about, and she was waiting at the back door. "Eat to da weeds," she said. "While you're already sweat."

Now, what you've got to understand is that my wife is Filipina, and English is not her first language. It's actually her fourth. Most Filipinos speak Tagalog, their national language, some sort of regional dialect, which in my wife's case is known as Visayan, and English. The fourth language? Well, they'll learn one of the languages native to their locations so they can talk about other Filipinos who don't speak it behind their backs, but right in front of their faces. Hey, it's just the culture. I'm not judging, I'm merely explaining, so you'll understand what my wife meant by "eat to da weeds." It's broken English for "get your ass to the weed eating I've been telling you to do."

We had company coming over in a couple days, and she wanted the place to look a little extra nicer than it usually does, and I'd been putting it off for a while, oh, about a month or so, so I went into the garage and came out with the weed eater. I told her I'd do it after my cooldown, but she just crossed her arms, and gave me a dirty look and told me to 'eat to da weeds' now! She's a tiny little thing, about five feet nothing and a hundred and nothing pounds, but she keeps a machete hidden in that garage, and she knows how to use it, so I got to 'eating to da weeds.'

She'd gone back in the house once she'd seen that I'd actually started the weed eater and went around the side of the house to 'eat to da weeds.' She came back out just a short while later when I was finished. "You're done already?" She said.

"Well sure," I told her. "It don't take long."

She mumbled some dirty words in Visayan and took off around the side of the house to inspect my work. "You come here!" I heard her scream a few seconds later. I walked around the side of the house to join her, and she's pointing down at all the weeds and grass going along the length of the house. "Why you do not do this?" she said.

"I did," I said, and I had. Part of it. I'd gotten about a third of the way down the side of the house and I saw a cute little toad. I was able to stop weeding just in time to not hit him. I started weed eating again about a foot past him, and I'll be damned if he didn't panic and jump almost right into my spinning twine. I was able to move it in time, and he didn't get hurt, but I thought, hell, I'm trying to help this little feller and he don't even realize it. Hell, he might be so scared and panic stricken and confused that he follows me all the way down the side of the house and at some point, he might jump right into my twine and I'll kill him.

Well, I didn't want to do anything like that, so I just skipped the rest of that side of the house and went around and started again at the front of the house. I told my wife all this, and she just said a bunch more words in her native language, I think they translated to damn my eyes, or something like that, and then she kept going around the side of the house for her inspection.

"You come here!" I heard her scream when she got around to the other side of the house. I guess I'd passed inspection on the front. "What this?" She said, pointing to a beautiful little piece of vegetation sticking out in all its glory. "Why you not cut this weed?" she said. "You cut whole side, but you leave one weed? One really big weed? How you not see this weed?"

"Well, hon," I told her. "That's not a weed."

"How this not weed?" she said.

"It's an edible wild. It's called plantain. And it's the biggest one I've ever seen in my life." And it was all true. If you don't know what plantain is, Google it. And by the way, I think it's wonderful to live in a day and age where you can be a descriptive writer by simply saying, "Google it." It takes a lot of work from the old days out of it all.

Anyway, plantain is a green leaf type plant that grows up among the grass. Okay, I know I'm being descriptive here, but it's only because I don't want to come across as lazy. So this plantain, it's shaped kind of like a spade, and it's usually about the size of the palm of your hand at maturity. Not your whole hand. Just the palm. Well, this plantain I'd found was huge! It was the size of a dinner plate. I'd never seen one that big in my nearly fifty years of living, and I just figured that if that little plant, that's not a weed in my book (or this one, which I guess is mine, too), was able to grow that big, I had absolutely no right to come along and kill it, just because we had company coming over.

"Are you serious?" my wife asked, incredulously.

"Yeah," I said, "Look." I bent down on my knees and found a little leaf of plantain in the yard and picked it and then ate it. My wife started damning my eyes and my ancestors, this time, all in Visayan, and then she bent down and plucked that big 'ol plantain leaf out of the ground there at the base of the house. Hell, I figured she was going to cook it. Maybe throw it in her next batch of chicken adobo, or something, but hell, she just ripped it up and threw it on the ground and kept going with her inspection.

"What's this?" she said, pointing at the base of the four trees she'd told me to trim around. "Why," I said. "Those are flowers. Aren't they beautiful?"

And they were. I'd gotten over to the trees and I noticed that what appeared to be weeds from a distance were not weeds at all. They were long, slim flower stems that had beautiful little pink and purple flowers on top. Not big ones. You couldn't even see them from the porch, which was only about forty feet away. You had to be right up on them. The flowers were only about half the size of a pencil eraser.

Well, my wife just started cursing my eyes, my ancestors, and my favorite college football team in her native language, and she just got down on her knees and started ripping all those beautiful little flowers up out of the ground. "You go!" she screamed at me. "You go take shower!"

"Okay," I said, and I did, and on my way to the shower I'd realized my mistake. Those flowers were so pretty, I should have picked some of them for her and put them in an old, empty jelly jar with water. Here this poor girl was now, out there picking her flowers for herself. I'd been so unthoughtful.

Anyway, a couple days after that, and after our company had come and gone, my wife comes out on the back porch, and it was a super hot afternoon (we live in Virginia, that's why I talk a little funny- so much so that it even comes out in my writing, somehow), and she points over to this old chicken pen where we used to keep chickens. We stopped keeping them in there a few years ago, because it was too close to the house. You could smell the shit in the summer, and if the birds saw you on the back porch, they'd just scream and scream at you to feed them or let them out to free range, so we started keeping them further away, and we'd just never gotten around to taking down the pen.

My wife points at the pen, and she says, "Take down to da pen."

"I was just sitting here, drinking this ice cold lemonade, thinking about how I need to get around to taking that chicken pen down."

"Then do it," she said. "You can wait till later. When not so hot. But take down to da pen."

"Well," I said. "I don't actually want to take it down, though."

"You just said you are sitting here thinking about taking it down," she said. "Now you change your mind. You crazy. You crazy from war."

"No hon," I told her. I mean, I probably *am* crazy from the war, but this had nothing to do with PTSD. This was a cultural thing, so I took the time to explain it to her.

See, this isn't so much an American cultural thing, as it is a southern American cultural thing. When you live out on a homestead or a small farm like ours, you've got to have that one project that you never get around to doing, so you can sit on the porch on those scorching hot dog days of summer, and stare at it, and say over and over, "I really need to get around to," and then you fill in the blank with whatever it is you need to get around to doing. But you absolutely, under no circumstances, get around to doing it.

"Why you never get around to doing it?" my wife asked me after I'd explained all this, and I told her, because if you did, you'd not have that one project there to say you needed to get around to doing while you're sitting around on the porch during the scorching hot dog days of summer.

"You make no sense," she said. She cursed my eyes, my ancestors, my favorite college football team (which are the Cavaliers, by the way, and definitely *not* the Hokies), but then she cussed something close to me that I couldn't quite make out. I used to speak her language somewhat fluently, because I lived over there on those islands for many years- it's how we met in the first place- but I rarely speak it with any sort of regularity any more, and I hadn't in years, so I'm not quite sure who or what it was close to me that she was cursing in her native tongue, but I'm sure it would have hurt my feelings a little bit had I known.

I told her, hey, she should respect my culture, even if she doesn't understand it, like I did my best to respect hers while we were over there. Hell, there was this one superstition they had, and they had a shit ton of superstitions, but this one, they believed that if you didn't make your kids put shirts on as the sun fell in the evenings, the ghosts would play with their skin and they'd get these red swells on their skin. When I tried to explain about mosquito bites, I was nearly banished from the village, so I learned to just respect the culture, and the superstitions, and keep my mouth shut.

Well, she just started to really let me have it. She went on and on again about how I talk so slow. "Why it takes you eighteen minutes and thirty three seconds to tell story that can be told in two minutes?" I told her that was a southern tradition, as well, but she didn't want to hear it. She just stormed off into the house cursing. I think she may have been damning my hiking boots of all things.

So the next day, I'd just come back from a jog. I'm sitting there on the back porch, staring at that chicken pen that I really needed to get around to taking down but not really take down when my wife comes out the backdoor and tells me she was going to one of her friend's houses to play tongits. That's a Filipino card game. My wife and about four of her Filipina friends we have here get together about once a week and play tongits and binge eat. They all cook a huge pot of one of their native dishes and take it to the card game, and they all eat three times as much as I ever could, and don't a one of 'em ever gain a pound. Hell, one of 'em's only four feet ten and weighs about ninety pounds. She's a sweet little forty year old lady, and I love to watch her eat, because I've never seen any college athlete put away food like that (I used to be a college athlete, so I'm qualified to speak on this), and she will never, in her life, tip the scales over the century mark, I'm sure.

"You take down to da chicken pen today," my wife said, just before she left.

"That's a lot of work," I said to her. "For one day, at least. How about I promise you I will absolutely get started on it today, before you get home."

"Okay," she said, willing to meet me in the middle, and then she left.

A few hours later, I'm awakened to what sounded like someone cursing some aspect of my life, or some aspect of the interests of my life, in a foreign language. I'd fallen asleep on the back porch, due to the heat, and simply having been worn out from my morning exercise, and when I opened my eyes, there was my wife, screaming at me.

"Why you not start on chicken pen?" she screamed, demanding an answer.

"I did," I told her. "I've been sitting here working on it the whole time you've been gone."

"You sit here sleeping," she screamed. "You do no work."

Well, I had to explain something to her about southern culture again. "You never just jump right into any project," I told her. "You've gotta study on it for a while."

"What? What study?" she said.

"Well," I said, turning my head to face the chicken pen. I could see that she followed my gaze with her own, her head turning in the same direction. "There's plenty of ways to go about taking that pen down," I said. "Certainly many more than one. So what you gotta do, is you got to sit here, stare at it, and think about it for a while. This is what we refer to as studying on it."

"You go!" she said, screaming at me. "You take too long to tell story. Too long to explain. What you could say in two minutes, you draw out for eighteen minutes and thirty three seconds!"

She started stomping off for the garage, and I feared she might be going in there to pull out that machete. I know she's got in there somewhere, so I took her advice, and I got out of there. I ran up into the woods behind my house, where we may or may not have a Bigfoot Sasquatch living, and started poking around to see if I could find that son of a gun.

After I'd been up in the woods for half an hour or so, I looked back down toward the house, and I saw that my wife had already taken all the chicken wire down off the t-posts that formed the frame of the pen, and hell, she was almost finished pulling all the old t-posts up out of the ground, as well. I had thought she was going in to the garage get her machete, but she'd just been going in there to get some gloves and wire cutters.

You know, there was one thing I was going to try to explain to my wife about southern culture. One more thing at least that I really thought she should know, but she ran me off and wouldn't let me finish, because it takes me so long to tell a story and all that. But I think it's something that she could appreciate if she would be willing enough to set her hot temper aside and be a little more patient in understanding, just like I was when we lived in her place. Maybe she'll figure it out while she's finishing up all the work she wanted me to do this time. With the chicken pen down there.

You see, here's another thing about us southerners.

We might talk slow.

But we think fast.

The End

October 12

Meeting Of The Minds

Here are some of the things I've learned so far in life. Never take parenting advice from people who do not have children. Never take financial advice from people who don't have money. And never talk about things that happened in combat zones with people who never fought in combat zones.

The first two issues, and issues like them, aren't too big a deal when people start flapping their gums about their opinions. But that last one, that's different. Because that is very personal and often painful.

You learn pretty quick after getting home from war not to talk about it with people who were never in war, because there's nothing like pouring your soul out to someone about maybe some of the things you saw, did, or heard of others seeing or doing over there, only to have the person you told these things to look at you and tell you that you're a liar afterward. And it happens. People will say, "my grandpa served in WWII and he never talked about it, so I think you are lying. Hell, you probably weren't even in the military."

The danger with this, is that when these people say these things, you want to punch them in the throat, but you're not in a combat zone anymore, and throat punching is looked down on by the police they'd probably call the police if you did punch them in the throat.

If they were able to get back up.

Anyway, you learn. It just isn't worth the negative emotions associated with telling someone who obviously suffers from veteran envy (by the way, that's a term that I believe I invented, because I've never heard anyone else use it) everything or even anything that happened while you were in combat.

And then, there are others who mean well, I believe, but who still tell you how they would have done it if they were there. How you did it wrong, and how they would have done things so differently. The thing is, you have *no clue* what you'd do in combat unless you were in combat, so that's never a pleasant conversation to have, either.

This is all relevant, because I have two best good buddies who served in war who I can talk to these things about. We don't get together frequently. Maybe once a quarter. But our get togethers always prove to be much needed get togethers, because every time we *do* get together and talk about all the things we can't even talk to our wives about (war related- none of us are into infidelity) we do something that can only be done by doing this.

We heal.

A little more each time.

My two friends (we'll call them Rick and Bob, because that's not their real names) and I recently got together for one such meeting of the minds. We grilled meat for dinner, as we always do (chicken, shrimp, squirrel and wild rabbit), and we did eat of the meat, and our bellies became filled with the meat that we did eat.

Then we went up to our family campground that we have at the top of my property, and we built a campfire, and we sat back and told each other lies and half truths and called each other on our bullshit, joked about war related shit that would make civilians cringe, and then, as is always the case…

…we started talking about Bigfoot Sasquatch and all things paranormal.

The Bigfoot Sasquatch conversation is pretty simple to explain. You see, I have a YouTube channel called

"Homesteading Off The Grid" where I make a lot of videos about Bigfoot Sasquatch. I won't bore you with the details here, because more than likely you already watch my channel anyway, but what I'll say is we've had some really strange things happen on our property and we believe, potentially, some of it at least, might be Bigfoot Sasquatch related. One of, or both of my buddies usually bring up a recent video I'd made, and thus starts the discussion of all things Bigfoot Sasquatch.

I'm always the one to bring up the paranormal stuff with these guys, because it only feels natural. I mean, we discuss one thing that may or may not be real- Bigfoot Sasquatch- and we're sitting around a campfire on a dark night, consuming meat, there's no one else around to hear how insane we might sound, so why not?

Pretty much, to give you the short version, neither of my friends believe too much in either. Bigfoot Sasquatch or ghosts. Like most nonbelievers, their reasoning for their disbelief lies in the fact that they've never seen either.

About the time we'd written off any possibility of strange things that can't be found in textbooks existing, I realized we'd run out of meat, so I took the platter we'd been keeping it on and I walked back down to the house to get more meat. When I got back up to the fire, I found that my friends' opinions on all things paranormal had changed.

Completely.

"We've got to get the fuck out of here, Kevin, and down to your house right now!" Bob, who's not really named Bob said.

"There's a fucking bear just inside the woods and it's going to eat our meat!"

See, my buddies weren't scared of the bear eating them. They were both actually eating squirrel meat for the first time, and they loved it, and they weren't about to share any of it with some bear!

"Yeah," I said. "We saw that bear a few days ago. It won't bother us."

Then, we heard something moving in the forest, just up the hill from us.

"There it is!" Rick, whose name isn't really Rick, said. "That's where we saw its eyes."

"You guys saw its eyes?" I asked.

"Yeah," Bob, whose name isn't really Bob, said. "We saw, like, this white flash in the woods. Just above the woodpile. Then we saw its eyes."

"Were the eyes green or yellow?" I asked.

"White," my friends said in unison.

"Okay," I said, taking the flashlight from Rick, whose name isn't really Rick. I'd actually gone down to the house and back without one. I keep my property well maintained, mowed, and free of unnecessary obstructions, so I can walk all over it in the dark without a light, as long as there's at least a sliver of moon, and I often do. "Animals' eyes reflect green or yellow at night," I said. "Not white. And have you ever seen an animal that can make a flash in the dark?" I started heading toward the woods where we'd heard the sound, flashlight turned on.

"What is it?" Bob, whose name really isn't Bob, asked.

"It's something paranormal in nature," I said, not even looking back, but continuing to move toward the woodline.

"Let's get the fuck in the house, Kevin," Rick, whose name isn't really Rick, said.

I stopped and turned to face in the direction of my friends, who were standing huddled together in the dark, their lawn chairs folded and tucked under their arms, and I said, "that is the absolute last thing we should do. The damn thing will follow us, and it might end up doing a lot more than take our meat."

My friends, obviously not even knowing how to respond, didn't. I walked into the woods, flashlight still lit, and I said, "we know you're here."

And that's when the flashlight went out!

And I hadn't turned it off.

"We know that this is *your* land, not *ours*," I said. "We welcome you here with us. I just ask you to please, stop scaring my friends, and you are not allowed to follow us home."

I then walked back down to my friends by the fire. "Did you turn off that light?" Bob, whose name isn't really Bob, asked.

"Nope," I told him, and then I clicked the power button and it came on just fine. "Hm," I said, and just to see if lightning could strike twice, I headed back into the woods, just behind the firewood pile we keep stacked with pine for our campfires, and I said, "We know you're here," and as soon as I was finished with the words, the light went out again. "You're welcome to stay," I continued, "but please, stop scaring my friends, and when we leave, you are not allowed to go home with us."

I walked back over to my friends, and said, "we could probably do this all night, but lets freaking eat meat instead."

We sat back down in our chairs, around the fire after Rick, whose name isn't really Rick, stoked it up really good by adding more wood, and I think more so for the light, which provided greater visibility of our surroundings than for the heat it put off, because it was a very warm summer night, and we did eat of the meat, and our bellies became full of the meat. And I told Rick, whose name isn't really Rick, and Bob, whose name isn't really Bob, one hell of a whopper of a ghost story that scared them more than the white flash and white eyes they'd seen in the woods had, and it scared them more than what they'd witnesses with the flashlight, so at time time we did go back down to the house. It was getting really late, anyway, and besides...

...we were out of meat.

The End

October 13

Night Of The Housecat

Dwayne was *not* a bad guy. Deep down on the inside, buried under addictions, addictions that had destroyed most aspects of his life, and far beneath his rocky past, destroyed relationships, the current toxic and dysfunctional relationships in which he was involved, and underneath a very lengthy rap sheet (all misdemeanors, mind you) was one of the most gifted, friendly, wonderful human beings anyone could know. However, the fact of the matter was that bad guy or not, Dwayne was an addict, and he was out of smack.

And he needed his fix!

Dwayne had given up on any hopes of recovery. They say that where there is life, there is hope, and Dwayne could buy into that. He just couldn't see it for himself.

Dwayne's first couple of rehabs had been court ordered, and the judge was really hoping they'd take. He did not want to send this kid to jail. Dwayne didn't want to be in those rehabs, and he didn't want what those people sitting around in circles in church basements had to offer him, so none of it took the first time.

Or the second.

Or the third.

Or the ninth!

Dwayne was no longer a kid. He was beyond middle age, and whether he was locked up in county for his latest offense, usually petty theft or robbery, and always rooted in getting his fix, or out and living in the only place he could go on the outside world, his dead mother's mobile home on a small patch of land barely large enough for the mobile home to fit on- but both paid for- was a crap shoot. It was anyone's guess. If you saw Dwayne down at the local convenience store buying a case of Pabst Blue Ribbon, you knew he was out. If you didn't see him, he might be out, but he probably wasn't.

By the time Dwayne had gotten around the point of actually wanting to get clean and sober, it appeared to him that the time had passed. It wasn't just the withdrawal he went through on the couple of occasions when he'd actually gotten thirty days clean, as much as it was the feeling of aloneness he got, because he'd burned all of his bridges. Even those people in the church basements didn't trust him anymore. Was he really trying to get clean for the sake of getting clean? Or was he trying to make it look like he was, in order to stay out of jail? No one knew, and even when he was being truthful, he understood why they couldn't trust him.

Dwayne had thought on several occasions about just ending it all, and on a couple of occasions he almost had. Never with a gun in his mouth or a rope around his neck. Always by way of taking way too much of the good stuff, when he could score it, in the hopes of passing the fuck out and never waking up. But he always woke up, either in the hospital or in jail. He couldn't understand why if someone had cared enough about him so much to get him help on these occasions, why they couldn't just care enough about him to simply let him die.

But Dwayne didn't have any of the good stuff tonight. He didn't even have any weed. All he had was beer, and it just wasn't doing it for him.

It had gotten really hard for Dwayne to score any of the really good stuff as of late, because of those times he'd worn a wire for the po-po and gotten his best good buddies arrested. Dwayne had fallen for the dirty cops' lies hook, line and sinker. They'd caught him once with a joint, once with a dime bag, and both times those crooked sonsabitches were able to convince him that if he didn't start narking out his best good buddies they'd make up a report that claimed he hated kittens and small children and the Fourth of July, and no jury would do anything less than sentence him to death by way of electrocution. Sure enough, all it did was get Dwayne sent back to county with the best good buddies he narked on, anyway, and effectively eliminated Dwayne's supply lines, because no dealers trusted him.

This would all lead, of course, to an entire new section of rap sheet for Dwayne.

Breaking and entering.

Dwayne was paying attention all those times in lockup. He'd gone in a petty pot smoker, back in the beginning, and came out, eventually, after a certain number of incarcerations, a bonafide conman and criminal.

Dwayne had shared cells with many addicts who knew way more about scoring the good stuff than he could have ever imagined. The hardest part of it all to believe, for Dwayne, was just how easy it was to do.

"Look for anyone who gets surgery. Or has had teeth taken out. They all get scripts, and few of them ever take 'em. Their bathroom cabinets are *full* of pain killers."

When he'd first heard those words from Scrubby, one of his cellmates from incarceration whatever number it was, it was as if a learned Christian had opened the Holy Bible and witnessed to a new, born again believer for the first time.

Dwayne's first scam was so easy it had him kicking himself in the ass for not having thought of it himself. All it took was a cheap push mower from the local Walmart and an even cheaper snow shovel from the same place. In the summers, Dwayne would go door to door, telling his story to the few residents of his small, shithole town who'd answer the door when he came knocking- the story of how he was trying to turn his life around, but no one would hire him because of his past, so by God he was taking his life into his own hands and starting his own lawncare and snow removal business. Most folks wanted to give him the benefit of the doubt, and so they gave him a chance, but pretty soon, after he'd finish up their grass, or their snow in the winter, some of these folks who actually *did* take their meds, started realizing they were running out of their pills a little too soon. Some of them a *lot* too soon. And they made the connection between Dwayne's last visit and their seemingly missing pills. And they noted how every time Dwayne came over to do his work, he always asked to use their restroom before leaving.

The jig was up.

And no one hired Dwayene to do their yard work or shovel their snow in the winters, anymore.

So Dwayne had taken to not so secretive petty theft. Technically, he never broke and entered into anyone's houses to steal their pills.

Or money.

Or personal effects he could pawn for cash.

He'd simply approach houses where it appeared no one was home, and he'd knock on the door. If, indeed, no one was home, Dwayne would simply walk into the home and take what he wanted, starting with the pills, of course, as long as the door was unlocked, and in many cases, that *was* the case.

Tonight, as Dwayne was needing his fix, and lamenting about how it was nearly midnight, he flipped through channels, figuring out how to justify, in his mind, not becoming an all out, kick the door in, total and complete piece of shit burglar.

"I'll go to houses where it appears the folks are sleeping," he said aloud, flipping through the channels of the old television his mother had bought years ago. It preceded modern flat screens, and Dwayne was surprised that it still worked. Even more surprising, to Dwayne, was that he could actually pick up three channels without having any sort of cable contracts. Unfortunately, they were old, shitty, and always played the same damn thing.

Tonight, shitty channel letter C was airing, for the second time this week, "Night of the Grizzly." Dwayne had thought that movie was scary when he'd first seen it, back when he was a kid, back when he'd been a good student, a promising athlete, and on everyone's good list. Back before the shitty little Appalachian town he lived it wasn't so shitty. It was before the Walmart went in on the other side of the county, killing the mom and pop retail businesses in his now shitty little town, and it was before the internet took away the rest of the educated middle class types, because they could work from anywhere now, mostly from home, and they were sick and tired of those nasty, mountain winters, and it was before the meth and the pills swept through next and took the hearts, lives and souls of almost everyone else who remained. The ones who never left the shitty little Appalachian town.

"This shit's only scary the first time," Dwayne said, watching the shitty actors who played the main characters of the B budget classic rush into the secluded cabin in the woods as the frothy, foamy, excessively salivating mouth of the Grizzly was shot in close up while the great beast screamed. "Or if you live where there's actually grizzly bears," he said. "Ain't got but black bears 'round here. And they're pussies."

Dwayne shut off the television and chugged the remaining half can of beer that sat on the end table beside him. He'd had enough booze to remove his inhibitions. It was dark enough outside now for him to move through the streets of his shitty little town, Methville it had been referred to by many, unseen, since the city stopped being able to afford keeping the street lights on more than a decade before, just a decade after they'd decided to only keep every other light on. And Dwayne had had enough of needing his fix to wait any longer, so he left his shitty little mobile home and went out into the dark of the October night, and he began heading toward his target. And at least there were a few jack-o-lanterns lit along the way to guide him. One in a yard here, one in a yard five houses later, there. Halloween was just a little more than two weeks away.

Dwayne had decided he was going to swing by the town's crazy cat lady's house. The woman had a couple dozen cats, and he'd heard she'd recently had some sort of surgery. Dwayne couldn't remember if it had been open heart surgery or hip replacement surgery, but hell, he figured either would require quite a bit of narcotics afterward, so he didn't care.

It only took Dwayne five minutes to walk the entire length of Main Street and reach the woman's house that was located on the far end, opposite end of his mobile home. He stood out front for a full five minutes once he arrived, watching and listening, and he heard or saw nothing except the occasional movement of something small and low to the ground in the woman's yard, which he assumed was a cat. Just to be on the safe side, he waited another five minutes, and then he walked up the porch steps and onto the porch to try the door.

Dwayne grabbed the door knob and turned it slowly. As he'd suspected, the door was unlocked, and this was going to be even easier than he'd imagined. He knew that the old folks of the town, like the crazy old cat lady, still saw the shitty little town as it had been when they were younger. They always went on and on about it making a comeback. The younger generation knew it was hogwash, and that these people just couldn't move on, mostly because they didn't have the skills to do so. They'd been big fish in a little pond back in the day, but the day had passed, and now they were of retirement age or older and understood little to nothing about modern technology, and therefore, they had nowhere to go. If they risked becoming little fish in that big pond out there called the real world, they'd be eaten alive, and they knew it, so they stayed in Methville and reminisced about it's finer days from years gone by, and lied to themselves about similar days returning, and being right around the corner. The biggest advantage to their pipe dream for Dwayne and his fellow druggies was their pipe dream, in that these idiots still did not lock their doors, and on a warm fall night, just like tonight, Dwayne and the likes of his ilk could walk right into their homes and take whatever the hell they wanted to take.

As Dwayne slowly pushed the door open, making sure not to allow it to squeak, he glanced to his right and saw that the crazy old cat lady had put a bumper sticker beside the door. Dwayne wasn't surprised to see a bumper sticker on the side of the house, because it *was* the crazy old cat lady's house, and those crazy old cat ladies will do the damndest things. He moved his head close to it and read what it said by the dim light of a lamp that was on in the living room. "Forget the dog," the sticker read. "Beware of the cat!"

These silly, crazy old cat ladies, Dwayne thought, and he stepped inside and closed the door behind him just as quietly as he'd opened it. Once inside, Dwayne made a b-line to the crazy old cat lady's bathroom. Like most houses in his shitty little town, Dwayne had been in this one before. He'd either done lawn work for someone, or had been friends with their children at some point in the past, or friends with the homeowner, or he'd already robbed them at least once.

After making it to the bathroom, Dwayne opened the medicine cabinet above the sink, and man oh man, did he score! The thing was filled with bottles, and from the dim nightlight in the bathroom, he could read the labels and he was elated to see that the bottles contained various flavors of the good stuff. Vicodin, Percocet, Oxycodone. Hell, Dwayne thought, there was enough here to stay high for a month and sell some on the side to get a little beer money.

Since Dwayne had been jonesing for some time, he shoved two each of three different flavors of the good stuff into his mouth and chewed them up like candy. Like all good druggies, he'd learned early on that the stuff enters your system and gets you high quicker if you just eat it, or let it dissolve in your mouth. Taking pills with water was for sissies who actually needed them for the medicinal value.

Dwayne could feel cats rubbing up against his lower legs as he stood in the bathroom, holding the weight of his upper body up by his arms on the sink, waiting for that feeling that made him feel like life was worth living.

Oblivion.

And it came quickly. So quickly, that Dwayne almost fell as he exited the bathroom. In trying to regain his balance, he stepped on a cat's tail, and the cat screeched and ran for one of the back bedrooms. Dwayne didn't care, because he was getting his fix he'd been needing for some time, so he somewhat loudly said, "fuck that cat!"

By the time Dwayne made it to the living room, he was really feeling the good stuff, so he decided to sit down on the couch and enjoy it. He turned the television on with the remote, and low and behold, the crazy old cat lady had been watching the same channel he had been watching when he'd left his mobile home.

Night of the Grizzly!

"This shit ain't too bad when you're fucked up," Dwayne said, and then he ate another pill.

As Dwayne sat, enjoying his high, and really getting into the movie, almost as intensely as when he'd match Pink Floyd's Dark Side of the Moon album with the movie The Wizard of Oz, he began noticing a foul smell. He'd not noticed it before, but he'd had his mind on other things. "Probably cat shit," Dwayne said, and tried to ignore it.

Dwayne heard a soft growl coming from under the entertainment center. He was so high, he feared the grizzly bear from the movie might be making its way out of the television, so he got down on his knees to investigate, and that was when a paw, much smaller than that of a grizzly bear's paw, came flying out from the bottom shelf. The paw's extremely sharp claws managed to catch Dwayne on the end of the nose, sending him flying backward in his attempt to get away.

"You fucking cat!" Dwayne said, returning to the couch, and just as he started really getting into the movie again, the cat under the entertainment center started growling again. It was really bringing Dwayne down off his high.

Dwayne popped the top off of one of the medicine bottles to take some more pills, and as he did, he got what he thought was a great idea. "You need to chill the fuck out, cat," he said, as he got up and made his way to the kitchen. There were bowls in the floor all over the room, and for some reason, they were all empty. No food, no water, but Dwayne was too high to notice. And it benefited him, anyway, as it made his idea work even better.

Dwayne pulled the milk out of the refrigerator and poured some into a bowl. Then, he crushed up one of the Vicodin pills with the back of a spoon and a plate. He put the now powdered pill in the milk and stirred it with the spoon.

Dwayne carried the bowl of laced milk into the living room and sat it on the floor in front of the entertainment center. Before he even had time to get back to the couch, the cat that was under the entertainment center came out and began lapping up the milk as if it hadn't eaten or drank in days. "There you go, you little mother fucker," Dwayne said, as he sat back on the couch to enjoy the movie, popping yet another pill for good measure.

Dwayne was at the best part of the movie. Just as the big nasty grizzly bear was about to break into the secluded cabin in the remote forest in the middle of nowhere, however, the cat he'd doped up came flying at him through the air and attacked him right in the face! Dwayne's high might have been great, but this cat's high wasn't. It was tripping, bad.

This cat was tripping balls!

Dwayne rose to his feet, trying to pry the cat off of his face as he did, but his efforts were to no avail. The harder Dwayne tried pulling the cat off, the harder the cat dug in so that he could not.

Dwayne began falling down, all over the living room, in his unsuccessful efforts to remove the attached cat from his face. Stand and fall and bleed. Stand and fall and bleed. That's all Dwayne was doing, and man, had it really killed his buzz. He was really going to be in need of those pain pills when this was all over, and for the medicinal purposes this time.

Thinking quickly, Dwayne decided he'd ram his face into the wall. It might hurt like hell, but it would hurt the cat more. Dwayne took off at a run and actually dove toward the wall, face first. The only problem? He didn't hit the wall. He hit a window. And he broke through it, and he fell nearly two hundred feet to his death below. Damned Appalachian hills and all these houses built on stilts so they won't slide off those hills.

The cat was able to remove itself from Dwayne's face just before Dwayne went flying into the window. It crawled back under the entertainment center and passed out and slept off the rest of its high. The next morning, it wouldn't even have a hangover.

The next day, the cops showed up at the crazy old cat lady's house, because someone had called them and told them that Dwayne was passed out in public again, this time down the hill back behind the crazy old cat lady's house. The police, upon checking Dwayne, ready to haul him in again, found that he was not passed out, but that he was dead.

They found the crazy old cat lady in one of the back bedrooms, as well. At least most of her.

She'd been dead for days, and no one had known, because no one checks on the crazy old cat lady.

But her cats, despite having not been fed cat food, milk or water while she'd been dead.

Had eaten well.

The End

October 14

There Are Angels Among Us

Or It Might Just Be Ghosts

I'd finally gotten around to taking down the Halloween decorations, but only because I was putting up the ones for Christmas. Nope, this did NOT happen in October, it happened in mid-December, and I did not throw in that little snippet about taking down the Halloween decorations in order for this story to qualify to be part of this anthology. That part really is true. But this story doesn't need to have anything associated with Halloween or the month of October to qualify for a collection of short stories about ghosts and ghouls and all things spooky during the Halloween season, because even though these events took place in December, this is definitely a ghost story, and it is one that is entirely true.

Our day had been a typical day. We woke up early, got the kid off to school, and then we, my wife and I, did our daily chores on the homestead and checked our watches every ten minutes to see how much longer it would be before the kid came home from school. And not because we wanted to know how much longer we had time to ourselves, and how much longer we could get stuff done without the constant interruptions, all of which start with the words, "hey, Mom," or "hey, Dad." But because we missed him. We always miss him every minute that he's gone.

We are one of those very strange families that love to spend every waking hour of our lives together. And it's not in any sort of codependent way. We simply and wholeheartedly love each other, and we understand how important we are to each other. We have never been able to understand so many families we see, the members of which go out of their way to find things to do by themselves, or with friends, in order to avoid being around their families. That is not us. Never has been, and hopefully (keeping our fingers crossed for our son's upcoming teenage years), never will be.

I finally got all the Halloween decorations down, and my wife and I got some of the Christmas decorations up. Our son finally made it home from school, and he helped us put up the rest of our Christmas decorations, and there was nothing wrong in our world. We had dinner, watched a movie, one of our favorite winter pastimes when we can't get outside and stay outside until dark, due to the temperatures, and then we went to bed.

We have a very old house. It was built in 1903. We have all amenities in our very old house, but it would be a stretch to say that they are modern. We have two bathrooms, one downstairs and one upstairs, in which I use the commode when I'm upstairs working out of my office, which is really a bedroom, and we've never used the shower in this upstairs bathroom. And of course, we have a downstairs bathroom that gets almost all of our bathroom usage and absolutely all of our bathing traffic. We have electricity and running water, and we are more than comfortable in this old house built in 1903, but what we do not have, per say, is anything remotely close to modern heating and cooling systems.

We do not have central air in our house, nor do we have the most modern heating and cooling system; ductless heating and cooling. Our first couple of summers in this house, we had no window unit air conditioners. We'd moved here from the Philippine Islands, where my wife had spent all 28 years of her life up until that time, and where my son, who was born there, had spent all five years of his until then. I'd been over there for nearly six years straight, myself, so even though it gets hot as hell and humid as hell here in central Virginia, where we live, in the summers, we were still accustomed to the hotter than hell and more humid than hell three hundred and sixty five days of the year in the Philippines, a subtropical region sitting only seven degrees above the earth's equator, and where we never had air conditioning, like more than ninety percent of that country's population. So, we just bought a couple of electric fans and never thought twice about it.

In time, we began meeting people and making friends, American friends who'd never left America, and who literally would not come visit us in the summer because they felt like they were dying in our house, after having spent a lifetime being spoiled by central air, and in recent times, ductless. Hell, they *looked* like they were dying, and I actually felt sorry for them. We broke down during the third summer in our house and bought window unit air conditioners, because we wanted our friends to come back and visit during the hot months of the year, and we didn't want to see them die while they were here.

As far as heating our house in the winter, we have two methods. We have baseboard electric heat, and we have an old fashioned wood stove which sits out about a foot from the wall in the middle of the living room. What we do is we shut all the doors to the upstairs rooms during the winter and we burn wood in the stove to generate ninety percent of our heat. The only time we use the baseboard heat is if we didn't wake up during the night, to put more wood on the fire, and it burned out, and the house is freezing. We'll turn the baseboard heaters on, jump under the blankets and wait about ten minutes, and then get up and build a new fire and then immediately turn off the baseboard.

Why are we so hesitant to use the baseboard heating system? As I said, it's expensive. We decided to find out how expensive, so our first winter here, when we ran out of firewood at the end of January, we decided we'd just use the baseboard heat for the entire month of February in order to see what the difference on the electric bill would actually be. It turned out, it cost us nearly five hundred dollars more to heat our house for a month during winter using baseboard heat rather than using the wood stove. Let's just say that I have learned to keep two years worth of firewood available, because five hundred dollars a month is a lot of money to me. I don't even like to buy firewood, though I have a couple times, just because I've found it so cheap during some of the summer months. I cut, split and stack ninety percent of the wood we burn in the stove to keep our house warm in the winter. And I love every backbreaking, full body workout, sweat like you're in a freaking sauna minute of it!

On the day I finally took down all the Halloween decorations and we began putting up the Christmas decorations I'd stoked the fire up before going to bed. I knew it would burn for three or four hours before needing more wood. It's so strange. Spring, summer and fall, I go to bed at bedtime and sleep until morning, barring the occasional awakening from my batshit crazy cat, Cleopatra, but in winter? Well, I've somehow trained myself to wake up every three hours to put wood on the fire, and I'm equally trained to fall right back to sleep after I've done so.

But this night was different.

Very different!

Around midnight, I got up to put more wood on the fire. We'd gone to bed at 9:00 p.m., because it was a school night, so I was right on schedule. However, I didn't put the same amount of wood on the fire as I usually did, and I didn't set the damper and arrange the stove doors the same way I always did. I had not set the fire up to burn for another three hours. I'd set it up in such a way that I would need to get up in only one hour to put more wood on the fire, because I felt something, in my gut, telling me to do this.

I never heard voices. I had no visions. It was like the knowledge that I needed to do this popped into my head like a random thought or idea- this is the best way I know of describing it- and my gut told me to listen to this random thought or idea type of message, because my heart told me that that was exactly what it was; a message- and I listened.

An hour later, around 1:00 a.m., my eyes popped open, and I was fully awake. It felt more like 1:00 o'clock in the afternoon. I knew I needed to put wood on the fire, and I knew there was a certain reason why it had to be now.

I went into the living room, and sure enough, the fire in the wood stove was nearly out. As I was putting more wood on the fire, building it back up, I heard what I would best describe as a popping sound, like those little white wads of gunpowder you can buy at carnivals, and that you throw on the ground to make the popping sound. The sound was coming from the kitchen.

I went into the kitchen, where our water heater is crammed between the electric range, and believe it or not, the washer and dryer (yes, it's cramped in there, but none of these appliances even existed in 1903 when our house was built, and the folks who would live in it during all the decades before us had just figured out how to cram all of these various appliances as they were invented in there and make it all fit, and we'd simply followed their lead after we'd bought the house), and sure enough, the popping sound was coming from the water heater.

It was on fire!

I immediately went into the bedroom and woke my wife. My son had fallen asleep with us while we'd been watching the aforementioned movie in bed, so we never moved him to his room upstairs, and I can't help but think this was part of tonight's divine intervention, or whatever it was that was going on, as well, and I woke him up, too. I didn't want them to panic, but I wanted them to be awake in the event I couldn't get the fire out. I told them the water heater was on fire, but that I could get it out, and that I wanted them to stay awake until I did in case we had to make a run for it.

I went back into the kitchen, ever grateful that we'd been wise enough to keep a fire extinguisher beside a rack where we keep the microwave and store food. I grabbed the extinguisher, and with one small squirt, the fire was out. I went outside to the breaker box and shut off the breaker for the entire kitchen so that we wouldn't have to deal with an electrical fire later in the night. Then, we all went back to sleep, and we slept soundly through the night.

The next day, we went to Lowe's and bought a new water heater. I was amazed with the customer service, as they subcontracted a man to come out to the house to hook up the new one that very day. We did not even go a single day without hot water, which was great, because it was December.

I told this story on our YouTube channel, "Homesteading Off The Grid," and I was amazed by the replies that came in by way of the comment section, from so many people who'd had similar experiences. One of them was so simply amazing that I went back up to our campground that evening, camera in hand, and told the story in order to share it with all of our followers.

The story came in from one of our viewers named Tamila. Tamila let me know that when she goes through stressful periods in life, she'll often sleepwalk. Tamila further told me of a time when she went through an incident eerily similar to the one I just told of.

Tamila, it seems, had been going through a divorce. As can be imagined, her stress levels were very high during this period of her life, and as a result, she began sleepwalking even more.

One night, Tamila walked into her living room, in her sleep, and she lit a cigarette and began smoking it. However, she returned to bed and lay back down to sleep before she finished smoking the cigarette. She was lying in bed, dead asleep, lit cigarette in hand.

Tamila, while sleeping with a cigarette in her hand, beginning to burn a hole in the blanket, had an amazing dream. In her dream, there was a mean, grumpy, curmudgeonly old man standing at the foot of her bed, screaming for her to wake up. He kept screaming, over and over, telling her that she had to get up. She would tell him to shut up, because she was sleeping, and he just kept screaming. Finally, in her dream, she sat up and asked the man who he was, and he said that he was her uncle John and that he was there to save her life. Wake up before the house burns down!

At this point, Tamila woke up, throwing the blankets off of her and sitting up quickly as she did, and when she'd flung the blankets she'd also flung the cigarette out of the bed. She could smell burning, and she got up and extinguished the cigarette and the bed clothing. The cigarette had burned through the two blankets she'd had on the bed as well as the sheet underneath and it had begun to burn through the mattress, which certainly would have set the house on fire.

A short time after Tamila had this experience, being visited by a man in a dream who no doubt saved her life and who claimed to be her uncle, she asked her father if she had an uncle named John. Her father thought for a moment and then told her that he had an uncle named John, and that John would have been her great uncle. John had been Tamila's mother's brother.

"Why did I never know about your uncle John?" Tamila asked her father.

"He died in 1957," her father said. "Before you were even born."

"How'd he die?" Tamila asked.

"He died in a house fire," her father told her. "He fell asleep with a lit cigarette in his hand, and it burned the whole house down."

You see, even though this story was *not* set in October, it was very much appropriate for a collection of stories such as these, and I know that it gave you chills, regardless.

You're very welcome.

The End

October 15

Dr. All Hallows' Eve

"You, Doctor. What do you think?"

"Huh?" the sophomore sitting in the first row of Dr. Holt's history of world cultures class said, realizing he was being called on.

"I asked, Doctor, what you think about any possibility of spirits actually coming back and walking the earth on All Hallows' Eve, a holiday we refer to as Halloween, and which takes place the night before All Saint's Day. Is it possible that this happens?"

"Oh," the kid said. He didn't come to class with a hangover, like usual. He came to class still drunk from the night before. "I guess anything's possible," he said, barely hearing his own words over the buzzing in his ears.

"Doctor, Doctor, Doctor," Dr. Holt said, shaking his head as if disappointed. "And I'd had such high hopes for you. You there," Dr. Holt said, pointing to a beautiful young girl in the third row. Though she was young enough to be Dr. Holt's granddaughter, he was keeping his eye on her, because she was smoking hot, and though he was old, at almost seventy, he was still a man, and he was still healthy, and unlike most of his counterparts his age in academia, he could still get it up, even without the use of the little blue pills. "What do you say?"

"Me?" the girl said, sheepishly. Dr. Holt thought her name might be Sarah, but he could never remember, because he never focuses on her name.

"Yes," he said. "You."

"I don't believe in any of it," the girl said.

"Finally!" Dr. Holt said, happy with her answer and making sure to be just over dramatic enough to flatter and groom the young co-ed in the hopes his perverted fantasies could materialize into more perverted realities. "Someone who can think!" He could see the girl perk up as a result of his methods. "And tell us, Doctor, why do you not believe any of it?"

"Because it's not in the Bible," the girl said, and Dr. Holt felt the slight stiffy that had been forming in his pants lose blood. "If it's not Biblical, I don't buy into it." She sat even more straight now, hoping for another compliment from the aged professor, but it was a compliment that didn't come.

"You then," Dr. Holt said, pointing to a redhead he *almost* found attractive sitting in the second row. What she lacked in face, as Dr. Holt saw it, she more than made up for in body, and he'd kept her as his plan b, in case little miss perfect, who obviously turned out to be little miss Bible beater, didn't pan out, and she hadn't. "Is it possible for anyone to come back from the dead for any reason at all, let alone to walk the earth and take revenge upon those who had wronged them in life on All Hallows' Eve?"

"I didn't know that's why they did it," the girl said. "I thought, like, they were just allowed to come out for three days. Like a vacation."

"What's your name again, Doctor?" Dr. Holt said.

"Tina," the girl said.

"Well, Doctor Tina," Dr. Holt said, "according to a Christian minister," and Dr. Holt made sure to look over at little miss Bible beater when he spoke these words, before looking right back at the red headed girl's breasts, hoping he was far enough away from her for her to think he was looking her in the eyes, "the reason the spirits come back, is to take revenge on those who'd wronged them in life. And it's the reason this Christian minister believed people started wearing masks. To hide from the spirits of the people they'd wronged."

"Wow," Tina said, and she was genuinely enthralled. Dr. Holt was confident he could get in this girl's pants before the Thanksgiving break next month.

"You, Doctor," Dr. Holt said, looking at a young man named Bruce who was sitting in the front row. "What are your thoughts?"

"What I want to know," Bruce began, "is why you call everyone Doctor?"

"Well, Doctor," Dr. Holt began. "We *are* in academia. And when in academia, when one does not know someone else's highest level of education, one calls one Doctor, out of respect, as it would be terrible to call a man or woman with a P.H. D. or an E.D. D. Mr., or Miss, or Sir, or M'am, and then find out they actually have a doctorate degree."

"Dude," Bruce said. "We're all sophomores. This is a required class in the history of world cultures. None of us have P.H. D.'s, and I think you know that."

Dr. Holt chucked to himself, making sure he did so just loud enough, however, for the entire class to hear it. "You, Doctor," he then said, "assume quite a bit. Why, there could be a Doctor sitting in this class right now working on a doctorate degree in another field."

Bruce stood up and said, "does anyone in this class have a doctorate degree? If so, please raise your hand." No one did, and Bruce sat back down and gave Dr. Holt a look that said *I told you*. "I think you're a pompous ass," Bruce then said, "and I think that if people want to believe that spirits come back and walk the earth on All Hallows' Eve, to get revenge, or for any other reason, that's their right. And I think if people don't want to believe it, because it's not Biblical, then that's their right, too."

Dr. Holt felt his blood heat up a notch. Not because he was being challenged, or insulted, but because he felt as if he knew exactly what Bruce was doing. Bruce was twenty years old, a member of the small college's football team, and by coming to the defense of little miss Bible beater, he was probably going to get that virgin piece of ass that Dr. Holt himself had had his eyes on, not even realizing it was a virgin piece of ass until today, if she actually lived according to her Bible beating beliefs, Dr. Holt thought.

"I disagree with you," Dr. Holt said, classic academic cop-out when unable to argue the facts.

"Then prove it," a girl in the fifth row said. Her name was Emily, and Emily was an emo. She had long hair, died black, because it was naturally blond, which was good, because she had the fair complexion of a blonde, allowing the dark eyeshadow and black lipstick she wore to stand out even more. "Join us tonight," Emily said. "On All Hallows' Eve."

"Join you for what?" Dr. Holt said, and he sounded incredulous, because though he thought Emily had a hot body, and felt that she was probably a natural beauty if she didn't mess herself up with that goth look, she *did* mess herself up with that goth look, and he detested the goth look.

"Join us in the old graveyard," Emily said. "We're going to do a ritual. We're going to call upon the dead. We're going to ask them to rise, before our very eyes, so we can see for ourselves."

"Yeah," Bruce said from the front row. "Join us!"

Emily felt her face flush. She did not know Bruce. The two had never even said hello to each other in passing. But Bruce was a hunk, and emo or not, Emily was a very healthy, very heterosexual female, even though she'd gone through her bicurious period the year before as a freshman, and she was excited about the idea of getting to know Bruce.

"I'll go if you go," a voice came from Dr. Holt's left. He looked over, and it was Tina. She's not so bad looking after all, Dr. Holt thought to himself, noticing her girlish grin.

"It's on!" Dr. Holt said, excited about getting into Tina's pants well before Thanksgiving break, now.

***

Emily wasn't just a goth, she was a wiccan, a modern day witch, in short. And Emily came from a long line of witches. She could actually trace her ancestral roots back to Salem. She'd had a great, great, and a bunch more greats before you get there grandmother who had been burned at the stake for giving birth to the illegitimate child of the local preacher who the community respected greatly, and since that preacher who'd been respected so greatly had been married, well, that meant the witch had to die.

However, the witch, before being burned alive, had given birth to a daughter who was raised by close family friends, and who'd continued the witch bloodline which ran down to Emily all these years later, and one thing this family of witches had always despised were arrogant, pius, better than though men with double standards.

Dr. Holt certainly fit the bill in that regard, Emily thought. He wasn't pious in a religious sense, because he was an atheist, like most good college professors, but he was self-righteous in regard to academia and what he thought of as intelligence, but was in fact, merely advanced degrees. The two, contrary to Dr. Holt's beliefs, didn't always go together. Emily and her ancestors might have referred to Dr. Holt as an educated fool, if asked, or, if not asked.

And double standards? Well, Dr. Holt had thrown his first wife out and filed for divorce when he'd caught her with one of the guys from the college football team back in the early eighties (just another reason Bruce had drawn his ire). Ironically, it was on the same day he'd snuck out of the freshman dorms after just having had all out dirty sex with a little cuty from upstate. But what was good for the gander was *not* good for the goose, in Dr. Holt's book, so he sent that whore wife of his packing. It was back to the farm for her, since she'd dropped out of college only the year before to marry him and had never finished her degree.

Through the years, Dr. Holt had had his way with many coeds. They'd all been willing. I mean, hey, what an easier way to get an A?

Except one.

Karen.

Karen happened in 1995, and Karen hadn't been too willing. Not willing at all, as a matter of fact.

If Dr. Holt were to be honest, if asked, he would say that Karen had been the hottest girl he'd ever seen walk across his or any other college's campus. She didn't stand out in any exotic way. She was a fair skinned girl with big brown eyes and dirty blonde hair, and she had a body made for porn, and man, did she just naturally sway her hips with every step she took in such a way that made every heterosexual or bisexual male, and even some of the gay ones, stop and stare as she passed. However, Karen was gay. And it wasn't just a phase. She really was a lesbian, and Dr. Holt hadn't stood a chance.

But after seeing this beautiful goddess sway those hips as she passed him in the halls, and on campus, day in and day out, and seeing her sitting in the front row of his class for the first half of the first semester of that year, Dr. Holt couldn't stand it anymore. He was going to have Karen, whether she had a girlfriend or not, and he was going to have her now! At least *now*, on that day back in 1995.

"I need to see you in my office, Karen," Dr. Holt had whispered to her at the beginning of class on that October afternoon back in 1995. "About your last paper. Come to my office at 5:30."

Karen was only a sophomore, and she thought that the time Dr. Holt had set to see her was after office hours, but she was afraid that perhaps he was going to accuse her of paying someone to write her last paper for her, because she had, so she didn't offer a rebuttal. All she said was, "okay."

Karen arrived at Dr. Holt's office at 5:20, hoping to make a good impression by being early. She wasn't surprised to see that there was no one in the entire building except Dr. Holt and herself, because it was Friday, and it was college professors who worked in the building, and they did have a tendency to go home at two o'clock Monday through Thursday, and even earlier on Fridays.

"I could tell a difference in the writing style of this paper and the last one you handed in," Dr. Holt said to Karen after she sat in a chair across from his desk in his office. He'd shut the door behind her after she'd come in, and unbeknownst to her, had locked it. "What are we going to do about this, Karen?"

Karen knew she'd been caught. It was the third paper of the semester, and all three times she'd paid different students to write all three of her papers. She never stopped to think that people's writing styles were different, and that she should have stayed with the same paid help.

"I can explain," Karen said, trying to figure out her lie as she went along.

"There's no need, child," Dr. Holt said, sitting down in the chair beside hers. He'd never even made it back to behind his desk. "We can work something out." He then placed his arm around her neck and leaned in to kiss her.

"I'm a lesbian," Karen said, pushing his chest with both hands. "I'm sorry. But you've got the wrong coed this time, you fucking perv!"

Without even thinking. Instinctively, Dr. Holt punched Karen in the face, surprising even himself, as he had always considered himself a pacifist. Hell, the whole reason he even got a P.H. D. and had gone into academia was because he wanted to stay in college long enough to avoid the draft during the Vietnam War. But here he was, punching this beautiful young lesbian, all these years later, and having his way with her while she was knocked the hell out.

When Dr. Holt had finished, he came to his senses, and he knew what had to be done. Karen must be killed and her body hidden.

And that's exactly what happened.

***

"How about we let you do the honors, then, Dr. Halloween?"

It was Emily. She, Bruce, Tina, Dr. Holt and about half a dozen of Emily's goth and wiccan friends were in the small graveyard that sat atop a hill on campus. It was the family graveyard of the family who'd owned the land and used it as farmland before the college bought it. Four generations of the family's members were buried here, as well as, and unbeknownst to anyone but Dr. Holt, the skeletal remains of a beautiful twenty year old girl who'd had her life taken from her way too early back in 1995. Her body had been buried on a dark night in October, four feet beneath the earth that covered the grave of one of the property's original owners' family members.

"I prefer Dr. All Hallows' Eve," Dr. Holt said, hoping to impress Tina. He looked at her after he'd said it, and he could tell she *was* impressed. She was looking at him as if he possessed great powers. Bruce and Emily were looking at him as if he were a fool.

Dr. Holt began reading from the script that Emily had handed him. It was an old spell that was alleged to call out, specifically, the spirit of someone whom the one reading the spell had offended or wronged in the greatest of ways during their lifetime. But Emily had conveniently neglected to tell this to Dr. Holt, who was now, in his arrogance, referring to himself as Dr. All Hallows' Eve.

The not so good doctor read the words in old Latin. It was well past dark, and the night air was chilly. A fog had set in, making for the all around perfect Halloween atmosphere.

"There," Dr. Holt said when he finished reading the spell. "I've said it. I've said it all, and there are no spirits among us. None have come back to walk the earth for three days, and certainly none have come back to exact revenge."

As Dr. Holt finished speaking, he glanced over at Tina, certain she would now be unbuttoning her blouse, inviting him to touch her breasts, as he'd been fantasizing about doing all day. But what he saw, was not a marginally cute red headed girl with a body built for sin undoing her blouse buttons. He saw a young girl with a face full of fright, and she was looking just over his shoulder.

Dr. Holt turned around, and there, standing in the dim light of the battery powered Coleman lanterns some members of the group had brought with them to the graveyard was an apparition. It looked like fog, or mist, but one thing for sure, it also looked like Karen.

"Karen?" Dr Holt said, unable to believe what he was seeing.

Karen said nothing. She moved forward, closing the distance between herself and her murderer. Soon, her nose was touching his nose, and she finally spoke. She said, "take me," and she parted her lips for a kiss, and as creepy as the whole thing was, Dr. Holt was such a perverted creep, he actually parted his lips and stuck out his tongue to French kiss the aparition of the young girl he'd raped and murdered so many years ago and he was starting to get a stiffy.

But then, Karen exhaled, breathing fire and poison down Dr. Holt's throat, stopping his heart instantly, and Dr. Holt, slayer of more than one hundred young coeds through decades of being a creepy, perverted college professor, dropped dead in the graveyard.

Bruce and Tina had no idea what they'd just witnessed, but they saw Dr. Holt lying on the ground, still twitching, so they both pulled out their smartphones to call 911. Emily and her wiccan friends knew exactly what they'd just witnessed, so they stood by idly, doing nothing but grinning and chuckling amongst themselves.

The paramedics would later arrive, and Dr. Holt was dead as a doornail when they did, and it was all written off to a sudden heart attack. Dr. Holt had been in relatively good health, for his age, but at his age, one can go at any time. Especially when one reads certain spells of witchcraft in graveyards on a dark, chilly, Halloween night.

The End

October 16

The Roadrunner

I have a long history of running. Running from problems, running from people, and mostly, running from myself. The problem is, with the last part, especially, is that wherever I go, there I am. Me always seems to get there before I.

But I've gotten tired, so I've done something differently for the past few years. I've stayed in one place. I've found there was no one or nothing chasing me. The people I'd run from were happy to see me go, and after some pretty serious spiritual discovery, (and more than just a *little* therapy), I've found that I'm okay with all of it after all.

I also have a history of running in the literal sense. I used to be a competitive distance runner, and one thing I can tell you about distance running is that once a runner, always a runner. There's actually a book somewhat titled on that premise called "Once A Runner," which is almost okay. Decent story, middle school level writing. But runners love it, because there's not much literature out there on running. It's a pretty boring sport, really, even if you are the runner.

Running is addictive due to the endorphins the brain releases from the pleasure center once you've done it long enough to get in good enough shape to reach that level of a run. It can take up to forty five minutes worth of continuous, non-stop running to get the endorphins to kick in, but once they do, you realize it's worth it. Back in my days of psychiatrist hopping, after the war, I had a shrink tell me that I was manic, and that the reason I had been such a good runner in my youth was because I was self-medicating with endorphins, and that the proof to this theory was that later in life I'd do the same with alcohol and drugs. "Here," she said. "Take these medications, and it'll fix it all." I got up and left and never went back, and when I got home, I went for a run.

I've learned that it's okay to just enjoy running, whether the endorphins are addictive or not, or whether I'm self-medicating some 'ism or not. I've certainly found that there are worse things out there to self-medicate with, but to be honest, the worst things I've found to medicate with are the drugs that come with prescriptions. But hey, that's legal, so let's all do it, right?

Not me.

It's taken me nearly half a century, but I've found that the best therapy is a healthy diet, regular exercise, and, if you're fortunate enough to find it, unconditional love from someone to whom you give unconditional love in return. I have been blessed with a wife and son who fit this bill. The three of us fit this bill for each other. We complete each other and we support each other like three legs on a stool and we don't need medication.

All the rest? The past? The problems, the people, the toxic relationships that should not have been in the first place and that led nowhere good?

Unconditional forgiveness. It's the only way. Whether the ghosts of my past ever forgive me unconditionally or not has nothing to do with it and it's none of my business, anyway, but I can assure you that I have forgiven them.

And most importantly, I have unconditionally forgiven myself.

This recipe has allowed me to stop running in the figurative sense. Stay in one place. Heal and be at peace with myself and the world around me.

I managed to come to this understanding all in time to not really be able to run so much anymore in the *literal* sense. You see, after thirty years of doing so, combined with a military stint that saw me jumping out of airplanes (and hitting the ground really, *really* hard), and being strapped down into a gunner's turret as the machine gunner for various, massive up-armored military vehicles in Iraq for a year, all while wearing thirty pounds of body armor, has led to what the docs down at the VA call a 'chronically inflamed swollen lumbar.' In layman's terms, I cannot take the pounding. My lower back begins hurting with the first stride I take when I run. It then loosens up and feels okay for about twenty minutes, at which point the pain returns, and I must stop, or I may not be able to get out of bed for the rest of the day.

No worries. I've found the alternative.

Cycling!

I've never been too excited about cycling, because it's just not the same, and I always worried about cars on the road. *I* always slow down for cyclists when *I'm* driving, and I trail them until I have a place that is safe for both me and the cyclist before I pass them, but I also know that not everyone else pays cyclists the same respect. I also remember times, as a runner, when I had to literally dive out of the road so as not to get hit by cars. Usually aggressive drivers, or in more recent times, people of all ages, both genders, and all racial makeups texting or scrolling on social media while driving. I know there are cars that have almost hit me, while I've been running, and the drivers never even saw me. And I've always feared that if I were on a bike, I would not be able to get out of the road, and the car would kill me. Or if I *did* get out of the road, I'd end up pretty seriously injured.

However, I've never been too excited about being fat and unhealthy, either, and with the ability to only run for twenty minutes at a time, every four or five days, due to the pain in my back, I finally chose to take up cycling. I refuse to become someone I do not want to be, in this case, fat and unhealthy, at the hands of an excuse.

This backstory of my athletic background now brings us to the main part of this story. The roadrunner. And no, it's not me. If you thought that was the case, I can see why, but the roadrunner in this story is a fat and unhealthy man, who appears to be in his early sixties, who not only does not run, but who cannot even walk.

I still don't know his name. I refer to him as the roadrunner because that's what he does. He runs up and down the road all day in his really shitting looking van. It's copper in color, and I've never seen one as ugly. He used to run up and down the road in a shitty old Ford Explorer that looked like it hadn't been washed since it came off the lot, new, twenty years before, but I guess it finally died in the road, somewhere (FORD does stand for Found On Road Dead), and he replaced it with the van.

I first started noticing the roadrunner as soon as my family and I had bought our place out in the country, literally in the middle of nowhere, but fortunately, only a half hour drive into several pretty good sized towns in pretty much all directions. It's a neat location. If we get burned out going into one town to eat or run errands, we can head the exact opposite way from our middle of nowhere location and be in a completely different town that offers the same products and services.

I remember, distinctly, the first time I saw the roadrunner driving by the house. He was going really slow, and he had his window down, his left arm hanging out with a lit cigarette in his hand. He looked over at me, and I waved at him, and he smiled and waved back. He came back the other way a short time later, and I waved, and he waved back, and I thought nothing of it. But then, I saw him coming back about an hour later, same thing; he was smoking, we waved, yada dada. And then, a short while later, here he came again.

I first thought that perhaps he was just being nosy. Wondering who the new neighbors were, as I would, in time, discover he only lived a few miles up the road from us. However, this wasn't the case. I found this out from another guy who lives a mile or so up the road who stopped one day because he was being nosey. Information gatherers, I call them. People who will stop, be friendly, act like they give a shit, when you know they don't. They're just trying to get as much info on the new people as they can so they can go running their mouths about them to everyone else, as if they win some sort of prize for obtaining information about the new people first. Bragging rights, maybe.

Oh, we shut this information gatherer down quickly, the best way I've learned how. You ask them where *they* live. You ask them about *themselves*. Then you tell them you're busy, and that you have to get back to work, and that you'll just stop by and see them at *their* place some time, since they were kind enough to stop by and see you at yours. Oh, sure, you get a funny look, but nothing as pleasurable as the look you get three or four days later when you go to *their* house, uninvited and unannounced, and try to take up *their* time talking about *them*. Trust me, you only have to use this method once, and it works. They never come around to bother you out of the blue again.

So, my information gatherer never returned after I implemented my method, and he and his wife make sure not to speak to me and my wife at our kid's school, out of fear, I believe, that we'll just show up again, and that's how we prefer it. We chose to live in the middle of nowhere, where we have no immediate neighbors, because we don't want neighbors.

Period.

However, while the information gatherer was standing at the edge of my property with me, where he'd pulled into our long, private driveway on the day he'd stopped by to grab his gossip fodder, we saw the roadrunner drive by, window down, lit cigarette in hand, and he waved at us.

"What's that guy's story?" I asked the information gatherer.

"Oh," he said, lighting up and smiling, eager to jump at the opportunity to gossip. Most folks like this man, I believe, in times past, where women, but in this day and age, there seems to be a lot of beta-males out there playing this role. "We call him the watcher."

"Why?" I asked, wondering just where this man's wife kept his balls that she obviously had in a jar. Did she keep that jar in her purse? Or perhaps she'd hidden the jar from him in the attic so he could not sneak it out of her purse and get his balls back?

"That's what he does," the beta-male said. "He drives up and down the road all day, watching what everyone else is doing."

"Why does he do that?" I asked, wondering if this man may actually have female parts inside the pleated pants he was wearing.

"Not sure," beta-male said. "I heard he had a stroke a few years back. He can't walk or something. So he just drives around all day."

"Hm," I said. "Interesting," even though it wasn't. "Okay," I said. "I'm busy as hell, and I have to get back to work, but I'll come by and see you here in a few days," and well, I already told you how that went.

As time went by, I came to accept the fact that I might have once been a runner, but now I was merely a guy who cycled a lot and ran occasionally. But it was keeping the middle age spread off, so that was all right.

For othe first couple of years on our property, I biked through all four seasons, amazed during the fall of how beautiful the colors were. Amazed in winter, when the leaves were gone, at just how many houses were actually out on these old country backroads and could only be seen that time of year because the leaves were gone. Amazed in the spring how beautiful it was to watch everything come to life at an average speed of twelve miles per hour and no windshield. You see so much more when you're on a bicycle than when you're going fifty miles an hour in a vehicle and you have a slab of glass between you and the world. And then, in summer, I'd be amazed at how all the green completely hid all of those houses I'd seen in the winter, and just how damn hot it gets in Virginia.

One hot, July morning this past summer I'd biked up to the only business in our part of the world. A small convenient store that had been family owned for more than ninety years. Sadly, the store is now closed, I believe, at the hands of Covid 19.

At any rate, I saw the roadrunner. His van was parked off to the side of the store, and he had his hand extended out the window, and he was holding cash this time, not a cigarette.

"Well if you can't get up off your ass and walk, how the hell do you get in your damn vehicle?" I heard a sour, bitter voice say, and the voice was coming from a sour, bitter old man standing only feet away from the roadrunner's vehicle. I'd seen this man around. He'd damn near run me off the road on my bike on more than one occasion. In my younger years, I would have walked up to him and confronted him, and probably whipped his ass, but I've outgrown such foolishness.

The bitter old bastard walked off and went into the store, leaving the roadrunner there in the lot by the store alone. I saw an opportunity to say hello for the first time after a few years of always waving, and potentially, practice a random act of kindness.

"Hi," I said, walking over to the roadrunner's van. I told him my name, and he told me his, and I asked him if he needed help. He told me that he wanted someone to go into the store and buy him a cup of coffee and the morning paper. He handed me a five dollar bill and told me I could keep the change. He explained that he'd had a stroke several years before, and that he could walk, some, but it was very difficult, and that simply the small amount of physical exertion that was required to get into his van to drive around and then get out of it once home was enough to keep him in bed the rest of the day.

"Buddy," I said, "you don't have to explain all that to me. I'll get you what you want, and I'm not keeping your change." I took his money, went into the store, and I bought him his paper and coffee. On my way into the store, the bitter old bastard who'd refused to help the roadrunner out was coming out, and he intentionally bumped into me. "There ain't nothin' wrong with that man," he said. "He's milkin' the system, and you're'a helpin' him do it!" And then he got in his truck and drove off.

I'd gotten a Gatorade for myself while in the store and I drank it while the roadrunner had his coffee in his van. It appeared as if simply raising the cup of coffee to his mouth took great effort. His hand shook so much that if he hadn't had a lid on his cup, he definitely would have spilled.

We both finished up our drinks, and I jumped on my bike to finish my ride, and he took off to only God knows where, to drive his endless loops for as long as he could before going home to sleep away the rest of the day.

There is one spot on my favorite bicycle route that absolutely scares the hell out of me. It's a series of kiss your ass turns that go straight down a mountainside. The spot is absolutely beautiful, and there are views to die for. The problem is that when people drive through these kiss your ass turns, they don't seem to slow down one bit. The turns are so sharp you cannot see around them, and I don't know how many times I've gone through them, ever so carefully, and ever so slowly, and had cars come blazing around the turn from the other direction and completely on my side of the road. There are so many skidmarks on the road here, you'd think people would have had enough close calls that they'd slow down, but obviously the close calls meant nothing to them.

I was at this particular part of the road, when guess who came barrelling around the turn, from the other direction, and on my side of the road? It wasn't the roadrunner. It was the old prick who hadn't helped the roadrunner with a cup of coffee and a morning paper. And I know the sonofawhore saw me, because just before he almost smacked into my bike, headon, the sonofawhore smiled!

I turned at the very last second, deciding to take my chances with the sharp dropoff into oblivion over the side of the hill rather than to take them with the front grill of a Ford F350 Supercab, as I didn't think it would be the Ford found on the road dead this time.

I learned two things. First, just like in airborne school, where they teach you for three weeks how to land properly when hitting the ground after jumping out of a perfectly good airplane, a method called a parachute landing fall, or PLF, and no one ever does a proper PLF after having jumped out of a perfectly good airplane, no matter how greatly they perfected it at ground level and from those stupid twelve feet high platforms where we swung from ropes, no one ever does a proper PLF when flying over the side of a mountain on a mountain bike after having been run off the road by an asshole in a truck, either.

Secondly, I learned that those bike helmets, the ones that are very expensive, and look so sleek and aerodynamic, yet brittle, are just that. Brittle. Because when my head slammed into the tree about halfway down the hill, my helmet shattered, and I was knocked the ever-loving fuck out.

***

Blackness. Silence. Bright light. Man standing over me, looking down. Looks familiar. Stubbled face. Dirty. Stinks. Blackness. Silence.

Dragged. Uphill. Steep. Big Man. Stops. Thrown over shoulder. Bad smell. Big man. Strong. Grabs Tree. Pulls. My weight on his back. Blackness. Silence.

Bright light. Asphalt. Flopped on back. Head rolls. Copper van. Shitty. Rustbucket. Big man. Dirty. Slides side door open. Lifted. Lain in van. Blackness. Silence.

Bright lights. Men in masks. Women in masks. Hell? Heaven? Blackness. Silence.

***

"Wakey, wakey, eggs and bakey," the nurse said. "Let's get some solid food in you."

"What the fuck?" I said. It wouldn't have been my first statement, had my mind been working, but I had a hell of a headache, and who the hell, in their fifties, says 'wakey, wakey, eggs and bakey,' to someone else the same age?

I was in the hospital, and that's where I stayed for two more nights. The doctor told me for observation, as I'd suffered a hell of a concussion, but miraculously no broken limbs. He said it was important I stay at least two more nights so he could keep an eye on my vitals. I'm not a dumbass. I knew that translated to *my insurance company would pay the hospital for me to stay for two more nights*. After that they'd stop paying, and I would be proclaimed miraculously recovered.

The doctor explained to me that I'd been in a bicycling accident. He said I must have been going too fast or something, because I flew over the side of the mountain and went headfirst into a tree. I told him that I'd been run off the road by a truck, and he looked down for a minute, thinking and then he said, and I quote, "you're probably just imagining that. From the hit you took. The police said there were no skid marks where you went over, so it couldn't have been a truck. Surely, if someone saw that they were going to hit you, they would have at least hit the brakes."

Not that asshole in the big Ford, obviously.

"How did I get here?" I asked.

"No one knows, really." The doctor said.

"How the hell can no one know?" I asked.

"You were lying on the sidewalk in front of the emergency room entrance," he said. "Someone found you and came running in. The medics rushed out to get you, and now here you are?"

"How did I get to the E.R. doors?" I asked.

"Who knows," the doctor said, and he stood up and left the room without even saying goodbye.

***

I've never lived in fear, and I never will. Because living in fear is not living. It is merely existing. It is sitting around, waiting on your turn to die. The very day I got home from the hospital, I started biking again. And I continued to go on my favorite routes, including the one where I'd been run off the road.

I would see the roadrunner occasionally, and I'd wave, and he'd always smile and wave back, but if I were to see him parked beside the road somewhere, taking in the beautiful view on the other side of his windshield, or parked down at the old store, I'd try to approach him, but he'd always speed away. It was the strangest of things. As if he didn't want me to ask him what I wanted to ask him.

I let it go and went on with life, and thought very little of it, until one day, a few months later, when I was biking through the very turns where I very well could have been killed. I came around the sharpest of the turns, with the steepest drop off over the mountain just off of the side of the road, the very spot where I'd been run off the road only months before, and there sat the roadrunner in his van.

And a state police patrol car.

And a wrecker.

I looked out over the precipice, and man, was it a beautiful view. Here we were. October again. Halloween in the air, as well as the smell of the falling leaves, and all was good with the world…

…and then I saw the Ford F-350 Supercab being pulled up into view by way of the wrecker.

"And you didn't see anyone else out here when you came up on this wreck?" the state police officer was saying to the roadrunner as I drew near. I'd gotten off my bike and left it by the road.

"No one but me," the roadrunner said. "A couple cars came by after I called 911, but they didn't stop to gawk. They just kept on goin'."

"And then the ambulance came," the state trooper said. "Yup," the road runner said. "Got here just before the wrecker."

"Well, what I don't get," the state trooper said, "is why when I go down over that hill, it looks to me like the man was trying to climb up, but someone kept kicking him back down. I saw the footprints. And if no one else was out here, who was it that kept kicking him down the hill?"

"You blaming me?" the roadrunner said.

"I'm not blaming anyone," the trooper said. "Just curious."

"Step back," the roadrunner said. The trooper did so, and the roadrunner opened the door of his van. He took one step out of the van...

...and fell flat on his face.

The trooper and I rushed to the aid of the roadrunner. "No!" he yelled, and slowly and methodically he rose on his own. He first rolled over on his back, and then, by grabbing the bottom of his van, where he was able to reach the floor well due to his open door, he sat up. Slowly and methodically he pulled himself up, using the van, and he stood. He took one feeble step, by way of holding onto the van's door, and got right in the trooper's face. "Would you like to show me the footprints? I'll put my foot in them, and let's see if they match."

"No," the trooper said, and he said it in a voice that let me know he felt like a total ass. He'd been accusing a man who could barely stand, let alone walk, of having walked partway down a very steep hill and then kicking a man, a man I'd soon find out had been a dying man, and a man who was now dead, back down over the hill as he was trying to climb back up to the road for help after having driven his truck over the mountainside and hit a tree. "I'm so sorry," the trooper said. "Just none of it makes sense. I know this man has lived out here his whole life, and I don't see how he could have gone off a road he could drive with his eyes closed."

"Excessive speed," I said. The trooper looked over at me, and it was the first time, I believe, that he even realized I was there. "This guy ran me off the road on my bike at this very spot months ago," I said. "I've seen him go through these turns so many times, fishtailing, I knew this was probably just a matter of time before happening, anyway."

The trooper looked at me, and I could tell he was trying to decide whether to believe me or not, and I knew that he did believe me, because everything I'd just said was the truth.

"Well," the trooper said. "I'll go inform the family. And I'm not looking forward to it, because his wife's as much of a miserable bitch as he was a miserable old bastard. Hell, she's probably going to be happy about this."

The trooper walked over to his squad car and drove off, and the wrecker took off down the road hauling the huge ass Ford F-350 Supercab that had nearly killed me months before and which, today, had killed its owner.

"Did you?" I said, turning toward the roadrunner, ready to ask him the question I'd been wanting to ask him these past few months, but he was already driving away as well. He had his arm out the window, a lit cigarette in his hand, and I could see his big, giant smile in his side view mirror as he waved to me.

The End

October 17

Revenge From Beyond The Grave

This story is short.

This story is sweet.

This story is true.

One of the most chilling stories I've ever heard in my life, came not from P.J. on top of Fork Mountain, back in Appalachiastan, during my youth, but after I'd reached middle age, and it came by way of a stranger in the comment section of a video on our YouTube channel Homesteading Off The Grid.

The first video we ever recorded and published that went viral was a video titled, 'How to get rid of an annoying neighbor with a crayon.' If you're reading this anthology, it's highly likely that you saw that video, and it's how you came to know of me in the first place.

A woman who simply went by the YouTube user id 'thereisgrace,' who we will refer to as Mrs. G in this story, commented on that video, and she told me the following story, which she swore was true, and I have every reason to believe her:

Mrs. G and her husband, Mr. G, lived in New York. Not the city, but the state, and out in the country. A very rural area. Much like where my homestead is located in central Virginia. Mr. and Mrs. G had two daughters, teens I believe, and an old bluetick hound, a male, named Rex.

Rex and Mr. G were the best of friends. How could they not have a common bond? Two males, living with all those females? They had to be close.

The G family also had an annoying neighbor. We'll call him Rocky. Not because he was a boxer, but because he loved to throw rocks at Rex at night if the dog made any sort of sound, or not.

Sadly, Mr. G's mother died one fall, in the month of October, and the family had to head upstate to attend the funeral. They were gone for a few days and a couple of nights. They'd made arrangements for a friend to come see to Rex in their absence, which that friend did. However, when the G family got home, they found dozens upon dozens of rocks in their yard from where Rocky had pelted Rex with rocks the whole time the G family had been gone.

Mrs. G was livid! Not just because she loved the dog, and because it had been a very mean and inhumane thing to do, but because she loved her husband so much, and she knew how much the dog meant to *him*. Mrs. G shared in her story with me that there were times when she'd put a doggy sweater on Rex just before Mr. G got home from work, and when he did get home from work and saw Rex in his cute little doggy sweater, he would light up like a Christmas tree, and the two of them would hang out the rest of the evening.

Mrs. G said she felt she was owed an apology, and Mr. G told her to calm down and that he would go talk to Rocky, which he did. Rocky offered no apology, and he'd simply bitched and complained about how Rex had barked and howled the whole time the family had been away for the funeral. Mr. G told Mrs. G to forget about it, and to simply ignore the spat.

Time went on, and sadly, about a year later, Mr. G passed away. The family mourned, and they continued moving forward, and then one day, a short while after, Rocky came knocking at Mrs. G's door. He told her he wanted to apologize for all the rocks that he'd thrown at the family's dog. And that it had to stop.

"Then stop throwing them," Mrs. G said, matter of factly.

"That's not what I mean," Rocky said. "I have. That's not what has to stop."

"What has to stop?" Mrs. G asked, confused.

"The rocks on the hood of my car," Rocky said.

As it turned out, after Mr. G had gone over to Rocky's and confronted him about all the rocks he'd thrown at Rex more than a year before, and Rocky had refused to apologize, Rocky continued to throw rocks at Rex, and at some point, either late at night, or very early the following morning, Mr. G. would collect the rocks that Rocky had thrown at his best friend, Rex, and he would lay them on the hood of Rocky's car. And the thing of it was, even after Mr. G had passed, it continued. Rocky woke up every morning with rocks placed on the hood of his car.

"But my husband passed away a few weeks ago," Mrs. G told Rocky when he'd told her all of this.

"I know," Rocky said, "and I'm sorry for your loss. And I feel like a jerk. And I've stopped throwing the rocks, but I feel like I had to come give you the apology that you always felt you deserved and that you *did* deserve, but which I never gave, or there's going to be rocks on the hood of my car every day for the rest of my life."

"Thank you," Mrs. G said, and Rocky left and he stayed straight, never throwing anymore rocks at Rex...

...and he never found another rock on the hood of his car again.

The End

October 18

P. J.'s Cabin

Every fall, when the changing of the colors of the leaves on the trees is at its peak, usually mid to late October, there's a special place I always go to in my mind. I went to this place, instinctively, in late October, even when I was living in Asia or the Middle East, and there was no changing of *any* leaves, but the heart knows when it's time to go, and it tells the mind, so though I may have been surrounded by desert sands, or walking along beautiful tropical beaches, in my mind, I was back in the mountains of Appalachia, at that special place, in that special cabin.

There is a small, handbuilt cabin that sits on top of a mountain called Fork Mountain, because it is in the middle of the two main forks of a river named Cherry. This cabin, P.J.'s cabin, is where I met a man named Philip James Ables, or P.J., as his friends called him, and P.J. was the greatest storyteller I ever knew.

Yes, we're talking about the same P.J. here, who in an earlier story, introduced us to 'ol Red Eyes. But long before he introduced some of my childhood best friends and me to 'ol Red Eyes, he'd introduced us to plenty of other ghosties and ghoulies by way of his tall tales, most of which we had every reason to believe were true. When P.J. would allow us to spend the nights, or the weekends, or even a week during hunting season in his old cabin that he and his family had lived in for years, before moving to the foot of the mountain it sat on due to harsh winters, he would always join us and tell us the most spine tingling tales we'd ever heard. P.J.'s cabin was a very special place, and it's only because the man who'd built it, and who'd allowed us to use it, and who joined us and told us his tales when we stayed there, P.J., was a special person, indeed.

The first tale P.J. ever told us is one that I still consider his best. It was a story, not that took place at his cabin, but at an old abandoned house in an old abandoned town about fifty miles away from his cabin.

Many folks don't realize it, but there are plenty of abandoned towns and communities out in the hills of Appalachia, the Blue

Ridge Mountains, and pretty much any secluded forested area across the entire United States. Many of them were old coal or timber towns, at least in Appalachia that had been walked away from, by all residents, after aforementioned resources were used up or fully harvested. There are also some old, abandoned towns out there in the middle of the woods that were started as Christian missions that never gained traction and were merely deserted after several houses and a town hall or other public building was built. They're out there, these small, abandoned and now overgrown hamlets, and P.J.'s first story took place in one such place.

Before we get to P.J.'s first story, however, I'd like to tell you a bit of a funny story about the first time that a couple of my buddies and I spent the night in P.J.'s cabin. We knew he and his family no longer lived in the cabin, and we knew he used it basically as a mancave, or a hunting camp. He'd told us as much before when we'd run into him out in the woods, which was regularly, because as boys, we lived in the woods, and as a man, so did P.J. Actually, it's how we'd met him. We were all just out in the woods at the same place and at the same time one day. I believe it might have been squirrel season and we'd all been out hunting.

Anyway, we fantasized about spending the night in P.J.'s cabin. Especially in October. It was hunting season. We could wake up in the morning and already be out there with the squirrels and the turkeys, or the deer if we'd taken our bows. And, as kids who lived in town, with all the modern conveniences and amenities towns have to offer, we fantasized of what it would be like to have to build a fire in P.J.'s old wood stove that sat in his living room before going to bed, because if we didn't, we'd freeze to death after the temperatures dropped, potentially into the thirties, or lower, after midnight. However, we were too shy to ask P.J. if we could camp in his cabin.

So, one day, we went up to his cabin, and we broke our backs doing a ton of yard work. P.J. kept a yard around his cabin, maybe twenty yards by twenty yards, cleared out. The rest of the area was forest. He mowed the yard portion with a push mower, and he had a weedeater, and we knew where he kept all this equipment, so we took it upon ourselves to go up and mow his grass. It looked like it had been a month since it had been mowed. We weeded after we mowed, and we gathered and stacked up any fallen tree limbs or branches that were within close proximity of his cabin, and we even went about and collected rocks and filled in holes on the small dirt driveway which we'd later learn always got washed out when it rained.

P.J. came up about the time we (there were three of us) were finishing up with all the work he never asked us to do, and needless to say, he was very pleasantly surprised. He went on and on about how great the place looked, the whole while, one of my buddies elbowing me, nudging me to ask him if we could stay in his cabin, and when I finally worked up the courage and did so, he laughed as hard as he could, and he said, "Well of course. All you had to do was ask. I hope ya'll fellers didn't come up here and do all this work thinking it was required in order to stay. You boys can stay up here anytime you want." And thus began our regular campouts at P.J.'s cabin.

That first night- the night after we'd done all that backbreaking labor that wasn't necessary- we would learn something about our new friend, P.J. Quite a bit, actually, as he came up and spent several hours with us before retreating to his new house he'd built down at the foot of the hill. We'd learn that P.J. had been born and raised on this mountain. We'd learn that he left the area for twenty two years to serve in the United States Navy. We found out he was a combat veteran of the Vietnam War. We found out that when he got back from the war, and after he'd retired from the Navy, he'd built this cabin with his own hands, as a way to have a place to live far from mankind, after what he'd experienced during his military career, and his wartime service, and one of us, the author of these words, would come to understand exactly what he meant and why this was so important years later after his own wartime service.

We also found out that P.J. had lost a son. A young man named Marlin, who was about twenty years old when he'd passed, and who had passed while building his own cabin on the hill just above the one in which we were staying. Over the years, we would stay in that unfinished cabin as well, but always reluctantly and only rarely.

And this is all part of P.J.'s first story.

That first night in P.J.'s cabin, after we'd heard many stories of P.J.'s life's history, he told us a hunting story. He, his son Marlin, and another man, Bobby, used to go to this abandoned town I mentioned earlier and hunt squirrels in early October. They were drawn to the location, P.J. told us, because the gray squirrels and fox squirrels there were not gray and red, like they're supposed to be, but black. We asked him how in the world all the squirrels could be black, and he said he had reason to believe that there were dark forces still living within this old, abandoned community.

P.J. explained that there were only half a dozen houses or so in the small community, which had been abandoned probably just before WWII. And inside the houses, it looked like nothing had been packed for a planned move. All the furniture was still in the houses, family pictures on the wall, and in one house, there was even the remains of a meal on an old dinner table. "It was as if," P.J. told us, "everyone just vanished into thin air."

P.J., Marlin and Bobby preferred to stay in one particular house when they'd go hunting there on the weekends, simply because it had been the house they stayed in on their first trip and they didn't see any need to change. And the stories P.J. told of this house? They were book worthy, but P.J. was not a writer. He passed stories on the old fashioned way; orally. And it's a true honor to have heard them, and now, thirty years later, put at least one of them, this one, in a book.

"The last time we went there," he told us, "we was all upstairs, and Marlin and Bobby were sleepin', and I just couldn't sleep. The whole upstairs had been gutted, so it was just one big room. And we was laying there, with our heads up against the wall, and I kept hearin' what sounded like scratchin' sounds coming from the other side of the wall. Like something was trying to get in.

"Well," he continued, seeing that we'd all been drawn in, and this was the part of our camping adventure we'd never planned on. Fire in the wood stove. Check. Already in a prime hunting location when the sun came up. Check. Hearing one of the creepiest tales we'd ever hear in our lives? Hadn't planned on it, but here we were, and the old storyteller had us hooked! "I just reached my fist up and banged on the wall," he continued, "and it sounded like these two little feet just took off running across a hardwood floor on the other side of the wall, ran about twenty feet or so and stopped. But the thing was, there wasn't no room on the other side of that wall. Just the outside was out there, because it was the side of the house.

"Just as soon as I started trying to figure out how that was possible," he continued, "I could hear what sounded like little feet scurrying back over to the wall. Sure enough, it got right back to the wall, and it started scratching again, and I pounded the wall again with my fist, and it scurried away. It came back, and I scared it again, but this time, after it scurried away, I didn't hear no little tiny feet scurrying back, I heard BOOM BOOM BOOM, giant feet coming back, like it had gone and got momma, and momma was mad!"

"What'd you do?" I said.

"I woke up Marlin and Bobby and told 'em we had to make a run for it, cause there was something on the other side of the wall, and they told me I was nuts and rolled back over and went back to sleep. I never heard no more scratching that night, and I eventually fell asleep.

"All kinds of weird stuff started happening after that," he said. "Like, the next day, I'd been out huntin' all morning, and I came back to the house for lunch, and after I ate, I'd gone upstairs to take me a nap. I guess I didn't get near enough sleep the night before, with the scratching and the footsteps and all. So after I slept for a right good while, I woke up, and I heard footsteps downstairs. I go to the head of the stairs and look down, and Bobby's down there making him a sandwich and heating up a can of soup on our Coleman camp stove for lunch. I asked him if he killed any squirrels, and he said he didn't see a single squirrel all morning. I told him to enjoy his lunch and I went back to sleep.

"Well, I woke up about half an hour later, and I went downstairs to fix me a cup of coffee before heading back out in the woods to kill me some of those black squirrels, and here comes Bobby walking through the door. He had four of those black squirrels with him, and he told me he was gonna skin 'em and clean 'em after he ate lunch.

"I said, 'Bobby, you was just in here eatin' lunch a little while ago,' and he said, 'I've been out all day, P.J. You drinking already?' And I wasn't. And I found the can of soup he'd heated up. It was in the trash. Someone or something had been there, but Bobby swore it wasn't him, and I watched him eat his soup and sandwich, and he was ravished. He didn't look like a man who'd just eaten lunch a half hour before."

P.J. took his twelve gauge pump action shotgun and headed back into the woods. He shot a few squirrels that afternoon, but what happened at sundown he said he'd never seen and he never could explain.

"Now, I know which way a shadow's supposed to fall," he said. "On the opposite side of you that the sun's on."

"Huh?" we asked, lost.

"When the sun started going down," he said, "it's like there was some kind of glitch. Like something you'd see on an old television after midnight, when the station signed off the air. And then, after that, all the shadows were being cast in the opposite direction they should have been. I'm telling you boys," he said, and he slammed his right fist into the open palm of his left hand, "I saw it, and it happened, and to this day I can't explain it!"

When P.J. got back to the house that evening, Bobby and Marlin were already there, and Marlin was out in the front of the house, just inside a massive brush and bramble pile you had to carefully cross to get to the front door of the house, carving his name into the side of a giant beach tree. "What in fool hell are you doing, boy?" P.J. asked Marlin when he saw what he was doing. "You don't want to let this place know anything about you." But Marlin giggled and finished off the bottom of the letter n.

"I always knew that'd come back to haunt him," P.J. said, and I could hear in his voice that he hadn't ruled out the idea that Marlin's carving of his name into the tree at this obviously haunted house and location may have caught up with him a year later. The year that he died.

That night, while Marlin and Bobby slept, P.J. lay awake, waiting for his little visitor to come back from the other side of the wall. But it didn't. Something else came.

Bats!

And lots of them!

The reason the men slept up against one wall of the upstairs, like they did, was because the other wall on the opposite side of the room had fallen out. There *was* no wall. Basically, you could stand on that side of the upstairs of the house and look straight out into the forest. If you were to look down, you'd see the big brush and brambles pile that had to be crossed in order to get to the front door.

P.J. noticed the first bat because it had flown into the side of his head. But the next thing he knew, there was a whole swarm of bats flying around the room. And not just up at the ceiling. They'd filled the entire room from the ceiling to the floor. And they'd done so instantly, as if they'd just appeared out of thin air.

Marlin and Bobby didn't need P.J. to wake them up this time, as the screeching of the thousands of bats flying about them woke them up instead. All three men stood, hands and forearms shielding their faces, and started walking backward. Rather, they were being *pushed* backward by the flying swarm of bats.

When P.J. realized they were being pushed backward, toward the opening in the wall where they'd fall two floors if they continued, potentially to their deaths, he pulled a handgun he always kept on his side out of its holster and started shooting at the bats. It took until his third shot, but he hit one, and it dropped dead on the floor, and the thousands of others vanished, instantly, as if they'd never been there at all.

"We're getting out of here, now!" P.J. said to the other two men, and no one stood around to debate. They ran over and got their sleeping bags and then headed downstairs and packed their stuff in record time.

P.J. saw Bobby working his way through the brush pile and brambles to get out of the house's yard and over to their truck and he followed suit. "And Marlin was just behind me, stepping on my heels, pushing me to go faster the whole time," P.J. told us. "And I just kept saying, damn it Marlin, just wait. I'm going as fast as I can. And about that time, Bobby says, 'P.J.,

Marlin's over here with me.' And about that time, I hear Marlin say, 'Yeah, Dad. I came over first.' And let me tell ya, I only *thought* I was gettin' through them brambles as fast as I could, but after that, I got through there even faster!"

The guys got to their truck, and they got in, and they drove the rest of the night. They were back at P.J.'s house just as the sun came up, and they were still able to get some sleep afterward, but not much. And as you might imagine, they never went camping, hunting, hiking or *anything* at that place again.

A year later, in October, Marlin was cutting down trees on the hill just above P.J.'s cabin in order to build his own cabin. He was a grown man now, and it was time to move out, but he didn't want to leave the mountain he'd grown up on, just like his father before him. One of the trees he'd been cutting down, for some reason, kicked back the wrong way when it left the stump, and it crushed Marlin, killing him almost instantly.

P.J. never said that he thought Marlin may have brought something home with them from the haunted hunting place, because he'd carved his name in the old beech tree in the front yard, but he *did* say that when he'd seen Marlin doing it, he'd gotten an eerie feeling that was impossible to describe in words, and he's just always wished his son simply hadn't carved his name in that tree.

My friends and I would go on to know P.J. for many more years, and we would go on to spend many more nights in that cabin of his, and we would go on hearing many more of P.J.'s stories. Stories, that I'm convinced, if I'd never heard, and if I'd never heard them told by the man who told them, I would have never become a storyteller myself. I would have never become a writer. This very book you hold in your hands right now, or which you may be viewing on your e-reading device during these amazing times of technology in which we live, can only be traced back to one source. P.J.s cabin and all of those October nights!

The End

October 19

The Legend Of Sleepless Hollow

You've no doubt heard The Legend Of Sleepy Hollow. But The Legend of Sleepless Hollow? Now *that's* a Halloween tale for the ages.

Whereas the classic by Washington Irvin showcased a Hessian soldier who'd had his head lobbed off during the Revolutionary War, The Legend Of *Sleepless* Hollow features a soldier as well, but one from a different war and one who, though having lost certain body parts, actually *survived* his injuries and lived out the rest of his days. In this legend, a confederate soldier who'd had his *feet* blown off by a Union cannon during the American Civil War is our man of the hour. And, well, that's pretty much where the similarities end. For you see, whereas Irvin's dead soldier allegedly comes back every Halloween night to try to find his head, or take anyone else's, for that matter, who happens to be in the wrong place at the wrong time, our Civil War soldier in *this* story, The Legend Of *Sleepless* Hollow comes back not to find his feet, but for something quite different, entirely.

A drink.

Moonshine!

I'm getting ahead of myself. Let me go to the beginning.

I have a couple of guys who come out to our house from time to time and do repairs that are way over my paygrade, namely plumbing and electrical repairs. My plumber's name, a young man in his early thirties, is Brian. This story comes by way of Brian, and only after me trying to convince him of something that *might* be real, but which Brian is pretty convinced is.

"Now if you see any large, dark figures staring at you from just inside the treeline," I'd said to Brian and his assistant one day when they were here working on our well's electric pump. They were actually replacing the old one that had burned out with a new one. "Just ignore it. They're just curious. They won't come close." Then, I went into the house, chuckling. Sure, I was warning them of the potential Bigfoot Sasquatch that may or may not live in the woods behind our house. It was kind of mean of me to do it, and even meaner to feel joy when I'd look out the window every now and then and see Brian and his assistant scanning the perimeter. They seemed a little paranoid all day, and I'm sure it slowed them down, but they eventually got the job done.

"I bet you had no idea what I was talking about when I told you about the large, dark figures in the treeline, did you?" I asked Brian once he'd finished up the job.

"I know *exactly* what you were talking about," he said. "I grew up with them."

"Grew up with what?" I asked, wanting to make sure we were on the same page.

"Bigfoot," he said, confirming that we were.

"You grew up with Bigfoot?" I said, shocked that he'd said it so nonchalantly. Usually these conversations are had with a note of skepticism, but Brian was not a skeptic. He was a believer.

"Yeah," he said, packing his tools in his van. "And ghosts. Mostly ghosts."

"Do tell," I said. "If you don't mind."

"I don't mind," Brian said. "I'll write up your bill, and if you'll bring me a glass of water, I'll tell you while I drink it."

"Okay," I said, and I went into the house and I brought bottles of water out for Brian and his assistant, and after he handed me my bill, he kept his word, and he told me his story.

Brain had grown up on land that had been in his family since the great depression. "Back when the Government ran us off the Blue Ridge Parkway," he said, and what he was referencing was when, back in the 1930's, the Federal Government designated all the land that ran for hundreds of miles along the top of a particular ridge of the Blue Ridge

Mountains, stretching from North Carolina through Virginia, as Federal Land. The Government would later build a beautiful biway along the top of the ridges running across the mountains, and it's actually a National Park. People come from all over the world to drive the Blue Ridge Parkway. My family and I do it twice a year. Once in the spring, and again in the fall once the leaves have changed colors, and let me tell you, it's worth the price of admission, which is roughly $25 per car, if memory serves.

But before our wonderful Government could build such a beautiful scenic roadway in such a beautiful place, they had to run all the families who lived on the top of the mountain off of their land.

Brian's great, great, great, great grandfather (who we'll simply refer to as Brian's grandfather going forward in this story, so I don't have to type the word 'great' so many times) had been run off his land for this massive roadway project. And Brian's grandfather is the centerpiece of this story. Yes, Brian's grandfather, a Civil War veteran who'd had his feet blown off during the war, would go on to become our ghost.

"They called him Stumpy," Brian told me, referring to his grandfather. "Because he just wrapped his stumps up in rags. He didn't have any prosthetics. And he walked around with a cane."

Brian said that 'ol Stumpy had a very distinctive sound to his steps. Thump, thump… wait for it… thump. There was a rhythm to it, and you could hear him in another part of the house, or even out in the fields, and you knew it was him.

"Now this is all according to the stories passed down," Brain told me. "He was dead long before I was born."

As it were, 'ol Stumpy didn't take too kindly to being told to get off his land, but he did as he was told, but not everyone else did. There were a few families so far out in the wilderness on top of those mountains, families who held out, and who the Government finally just gave up on, because, well, they were too afraid to go that deep into the woods where the families lived to run them out, and it wasn't so much because of the families.

"What were they scared of?" I asked Brian.

"Bigfoot," he said, with no hesitation. And he'd looked me square in the eyes without blinking when he said it. The man was telling the truth.

"Bigfoot Sasquatch?" I said.

"One or the other, but it doesn't matter which you call it. Same difference. But yeah. Bigfoot Sasquatch."

"Go on," I said.

"There's been clans of Bigfoot Sasquatches up in these mountains forever. Long before the white man came here and killed all the indians. And some of those old mountain people up there, before getting run off, had learned to live with them, peacefully. And when the Government men came around trying to run these families off their land, they'd have run-ins with the Bigfoot Sasquatches."

Brian went on to tell of how the Bigfoot Sasquatches never physically confronted the Government men, because they hadn't needed to, because they simply terrified the living shit out of them.

"Mostly they'd just scream," Brian said. "When they saw the Government men coming in to threaten the people, they'd just howl and growl, and the Government men had never heard *anything* like it, and they'd usually just turn around and run off the mountain. Sometimes the Bigfoot Sasquatches would throw rocks. But whatever they did, it worked, and the Government men finally gave up on about half a dozen families. They let them stay, and the road wasn't going around close to their place anyway, so it all worked out."

"Well, one of those families who were able to stay," Brian continued, happened to be real good friends with grandaddy, and they happened to be the biggest bootleggers on the mountain. You see, the decade before all those families had been run off their land was the period of prohibition. And this one family had a speakeasy in their house. You know. A private bar."

"Uh, huh," I said. I remembered learning about the old speakeasies. They're in just about every movie set in the twenties.

Brain went on to explain that the family who ran the speakeasy lived at the top of the hollow, above the land he'd grown up on. He said that even after his great grandfather had been run off his land, and forced to live down in the valley, and even though alcohol was then permitted in the U.S., his grandaddy loved to take all day hiking up the side of the mountain, thump, thump… wait for it… thump, to hang out with his friends and drink their moonshine, because he thought it was better than anything you could buy in the stores anyway.

"So here's the weird part," Brain said. "After grandaddy died, everyone who ever lived in our house- my father, my father's parents, their parents- all claimed that they could hear grandaddy coming home drunk in the middle of the night from time to time. They'd hear thump, thump… wait for it… thump, out in the field. Thump, thump… wait for it… thump, out on the porch. Sometimes you could be up in the woods hunting, up the hollow above our land, and hear it. I used to hear it up there when I was a teenager.

"And sometimes," Brain continued, "if you went far enough up the hollow, up to where you can still see the foundation of the old speakeasy house, if you wait 'till dark, and you're really quiet, and you're really lucky, you can hear music. It's really light. That big band stuff they used to listen to back in the twenties."

"Wow," I said, amazed.

"Seems that 'ol grandaddy still likes hanging around, and he still likes his buddy's moonshine up there," Brain said.

"Now this Bigfoot Sasquatch," I said, totally satisfied with the ghost story, but wanting a little more. "You said you saw one."

"Oh," Brian said, realizing he'd left a hole in his story that he needed to fill. "Sometimes, late at night, you'd hear thump, thump… wait for it… thump. Thump, thump… wait for it. Flop! And then you'd her. Boom, boom. Boom, boom. Boom, boom.

"What the hell was that?" I asked.

"It's what I used to wonder, myself," Brain said. "So one night when I heard it, I sneaked out the backdoor to see what it was?"

"And?" I said.

"That's when I saw it. It was a Bigfoot Sasquatch carrying the ghost of great, great, great, great grandaddy home, because he'd passed out drunk in the field again.

"Damn!" I said.

"Yeah," Brian said. "I moved after that. Like, seriously, the next day. My wife and I had just been married, and we were staying back at my parents' while we were trying to find our own place. After that, I went into town and rented an apartment at a complex just to get the hell out of there."

"Do you ever go back?" I asked.

"Of course," he said. "My parents still live there. But I never stay the night, and they're old, and I've already told them, as far as any will goes, they can give me whatever they want, but they better not give me the land, because I'll sell the damn place."

"Really?" I said.

"Yeah," he said. "I never felt threatened. I never felt as if I was in any danger. But that stuff freaks me out, and I don't want to have any part of it."

"Well," I said, putting my head down and thinking for a hot second. "You'd better make sure of something else then," I told him.

"What's that?" he asked.

"If you're ever out here working for me, make sure you're out of here before dark."

We both looked to the treeline, as did Brian's assistant. The sun was just setting behind the horizon, and all three of us could have sworn we saw a large, dark figure duck into the treeline, and as an empath, I got the feeling that this large, dark figure had enjoyed Brian's story.

The End

October 20

Murder By Mail

Mike the mailman walked up the courthouse steps, removing his cap as he did, ready to enter the building, admiring the beautiful autumn leaves twirling around on each step. Little tornadoes of color. Red, yellow, purple and orange. Fall had always been Mike's favorite time of year. He'd learned, after delivering mail, mostly on foot, for more than three decades, to appreciate the cooler temperatures of fall after the blazing, southern summers he'd endured, and since he'd only ever delivered mail in small, quaint communities, the blending of the fall colors on his daily routes made him feel as if he were truly living inside a Norman Rockwell painting.

After entering the building, Mike was guided into the courtroom by a bailiff. Mike had been ten minutes early, as he'd learned to do back in his Army days, where he served for four years before dedicating his life to the U.S. Postal Service. He'd seen one tour of Nam while in the Army, and one tour to any third world country to fight people he didn't know for reasons he couldn't understand was enough for him, so he hadn't reenlisted. However, Mike had always felt called to contribute, and serve, and he felt that his long stint as a mail carrier had answered that call.

"Will you state for our grand jury members, your name," the prosecutor said.

"Mike Planters," he said.

"And what is your occupation, Mr. Planters?"

"I'm a mailman," Mike said. "And please, just call me Mike."

"With your permission," the prosecutor said. "And with respect."

"Thanks," Mike said, thinking this guy should have been in sales, but hell, Mike had been around the block (thousands actually), and he knew *all* professions were sales.

"How do you know the accused?" the prosecutor asked. "Missy Pale?"

"I've delivered mail at her place for the past couple of years," Mike said. "Well, she moved, of course, a couple months back. I still deliver to that house, but someone else is living there now, of course. After the murder and all."

"Thank you," the prosecutor said. "And how often did you ever come into contact with Miss Pale?"

"Oh, almost everyday," Mike said. "She was one of my favorite customers. She was almost always home, with her baby and all. And she spent a lot of time out in her yard. Always working in her flower beds, and in her garden in the Spring. She is a real sweet kid."

"Thank you," the prosecutor said. "I'd like to state for the record," he then said, facing the judge, "that Miss Pale is actually twenty eight years old. I know that to Mr., um, Mike, that is very young, but the court needs to understand she was no child. She was fully an adult."

"That's fine," said the judge.

"Mike," the prosecutor said, facing his man on the witness stand again. "Would you consider yourself a good judge of character?"

"I would," Mike said. "I've been carrying mail for thirty four years, and I've come into contact with probably hundreds of thousands of people throughout the years, because I've carried the mail in three different cities, and I've met all types. You learn to read people when you do what I do."

"How so?" the prosecutor asked.

"Well," Mike said, looking down and taking a second, and then he said, "you can tell a lot about a person's character based on how they treat people from whom they stand nothing to gain."

There were light sounds of agreement from the grand jury members. An *um, hum,* here, and a few, *that's rights* there, and even an *amen* from somewhere. The judge said nothing to admonish them, but he *did* give them a stern warning by way of a look.

"Miss Pale had nothing to gain from being nice to me," Mike continued. "Shoot, if you knew how many people are out in their yards, and then step inside or go around the corner when they see me coming, just so they don't have to be inconvenienced with saying hi, it would blow your mind."

Gasps from the grand jury, and an even sterner look from the judge. If they kept this up, Mike was sure, the judge would eventually give them a verbal warning.

"Miss Pale, when she'd see me, if it was hot, she'd run in the house and grab a glass of cold water and have it waiting on me. And she was always giving me snacks. And it was stuff she'd cooked or baked herself. I mean, she was a pure angel in every sense of the word."

"And what about her domestic partner," the prosecutor asked, switching gears. "The deceased. Mr. Edward Given."

"Now, I'm not one to speak ill of the dead," Mike began, "but I got to today. That man was no good, and he'd been tuning up on that girl for some time, and I tell ya, I have suspicion he was on drugs. Probably pills."

"And this is based on?" the prosecutor asked, leaving it open.

"Well, again," Mike said. "Over thirty years carrying the mail. You see it all. You see the deals going down in broad daylight no one else would see, because they're not paying attention. Tunnel vision I call it. If it don't happen right in front of 'em, they don't see it. You'd be surprised to see all the nonsense going on all around you everyday, if you simply looked left and looked right a time or two. Of course, I learned to do that in the infantry, back in my Army days. And it kept me alive in Nam."

"Thank you for your service," one of the jury members said, a woman about fifty years old. She caught the words coming out of her mouth and quickly put her hand over her mouth and looked at the judge. The judge could see the fear in her eyes, and though he'd already opened his mouth, prepared to speak, he decided against it. This judge was good. He'd mastered the art of giving intimidating looks and stares, and he pulled out one of his best, and the woman almost started crying. She did not speak out of line again.

"Thank you," Mike said, facing the woman, happy the judge hadn't scolded her for having the audacity to be patriotic.

"Did you ever see any marks or bruises on Miss Pale?" the prosecutor asked. "Any physical evidence of your claim?"

"Well, sure I did. And it was getting more and more regular there toward the end. Before she left town and all. Left the state, according to her mail forwarding form she filled out. Looks like she went back to her parents' place up in Pennsylvania."

"That's correct," the prosecutor said. "She's up in Pennsylvania."

"And of course," Mike said. "That boyfriend of hers. That baby daddy the kids call 'em these days, who thought she was good enough to cook and clean for him, and I'm sure perform other wifely duties, but wasn't good enough to be asked for her hand in marriage, well, I guess that was unfortunate he passed on just a couple days after she left."

"He didn't pass away," the prosecutor said. "He was shot in the face at point blank range."

"Well," Mike said. "I just didn't want to come across as graphic. That's why I even used the term other wifely duties instead of talking about sex."

This drew chuckles from the grand jury, and the judge would have admonished them this time, but he was too busy giggling himself. He *liked* this Mike the mailman guy. He was folksy. The kind of guy you could sit on the porch with and have coffee in the mornings, iced tea in the afternoon, and a beer in the evening. All in the same day, too, the judge thought.

"If you ask me," Mike said. "And I figure you're probably gonna. It's why you called me in here today. If you ask me, I'd say 'ol boy had been making some deals that he hadn't been paying up for, and the money collector had gotten tired of not collecting his money. I tell ya, it's just my opinion, but I firmly believe the one you want for murdering this man is a drug dealing scumbag that's still at large somewhere here in our community. Not some innocent, single mother, whose baby's just become fatherless, and who's three states away!"

Mike had said this last part with such force that it drew the man who'd shouted *amen*, earlier, to his feet to shout a lofty *hear, hear!*

"Silence from the grand jury!" the judge said, finally getting vocal, and he'd steadied his hand over his gavel, letting the grand jury members know that if they kept it up, he'd pick that son of a gun up next. And if they kept going after that, he'd raise the sucker. And if push came to shove, and they continued to disrespect his courtroom, he'd slam that sucker hard. He'd show 'em. All those moms who always threaten to count to three and never made it past two and a half had *nothing* on him!

"That's all I have," the prosecutor said, addressing Mike. "Feel free to leave the stand, and you're welcome to stay if you'd like, or you can get back on your route."

"Well," Mike said, rising. "I'd like to know what's gonna happen to Miss Pale. But I do need to finish my route."

"Have a seat," the prosecutor said, pointing with his open hand to the first row of seats in the gallery. "Your honor," he then said, facing the judge, "and members of the grand jury," he said, facing the grand jury members. "I am a prosecuting attorney. It is my job to prosecute criminals. I know that Missy Pale committed no crime. In fact, I believe, after reviewing the investigator's notes, that Missy Pale was a victim of domestic abuse for some time, just as Mike the mailman stated today. I know that this *does* make her suspicious. It *does* give her motive. But Missy Pale had, indeed, moved to Pennsylvania three days before the murder. We checked her alibi, and it fit. Therefor, I move to dismiss any and all charges against Missy Pale in the murder of her former domestic partner, Edward Given."

Just as the judge began giving the grand jury their instructions, the appointed leader of the group, the foreman, looked at his peers, and whispered "acquit?" and all of his peers whispered "yes," and some gave thumbs up and they all nodded their heads.

"Judge?" the foreman said, looking at the judge. "Sorry to interrupt you, but we'd like to save us all the time. We're already in unanimous agreement to acquit this girl."

"So be it," the judge said. "All current and future charges against Missy Christina Pale for the murder of one Edward Jermane Given are hereby and fully dropped." And with that, he grabbed, lifted and then pounded his gavel, and the grand jury members all watched him do it as if they were witnessing a living legend. The man had been county judge for nearly as long as Mike had been delivering mail, so it was fitting.

Mike exited the courtroom and walked back down the steps, heading for his mail truck. The leaves were no longer swirling around in their little colorful tornadoes, but they looked beautiful, lying there, still, in their full autumn blaze, anyway.

"Just like back in Little Rock," Mike said to himself, aloud, as he drove off, heading for his route. "That beautiful young woman," he said. "Janet. Boy, was she a looker. And that piece of shit husband of hers, always getting drunk and tuning up on her." Mike took a right and drove, slowly, into the next neighborhood in which he'd be delivering. "I have *never* regretted shooting that son of a bitch!"

"And Savannah," Mike said to himself, slinging mail into the first box on the street. Like anyone else who'd delivered mail for any considerable period of time, Mike had developed the habit of talking to himself during the day a long time ago. He was, however, sure to make sure he wasn't saying the wrong things when people might be around, listening, which was not the case here, so he said, "I'll *never* regret having slit that man's throat. After the way he treated his girlfriend? I mean, she was *beautiful*!"

Mike completed his route for the day, and since the mail was light, he got finished at the regular time he usually did, despite having taken half an hour off his route to go to the courthouse. After taking in his outgoing mail and telling the desk manager no, he would *not* go out and drop off a dozen packages that the handlers hadn't thrown into the route baskets on time that day, he walked out of the post office and he went home.

"How'd it go at the courthouse today?" his wife asked after he'd gotten home. They'd been together for almost thirty years. Mike had met her on his route back in Savannah shortly after he'd become a mail carrier.

"Went great," he said, giving her a kiss on the forehead after he did. "They dropped all the charges against that poor girl."

"And do you think they suspect?" his wife said, leaving the question open, knowing that Mike knew exactly what she was getting at.

"Nope," Mike said. "Not any more than anyone has ever suspected anything in regard to that piece of shit you were married to when we met."

"Do you think they ever will?" she asked, concerned, but trying not to show it.

"Nope," Mike said, walking to the refrigerator and pulling out a cold can of Coors Light and then cracking it open and taking a long swill.

"How can you be so sure?" she said, walking up to him and lightly placing her right hand on his left art.

Mike shut the refrigerator and turned to his wife and said, "because everybody trusts the mailman."

The End

October 21

Jim Brown's Return

Here it was, almost October, and I was working on one hell of an anthology that I'd been writing, off and on, for pretty near seven years…

...and I got writer's block.

Again!

Well, no big deal, I thought. Sometimes ideas come to me when I'm being physical. I'd already exercised for the day, but it wasn't too hot out, which is really saying something for Virginia, in August, so I figured I'd just go outside and split some firewood. I got three truckloads recently from a good friend of mine who'd cut some trees that had fallen on his property up into stove lengths, but he hadn't split them, so I had plenty of work waiting on me, and so I went outside to get to it, and I'll be damned if it wasn't raining!

So here I was, suffering from writer's block, unable to come up with a word to write, let alone a whole story, and I couldn't split and stack firewood, because it was raining, and I was feeling at a total loss of what to do, so I sat down on the back porch and stared out into the rain, feeling completely defeated, and egads, and gad's be, and damned my eyes if I didn't look out across the field and see, the almost translucent potential spook of spooks, 'ol Jim Brown, himself, for the first time in a long while, and he was hanging out under one of my big maple trees to get out of the rain.

"Jim Brown!" I yelled out across the field. "You come on up here on the porch and get outta the rain!"

Jim Brown left that old bicycle of his down there under the tree, and he put that big black hat of his on, and he came walking up to the back porch to join me, and I swear, if he still didn't look just like that creepy kid from that Children of the Corn movie, just like last time I saw him.

"Where you been, Jim Brown?" I said when he stepped on the porch. I shook his hand, and man was it cold. Felt like ice. He was gonna catch his death out in that rain. I guess maybe it was a good thing I was suffering from writer's block, afterall, or I might not have come out here and seen him and gotten him to a place that was dry.

"I reckon I've been around," Jim Brown said, sitting in the chair I'd pulled up for him and put beside mine. "A little over here. A little over yonder. Got anymore of that purple Gatorade?" he asked, and I wasn't surprised.

"No," I said. "But I've got some sweet tea. Want some?"

"Reckon I'll have a glass," he said. I went in the house and brought it right back out to him, making sure to take my wallet off of an end table in our dining room and hide it in the drawer of that table while I was inside. Again, I got those weird vibes off of Jim Brown, last time he'd been here. I'd felt like he was planning to knock me over the head and see what he could take from my place, and I *did* happen to have a crisp, new, twenty dollar bill in my wallet. I didn't want Jim Brown a takin' it.

"Where's the Mrs.?" Jim Brown asked me as I handed him his glass. This question alone made me feel good about having hidden my wallet.

"Now Jim Brown," I said. "Don't you go trying nothing. I still don't know exactly how I feel about you."

"Then why'd you invite me over?" he asked, taking a sip of his tea.

"Because I'm a southerner," I told him. "Just like you. We see a man in need, we help. Don't mean we trust 'em, though."

"Fair enough," Jim Brown said.

"And why'd you run out of here like you did last time you was here?" I asked him. "My wife never even got to meet you, and she was fixin' to feed you. Can't help but point out that made you look a little suspicious."

"Fair enough," Jim Brown said, taking another sip. "Tell you what," he said. "How about I help you out right now. Earn your trust."

"Well how is it you think you could help me?" I asked.

"I don't know," he said. "If it weren't pissin' the rain down, we could split and stack firewood or something."

"Why, Jim Brown!" I said. "Were you standing down there under my maple tree reading my mind this whole time?"

"Come on now," Jim Brown said. "That's crazy talk. You don't want your wife catching you talking that way. Where is she, anyway?"

"Why you so interested in the whereabouts of my wife, Jim Brown?" I said, and I was starting to get that feeling like I wanted to fight this guy again, just like last time he was here. Man, did he ask a lot of personal questions. And something about the vibes he put off. Just made me angry.

"Forget it," Jim Brown said. "I didn't mean nothin' by it. Sit down and let's figure out what I can do to help you out and maybe start to earn some of your trust."

I sat down, and I got to figuring, and the first thing I did was tell Jim Brown that I wasn't paying him no money to convince me that my house wasn't haunted, because I already knew it was.

"We've already covered that ground," Jim Brown said. "No need going back to it."

"Okay," I said. And then we both sat in silence for a right good while.

"What kind of work do you do, anyway?" Jim Brown finally asked. "I mean, how do you pay your bills?"

"With money," I told him. "Same as anyone else."

"But how do you make your money?" he asked.

"Well," I said. "I'm a YouTuber and a writer."

"A what?" he said.

"A YouTuber."

"What in tarnation is a YouTuber?" he asked.

"That's it, Jim Brown!" I said. "What kinda fool you taking me for? You gonna try to make me think you don't know what YouTube is? The world's largest platform for selfmade videos. And that you don't know that the people who make those videos are called YouTubers? Jim Brown, do you come around here trying to pick fights?"

"Nah, sir," he said, and he put both palms of his hands up. I could tell he was being genuine, but how in the name of God's green earth had he never heard of YouTube? I got to thinking about that hat he wore, and that bicycle without gears that he rode, and the fact that he *did* look like that creepy kid from Children of the Corn, and I thought maybe it was possible that he belonged to one of those religious sects that don't use modern technologies. "But how do you really make your money?" he said, and man, did I feel my blood boil.

"Doggone it, Jim Brown, that's the same damn thing everyone else says when they ask me what my job is. I tell 'em I'm a YouTuber and a writer, and then they smile and chuckle and ask me how I *really* make my money, like I'm living off disability or something, which I am not! I'm just one of those people in the top five percent of YouTubers and self publishing authors who are actually good enough at it to support themselves doing it full time, and it took me many years of hard work to get here, so that response just absolutely infuriates me!"

"Okay, okay," Jim Brown said. "Take it easy. I didn't mean to offend. Let's get over this bridge here. Let me help you."

"Well, unless you know a good story I could pass on, without you comin' around with your lawyer down the road and suing me for doing it, I don't know how else you could help me," I said.

"A story," Jim Brown said, and then he sank back in his chair a little more, and you could tell the man was thinking. "What kind of story?"

"Well," I said, eager for any help I could get out of him. Let me tell ya, writer's block sucks. And the terrifying part? You never know how long it's gonna last. I've had it last as short as a day, and I've had it last as long as two years. "I need a scary story, I guess. I'm working on a Halloween anthology. I need thirty one scary stories. One for each day of October. They're all gonna be compiled together in a book I'm thinking about calling 'October Nights.'"

"Nice concept," Jim Brown said. "Creative." And I could tell he was being genuine again. There was no hint of smartassness about him as he spoke.

"I got it!" he said, coming alive. I almost fell out of my chair, because I have PTSD from the war and all, and loud sudden noises don't suit me.

"Look out across your field there," Jim Brown said, pointing as he did, and my eyes followed his fingertip. "Look across the road at your neighbor's place. See all those cows?"

"Yeah," I said.

"Black angus," he said.

"Yeah," I said.

"You know those bulls weigh more than two thousand pounds?"

"I know they're big," I said.

"How terrifying would it be," Jim Brown said, "if they all of a sudden realized how big and strong they actually were. What if they decided they weren't gonna be kept in by that little piece of wire with the barbs on it, and they were gonna step over it and come over here and make mincemeat out of us?"

I had to hand it to Jim Brown for his idea, because you have no idea how many times I've thought the same thing. Even though we've got enough land for it, I'll *never* own horses or cows, and it's for the very reason Jim Brown had said. I am not comfortable trying to continue holding the illusion over an animal that weighs more than my truck that *I* am superior to *it*. I've always wondered what might happen if these beasts were to realize the truth. Would the gig be up?

I told Jim Brown as much, but I said I don't think the story would work so good in my anthology, because I was trying to keep it more paranormal based, not so much actual horror, and I'd already written a story about a serial killing mailman, and I didn't want to push the envelope too far.

"Well, why didn't you just say so?" Jim Brown said, like I'd been holding back the obvious.

"How do you mean?" I asked him.

"Well, you've just made it too easy," he said.

"I'm not following you, Jim Brown," I said.

"How about you write a story about interviewing a ghost?"

"What?" I said.

"Yeah," he said. "Like, an interview with a ghost?"

"Hm," I said, and then I sat back to study on it a while. That Anne Rice woman did okay with a book called An Interview With The Vampire. And the movie was okay. Had that Brad Pitt guy and that Tom Cruise guy in it. Maybe enough time had passed since then that I wouldn't look like I was trying to pull off a knock off. I'm sure the millennials haven't even heard of that book or the movie based on the book. Why, Jim Brown might have been onto something, and I let him know it.

"How would it look?" I asked. "I mean, the setting?"

"Well," he said. "It could look like it looks right here," he said.

"How's that?" I asked.

"Like you're just sitting here on the back porch of your house, talking to a ghost while watching it rain."

"That's not very believable though, Jim Brown," I told him.

"Why not?" he said. "This is a very old house."

"Built in 1903," I said.

"Yes," he said. "We went over this last time I came around."

"And your point?" I said.

"My point," he said, "is just that. It could be that you're interviewing a guy, say, who was one of the original inhabitants of this house. One of the sharecroppers it was built for."

"That's not half bad, Jim Brown," I said, and I wasn't trying to fluff him. It was true. This house has a long history, some of it we know, some of it we still don't. And with the way Jim Brown dressed, and with that old black bicycle without gears that he was always riding around on. Why, he'd even pass as one of the sharecroppers who lived in this house nearly a hundred and twenty years ago, as of this writing.

"That might work," I told him. "What would we talk about?"

"Well," he said. "We could talk about all the stuff you and I've talked about here today. You could just write the story just like it's all taken place. Like I'm a ghost. Of one of the sharecroppers."

"Hm," I said. I looked down, studying on it some more. It seemed doable, but the subject matter seemed boring. I told Jim Brown as much, and I asked him how we could spice it up some.

"Well," he said. "You could always have an interview about how the ghost died in life."

"That's it!" I said, and I slammed my right fist into my left palm. "How'd you die, Jim Brown?"

Jim Brown looked at me as if he had pain in his eyes, and I thought of what I'd just said, and realized I was talking crazy talk again, and Jim Brown just didn't want to bring himself to tell me not to be talking crazy talk in case my wife heard me, so I corrected myself.

"Sorry, Jim Brown," I said. "I know that sounded like crazy talk. Okay, let's say if we were to do this story, what would the ghost's story be for how he died? This original inhabitant of the house? This sharecropper from back in 1903?"

"Well," Jim Brown said, looking down and sounding a bit resigned as he spoke. "It has to do with my dog."

"Your what?" I said, and all of a sudden I started thinking Jim Brown might put me out of business should he go into writing and YouTube'ing, because we do have that ghost dog around here, and he knows about it, and being able to just use that as a writing prompt so simply? "Jim Brown, I think you might be a genius."

"Just hear me out," Jim Brown said. "You know, back in 1903, there weren't as many people as there are today."

"Uh, huh," I said, listening.

"And a lot of times, these young men who went around sharecropping, well, the only family they had was their dog. And if someone was mean to their dog, why, one man would kill another over such things. And, well, let's just say that my dog, I mean, this ghost's dog, had gotten old and forgetful and didn't hear too good anymore, and because of that, he got clumsy, and maybe he went into the wrong room at night and woke up one of the other sharecroppers, and maybe that man got mad enough after it happened so many times that he kicked the dog, and then maybe the dog's owner caught that 'ol boy out in the fields alone the next day and kicked hell shit out of him, and then maybe…"

"Look at that," I said, interrupting Jim Brown. "Here comes my wife up the driveway."

"Just as the rain's stopped, too," Jim Brown said.

"You finally get to meet my wife," I said, standing and walking over to the end of the driveway to greet my wife.

"Honey," I said as she got out of the car. "Jim Brown's back."

"Who?" she said.

"Jim Brown," I said. "Remember? The quaker looking guy on the black bike? He's out here on the back porch with me. He's helping me write a story for my anthology."

My wife reached back into the car and grabbed her purse and then shut the door. We walked around to the back porch together, and I'll be dipped in monkey turds, if that son of a gun Jim Brown and already run off *again!*

"Where is this Jim Brown?" my wife asked. I raised my hand and pointed to the big maple tree on the other side of our field, down by the road, and said, "there. Getting on his bike to leave, gosh darn it."

My wife got up in my face and did that whiffy thing again and then went in the house like I'd never said a word about Jim Brown. I sat back down in my chair, grateful the rain had stopped, but no longer feeling like splitting and stacking firewood, because now, all of a sudden, I had a story to write.

The End

October 22

Have A Very Fairy Halloween

When we bought our house, out in the country, far enough out of the city to have plenty of peace and quiet, yet close enough to take advantage of the city's conveniences without making a day trip out of doing so, there was the strangest of conditions written into the contract via the seller's agent. It read thus:

Buyer agrees to never mow or plow the lower field, roughly a quarter of an acre in size, which borders the forest, or, to manipulate or molest this portion of the property for any reason under any conditions.

Of course, as you might imagine, this piqued our curiosity, so we asked our agent about this stipulation, and he told us that the seller's agent had told him that the old couple who'd lived in the house for more than fifty years, before dying within six months of each other (first him, and then her), had set the area up as a butterfly sanctuary, and that they wanted it to be preserved it as such, even after their deaths. My wife and I had no problem with this, so we accepted the agreement and bought the property. The close was relatively simple, in comparison to how these things often go, and we moved into our new house in pretty short order and quickly made our house our home.

We'd moved in during the fall, late October, actually, and we noticed that in the butterfly sanctuary, there were many long pumpkin vines, and the vines were absolutely loaded with pumpkins of various sorts. "The old woman must have planted them this past spring, just before she died," I said to my wife while we were out admiring the pumpkins and the crisp October air.

"She didn't plant them," a voice came from the road. I looked over, and there stood an older woman, close to eighty years old, who seemed to be out for a morning walk. This portion of our property is pretty close to the road, and we spend little time here, because of that fact. We do enjoy our privacy and spend the majority of our time back on the far part of our property so that we can have it.

"Who did?" my wife asked.

"You'll find out in time," the old lady said, and then she continued on her morning stroll.

We didn't harvest the pumpkins, and not because we were afraid to be in breach of contract, but because we figured the garden, Eden style, mind you, had been very dear to the old lady who had lived here before us, so we basically didn't harvest the pumpkins out of respect for her. Fall passed quickly, and then winter came and when it did the vines died off, as did all the wildflowers in the garden, and by January, the soil beneath the dead brush could be seen. As could all the little clay fairy houses that the woman had obviously put out at some point.

"Look at that," my wife said, the first time we noticed the small, brightly painted houses in detail since they were no longer covered with weeds, flowers and pumpkin vines. "It looks like there are underground tunnels connecting them all," she said. I followed the direction in which she was pointing with her finger and I saw that she was right.

"Huh," I said. "Must be rats or groundhogs. Maybe chipmunks or gophers."

"Good thing we don't walk in there. Or mow," my wife said. "Looks like we'd be destroying a small community."

"Yes," I said. "And we wouldn't want that." We both laughed and continued our afternoon stroll around the property. That night, as I lie in bed, just about to go to sleep, a sudden thought hit me. I'd never seen any groundhogs, rats, chipmunks or gophers on our property. Hm, I thought. I just haven't been paying enough attention. Obviously, they're here, I convinced myself, and then I fell to sleep.

Winter passed, and spring came, and my wife and I started a small garden on the opposite side of the field where the butterfly sanctuary is located. We planted corn and green beans, and yellow crookneck squash and lettuce. A few cucumber vines and a couple eggplant plants and okra plants. We'd never had a real garden before, having lived in the city, but we did container gardening at our old condo, planting tomatoes, corn and beans in five gallon buckets we got from a local deli. One must make sure to get plastic buckets that are approved to contain food, because not all plastic buckets are the same, and a simple five dollars bucket from Lowe's might end up getting impurities in one's food that one does not want in one's body. Our garden, out here in the country, did extremely well, and we were pleased, but we were also confused.

Because the garden in the butterfly sanctuary did better.

And we'd never planted one there.

As we strolled past the butterfly sanctuary throughout the spring, watching for flowers that might draw the beautiful butterflies later in the year, during summer, to begin budding we did notice several patches of wild flowers, but we noticed, too, that between the patches of flowers, there were vegetables. And they were the same type of vegetables we were growing in our garden.

"How do you explain this?" my wife asked.

"Well," I said. "I know most of this stuff will reseed itself. Maybe she had a full garden over here last year, and it reseeded. If that's the case, there will be less and less vegetables here with each passing year."

"But," my wife said, confusion heavy in her voice. "How is it that they are the exact same types of vegetables that we grew?"

"Hm," I said. "Must be coincidence."

That night, as I lay in bed, drifting to sleep, my wife startled me, jumping up on her elbows and saying, "Hay!"

"Good God, woman!" I said. "What did you do that for?"

"Remember when our seeds went missing?"

"What?"

"This spring," she said. "After we planted our garden. We still had lots of seeds left over, but we couldn't find them. Remember?"

"Yeah," I said, my heart rate slowing back down to normal.

"I bet those gophers, or groundhogs, or rats, or chipmunks that have those tunnels in the butterfly sanctuary took them and buried them over there and they grew."

"That must be it," I said, and then she lay back down and fell asleep much quicker than me, not because I was still getting over being startled, but because I was laying there, trying to think of any time I'd seen any of these small rodents, and I still had not, and I had very actively been looking for them. And how could rodents plant the rows of vegetables in such straight, true lines, just as if they'd been planted by a professional gardener?

Another scorcher of a summer came, and we spent a lot of time staying in the house, hiding from the sun, and becoming spoiled by the air conditioning. We kept our windows very clean, and we'd placed sitting chairs in front of the windows that offered the best views, and this is where we would read, and drink coffee, and have a beer in the evening, and it was in one of these chairs, the one in which I can sit and view the butterfly sanctuary, that I first believed my eyes were deceiving me.

"Honey," I said.

"Huh," my wife said from the middle of the room. "Can you come look at this?"

She put down the book she was reading and came to the window. She glanced out across the field to the butterfly sanctuary about one hundred yards away.

"What are those?" I asked.

"Butterflies," she said.

"Are you sure?" I asked.

My wife squinted her eyes and moved her face closer to the glass, to the point where she was actually touching it with the tip of her nose, and she said, "oh, my God."

We raced outside, and we didn't even close the door behind us. We ran to the butterfly sanctuary, but they were gone by the time we got there. Tiny blond, brown and red headed creatures about the size of butterflies, but which clearly had *not* been butterflies. Neither of us spoke the words, but we knew.

We made our way back inside post haste. The heat, which we'd forgotten while enthralled with our little visitors, reminded us about itself quickly once the girls were gone. Once back inside my wife raced upstairs to one of our spare bedrooms that we were using for storage and started digging through boxes. She pulled out some small dollhouse furniture and dollhouse dishes.

"What are you doing?" I asked her. We were in the room we'd hoped to turn into a nursery, but sadly, just as we were closing on the house, we'd gotten word that there would be no babies in our future unless we wanted to adopt. We had an agreement that we didn't want the doctor to tell us who was deficient. I didn't care if I was shooting blanks, but my wife didn't want to find out she was infertal. Maybe not the best choice, mental health wise, but I love my wife so I agreed.

"Gifting!" she said, excited, and then she rose to her feet and brushed past me like I wasn't even there. Before I could get downstairs she was out the door. I know, because she thought to close it this time, and I heard it shut.

Having gone outside in the summer heat once already was enough for me, so I watched from the window where I'd originally seen the small, flying creatures that looked kind of like butterflies from a distance, but which one could still tell clearly were not. I watched, as my wife made her way over to the edge of the butterfly sanctuary and knelt and placed the small dollhouse items she'd gotten out of storage, toys she had when she'd been a girl, and placed them in the grass. She rose, and began to turn to come back to the house, but she hesitated and turned back to face the road. I looked, and in the road I saw the old woman we'd seen some time before. She was in her car, but she'd stopped and rolled down her window and was saying something to my wife. Something brief, as she was only there a few seconds before driving on.

"What did she want?" I asked my wife when she came inside, sweat from the extreme Virginia summer heat already running down her forehead.

"She asked me if we'd seen them," my wife said.

"Seen what?" I said.

"I think you know," she said.

"What did you tell her?" I asked my wife.

"I said I think we have."

"Why did you say that?" I asked, fearing we'd be the new laughing stock of the area.

"Obviously," my wife said, "she already knew about them."

My wife had a point. Why else would the old woman have stopped and asked if we'd seen them?

The next day, the little dollhouse effects my wife had left were gone.

"They took them!" my wife said, sounding as pleased as a child on Christmas morning, having realized that Santa had eaten the cookies left out for him.

"Are you sure we have…" I said, not even wanting to allow myself to say the word.

"Fairies," a voice came from the road. We looked over, and there was the eighty year old woman who obviously knew more about what was going on on the little half acre plot on our land, which was obviously more than just a butterfly sanctuary, than we did.

"Come again?" I said.

"Fairies," the old woman said, stepping into our yard. "I hope you don't mind me coming over for a second to say hi."

"We're in the south, but we're not gonna shoot ya," I said, and laughed, and the old woman laughed.

"Just thought I'd ask first," she said, "because you're right, we are in the south, and you never know. Especially anymore."

The old woman introduced herself to us as Rebecca, but she said to call her Becky, because everyone else did. It turns out she had been friends with the old couple that had lived in the house before us. She and her late husband used to come over to visit often, and while the men sat on the front porch in the evenings and drank beer and told lies, the women would sit here, by the butterfly sanctuary, which is so much more, we know understand, and simply watch the fairies. Sadly, Becky's husband passed away shortly after we bought our house, and we never had the honor of meeting him.

"How did they get here?" my wife asked Becky. "I mean, I've always wanted to believe, but I never thought I'd see."

"It's a sad story, actually," Becky said. "You see, the couple that lived here before you, our dear friends, never had children."

My wife and I gave each other a look that we think Becky would have picked up on quickly if she hadn't been scanning the fairy garden hoping for a sighting.

"Well," she said, beginning to correct herself. "They *did*, but they didn't *live*. Margorie, that was the lady's name, God rest her soul, had given birth to triplets. And they were four months premature, and none of them lived a day. She and Ralph, her husband, buried them here."

"Wait a minute," I said. "You mean this is actually a cemetery?"

"A small one. Yes," Becky said.

"Why didn't we see the headstones this past winter, when all the flora and fauna was gone?" my wife asked.

"Because," Becky began. "Margorie didn't want to have a depressing old cemetery over here, where she'd be forever reminded of her three babies who hadn't made it. She was never able to get pregnant again after that, by the way."

My wife grabbed my hand and gave it a light squeeze, and I gave a light squeeze back.

"She made a little fairy village here," Becky said. "She put out clay houses that she'd hand painted herself. And instead of leaving flowers for the children, she planted some, and she'd plant a garden off and on, and she would leave tiny trinkets for them. Mostly just little shiny objects that might draw a baby's attention. Like little bells. Or those bouncy plastic balls.

"And then," Becky continued, "they just showed up."

"The fairies?" my wife asked.

"The fairies," Becky said, matter of factly.

Becky started coming by regularly after that, and she and my wife would spend many evenings sitting out by the butterfly sanctuary, which we no longer called a butterfly sanctuary, rather, what it truly was; the fairy garden. Both of them would leave little gifts when they visited the garden, and sure enough, the next day, the gifts would be gone.

Summer turned to fall quickly that year, last year, actually, and we were happy to see the heat move out and watch the leaves change colors. Again, quite a few pumpkins had grown in the fairy garden, though we hadn't planted them. We had, however, gifted the seeds.

A week before Halloween, we took a pumpkin we'd bought at the grocery store over to the fairy garden. We'd planted pumpkins in our garden, but none of them grew. We didn't water them enough.

But we didn't just leave this pumpkin as a gift. We had also purchased one of those little jack o'lantern carving kits, and my wife and I sat there, at the edge of the fairy garden, and we carved a jack o'lantern. This, we left as a gift.

We finished the jack o'lantern just before dark, and in our haste to get inside, we left the little carving tools outside as well. We had never intended to do this, but when we woke up the next morning and looked outside, we were glad we had, because we were amazed by what we saw.

Overnight, the little fairies had taken our small carving tools, obviously thinking we'd left them as gifts, and they showed that they'd obviously been hiding, watching us carve our jack o'lantern, because every pumpkin that had grown in their garden that year- and there were at least a dozen- had been carved up as well!

There were images of flowers carved into pumpkins. There were images of pumpkins carved into pumpkins. There were images of fairies carved into pumpkins, and there were even two busts, one with a likeness of my wife, and the other a carved likeness of myself.

My wife and I, fearing we may be overstepping our bounds, rearranged the jack o'lanterns. We were able to find three that had fairies carved into them, and we put them close together in the center of the arrangement. Then, we placed the jack o'lantern with my likeness carved into it on the right of those three, and then we placed my wife's jack 'o'lantern on the left of the three little fairies. The rest, we evenly placed on both sides.

We took joy in going outside and viewing our fairy carved jack o'lanterns that last week leading up to Halloween, and even Becky had been amazed when she saw them. She said the fairies had never done anything like that before.

Trick or treat came and went a week later, on Halloween night, and as we'd suspected, we didn't get anyone at the door. We live out in the middle of nowhere, and we figured people who had kids probably took them into town where there were subdivisions to trick or treat.

"Oh, well," my wife said, turning off the porch light at 8:00 p.m., the official end of trick or treating county wide. "More snack sized candy bars for us."

"Yeah," I said. "Like all of them." I'd already eaten *half* of them.

"Honey?" I heard my wife say as she was carrying the bowl of candy bars to the kitchen.

"Yeah," I said, mumbling, my mouth full of Snickers. I was on Netflix, already pulling up the original "Halloween" with Jamie Lee Curtis, one of our Halloween traditions.

"You need to come see this," she said.

I rose and walked over to my wife. She was at the window which looked out across our front field to the fairy garden.

"Oh, my God," I said, and I stopped chewing.

My wife placed the bowl of candy bars down on an end table we keep by the window. She and I went outside, keeping the porch light off, as not to disturb the scene with artificial lighting. We made our way across the field and to the fairy garden.

And there, lit brightly by the tiny little lanterns of so many tiny little creatures, all of the jack o'lanterns were in full glow. And the ones that shone the brightest were the three in the middle, the images of three little fairies carved into the side of pumpkins, and the two jack o'lanterns beside them, the likenesses of my wife and myself.

Our family.

The End

October 23

Pumpkin Munchers

This is going to sound like something straight out of an H.P. Lovecraft story. And not because these creatures, or spirits, or monsters, or, hell, whatever you call them, resemble fish in any way. They don't. But because I've only seen one other creature on earth that lives in a similar way as they do, and those creatures happened to be fish. The ones here, in this story, resemble rabbits.

I'm getting ahead of myself, as I have a tendency to do, so once again, let me start at the beginning.

I lived, for many years, in the Philippine Islands. And during my first full year there, after having gone back and forth a couple times, I decided to truly learn about the native culture. My wife, who is Filipina, and I left the city, with our ten months old son, and we went to my wife's native province. What we might call here in the U.S., living out in the country, but there, of course, we were living out in the jungle.

Now, I could compare and contrast our cultures, the U.S. and the Philippines, and I could even compare and contrast in regard to country living here vs. there all day long, but I don't have time, and that has little to do with this story. You see, the part that has to do with this story is the Hito, a type of fish that closely resembles an American catfish and that I'm sure is in the catfish family. It looks just like a channel cat, except it's black and it doesn't have whiskers.

During the time we lived in my wife's province, nearly two years, we stayed in a bamboo hut with a leaky roof and no electricity or running water. The hut belonged to her lola, or grandmother. Lola had about three acres of land, and there were roughly three generations of her family living on it. Roughly five hundred people. And no, this is no exaggeration. We're talking about a culture where women pretty much start having babies shortly after they start their menstrual cycle and don't stop until they hit menopause. My wife's mother had twelve children, one of which died, a little boy when he was four years old, and the other eleven of which are still alive. Some of my wife's sisters already have four or five children, even though they're still in their twenties, and I'm sure they will continue to give birth to children for another twenty years. Do the math, and you'll see that the number five hundred might actually be an *underestimate*. And I say all these things without a hint of disrespect. It's simply how life is in the Philippines, and I think once upon a time in America you could simply state facts about other cultures, without it being viewed as hate speech, but I think those days are over, hence this disclaimer.

At any rate, on my wife's lola's land was a pond. Rather, what they referred to as a pond. What it actually looked like was a field of standing water. As if it had rained hard the night before, and the field was sitting at a low place on the property, and the water was going to take a couple of days to drain. It was about half the size of a football field, not big at all, and at its deepest point, it appeared to be about a foot deep.

"There are no fish in this," I said to my wife's little brother, the first time he took me to Mud Puddle Pond (that's what I named it, for obvious reasons) to go fishing. We had bamboo cane poles that we'd cut that morning and about six feet of line on each one, the end of which had a hook baited with a coconut worm. These are short, fat larvae that look like just about any type of larvae you might dig up in your yard back in the U.S. Either the larvae of an oak or pine beetle, or a Japanese beetle about to come up in a month or so and eat your rose bushes.

"Unsa, dai?" he asked his sister. This kid, about fifteen years old, didn't speak a word of English. He was pretty good at nodding his head though, as if he were following along, when you spoke to him in English.

My wife translated, because this was before I'd learned to speak their language, Visyan- and let me tell you, living two years in the jungle where you either learn to speak the language of the locals or talk to no one but your wife is the greatest crash course in learning to speak a foreign language I could think of. When I left that jungle village two years later I was fluent in VIsayan.

My wife's brother laughed, and he flung his worm out into the water and stuck the end of his bamboo cane pole in the ground. I did the same, and then said, "how deep is this? A foot?" And then I started to walk into the pond, again, which appeared to simply be a giant mud puddle.

"No!" my wife and her brother said in unison, each of them grabbing me by both arms and pulling me back.

My wife explained to me that the pond was underground. All we were seeing was the surface water. There was a type of fish that lived in the pond, this Hito, or Filipino catfish, that made tunnels under the surface of the mud. Some of these tunnels, she said, could be twenty feet deep, and at the ends of the tunnels there were giant, underground caves where the fish schooled, she believed, by the hundreds. She warned that if I were to walk into the pond, I could collapse one of the tunnels and fall into one of the caves and drown. She said drunk Filipinos did it all the time.

"Damn," I said. "Are there really that many fish in here?" My wife and her brother said yes, though I don't really know if he was sure what he was saying yes to, but I'd find out in time that I didn't need to take their words for it. We walked away from our poles, so the fish wouldn't see us standing there when they came up out of their tunnels to take the bait, and then we went back to check them fifteen minutes later and my wife's brother and I both had a Hito on the line. They'd set their own hooks when they grabbed the coconut grubs and tried to make a run for it, so all we had to do was lift them out of the water. They were about a foot long each, which seemed to be the average size for Hitos, though I'd go on to break the village record some months later by catching one that was about two feet long. And we would catch those things all day long, as much as we wanted. We'd simply toss our baited hooks into the water, stick the poles in the mud so the hitos couldn't drag them away, and then go back in fifteen minutes and get our fish. And man, were they some good eatin'! Tasted *just* like catfish I'd eaten so much of here in the southern U.S.!

Fast Forward about six years. My wife and I, and our son, are living on a small, six acres homestead in central Virginia. And man, are we excited to grow and raise our own food!

One of the first forms of livestock we started with on our Virginia homestead was rabbits. We tried to breed them in the Philippines, but between the hot and humid environment (rabbits are not indeginous to Southeast Asia, and though you can find them there, the death rate of the newborns is so high it's near impossible to be successful unless you start in sheer bulk and charge extremely high price upon selling, which were two things we never did), and our friendly Filipino neighbors helping themselves to our rabbits at will, we were not successful. But things would be different here in the U.S., where people, for the most part, don't take what isn't theirs, and the temperatures are perfect for rabbits, and where they are indiginous.

When we started, we went through the very difficult trial and error stage, which lasted several months. Let me tell you, all those YouTube videos that show how easy it is to breed rabbits aren't very accurate. We tried the whole "put the mother and the kittens (actual name of baby rabbits) into a nursing box, and blah, blah, blah…" It was all crap. All of our kittens kept dying, and so we eventually gave up. We turned our rabbits loose- we only had three females and one male- and figured they'd either get eaten by predators, or they would make it on their own in the wild.

A month after we'd set our rabbits free, and during which time we'd always see them lingering around in the yard, I walked into our woodshed. It was winter, and I'd gone in to get more wood for the woodstove. One of our female rabbits ran in behind me and scurried into a pile of hay that we had in there, and I immediately began hearing what sounded like suckling. I pulled the top portion of the hay back, and I saw that the mother rabbit was nursing six kittens.

And the other two females, I'd soon find, also had babies hidden under the hay!

We had a total of twenty two rabbits now, all alive and healthy, and we were back in business!

Realizing that we simply had to let nature run its course, we fenced off a one hundred feet long by twenty five feet wide section of one of our fields. We buried two inch by two inch wide chicken wire two feet deep around the bottom of the fencing so that no rabbits could burrow out, and no predators could burrow in. And then we simply put up natural structures, like stick piles, firewood piles, haypiles, etc., and we turned our new fleet of rabbits loose. In time, we would have as many as fifty rabbits at any given time, even though we were selling, on average, twenty rabbits per week, at ten dollars a pop, on Craigslist. Yes, it turned out we thought our rabbits were too cute to eat, so we never did eat them, and everyone we sold them to were buying them as pets.

But then the spring rains came around in April, and we were heartbroken.

I will never begin to understand the magic of nature. When female rabbits first get pregnant, they know, and what they do is dig a tunnel about two feet underground and then make a tiny cave where they'll give birth to and feed their young. I can't think of any better way to explain the structure than by describing the Hito structures I'd learned about while fishing in the Philippines.

After tunnelling down two feet, and making their little caves, the female rabbits will then return to the surface and bury the opening, as if they're hiding it, and then they'll never go back to it until about three days before they give birth. At this time, they reopen their tunnels and they begin preparing their nest. They actually chew the fur off of their breasts and roll it up with grass and make what looks like a bird's nest down in their underground cave. Three days later, they give birth, they nurse, and about twenty one days after this happens, you walk outside and look in your rabbit pen, and you see anywhere from four to eight little baby bunny rabbits bouncing around that you never even knew you had. It is all so magical and exciting.

But when the rains came in April, all the underground bunnies died.

It was our first spring on the homestead. We had no idea about the water runoff worked on this land. Where the land drained well, and where it didn't. It turned out that where we'd constructed our rabbit pen just happened to be at the worst possible place. The area sits at a low level, just beneath the steepest grade on our land, and it's riddled with underground springs that you'd never know where there unless you'd lived through at least one rainy spring on the land and had already observed it.

Our little bunnies took a toll, and by the end of that summer we were out of rabbit breeding once again, and for good this time. Not because we didn't want to reconstruct a new pen elsewhere- fearing hard work has never been our way- but because of dealing with people. You have *no clue* how many times people would contact us by way of Craigslist and claim they were coming out at a certain time to buy rabbits, and then just never show and never call. Since we live so far out from the city, we would often set our entire day aside to be here to sell a rabbit for ten dollars, and it was ten dollars we didn't even need in the first place, and then the buyers never came. Our entire day had been rearranged for not.

So we stopped.

We began using our old rabbit pen as a garden spot. And let me tell you, nine months of rabbit poo going into the soil increased the nitrogen content to the perfect level for growing vegetables. We were getting record sized zucchini and squash at harvest, and the corn was the sweetest I'd ever eaten. The following winter we put some of our chickens over there to till up and fertilize the soil for the next season, but they didn't live through the winter, that damned old Bigfoot Sasquatch! But that's another story for another time.

The following year we planted pumpkins on one half of the garden spot where we'd kept the rabbits, and let me tell you, did we get a bumper crop! I've tried to grow pumpkins every year, and it's hard work, because they require a lot of space to vine out and a lot of water to grow their gourds, which are actually a type of squash, but I'd never had success. But that year, the conditions were perfect. The space, the soil, the water. And we had dozens upon dozens of pumpkins.

Until…

…the pumpkin munchers came along.

I noticed the damage they were doing long before I ever saw them. And, technically, I've still never seen them. Well, with my naked eyes, at least. I'm getting ahead of myself again, so let me explain.

I was so excited for our pumpkins that year, that every morning, after I did my morning run, or took my morning bike ride, part of my cool down would include going into the pumpkin patch and seeing how much the pumpkins had grown compared to the day before. I'll never forget that first day, sometime in October, when I walked into the fenced off pumpkin patch and saw that half of my pumpkins had been halfway eaten.

"How could this be?" I asked myself, aloud. The garden was completely fenced in. We shut the gate every night. I got down on my knees to investigate the teeth marks, and I'll be damned if they weren't rabbit teeth marks. "How can this be?" I said, aloud, again. We'd buried chicken wire two feet deep around the entire perimeter of the cage when we'd built the rabbit pen, and with all the rabbits we had at one point, none ever escaped, and not a single predator ever burrowed in. And we had *not* removed the wiring.

I walked around the entire perimeter of the pen and I did not see a single breach. It's as if whatever had come into the pen and eaten the pumpkins had flown over the top. But rabbits can't fly, and though they can jump, they can't jump *that* high.

I knew that if I didn't figure this thing out quick, I was going to lose all my pumpkins. They were almost ripe enough to harvest, but not quite. They needed only a few more days. We were well into October, but not quite to Halloween, and I wanted these pumpkins to be perfect so they would become the perfect jack o'lanterns.

That night, I set one of my trailcams out in the pumpkin patch. I was certain I'd catch whatever was eating my pumpkins on film, and the next morning, to my sheer horror, I found out that I had.

Okay, so here's the deal. These things, though they looked like rabbits, did not move, in any way, like rabbits. I watched in fright, as the camera footage revealed creatures that looked like rabbits, but with supersized heads, like three times the size of regular rabbit heads, crawling out of the soil, like Hito coming out of their tunnels to take the coconut grubs, and making their way to the pumpkins and munching on them.

They did not hop, and they did not walk. They slithered, like a snake, even though they had four legs. Their legs simply lay out to their sides as they slithered along, much like fish fins. They'd even flap from time to time, as if these creatures (or at least, what I *thought* were creatures, at first) were swimming across the ground's surface.

We have a live and let live policy on our homestead. We do not kill the wildlife here, nor do we allow others to do so, even though we have an abundance of it, and it's been hell at times trying to garden and grow flowers and trees and ornamental bushes because of all the deer, but our attitude is that we've invaded their land, they didn't evade ours, so we've spent a shit ton of money on fencing and environmentally safe repellents, etc., and yes, I know this makes me sound like a passivise hippy, but let me tell you, I'm anything but. I just respect life, and perhaps it's because I've fought in war zones is why.

But I'm not an idiot.

I have weapons.

Because though I *do* love animals, I have very little trust and faith in people.

The next night, I took my twenty two caliber rifle into the pumpkin patch with me and I sat and I waited. And just as I was about to fall asleep, I heard munching.

I looked to my direct left, where I heard the sound, and damned if I didn't see one of my pumpkins being eaten.

But I couldn't see what was eating it!

That's right. I could see the pumpkin getting smaller and smaller, and I could see the teeth marks of whatever was eating it being left behind, but for the life of me, I could not see what was eating the pumpkin, even when shining my really bright tactical flashlight on it.

I'd been on my land long enough by this time to have seen some really strange things, things that I couldn't even begin to explain, things that would completely change my way of thinking, and at this time, the thought that instantly came to my head was to pull out my iphone. I did so, and I switched it to camera mode. I aimed it at the pumpkin that was being eaten, and there, in the center of the phone, I saw it.

A pumpkin muncher!

Something with the body of a rabbit, and a head three times larger than it should be, lying on its belly, its four legs fluttering back and forth, lightly, as if it were a fish trying to maintain its position in a stream with a light current.

I looked around the camera, with my naked eye, and again, I could see the pumpkin being eaten, but I could not see the pumpkin muncher that was eating it. I looked back into the camera, and sure enough, there it was.

A pumpkin mucher!

My first instinct was to aim my rifle, by using the camera to do so, at the pumpkin muncher and shoot it. But my better intentions kicked in.

"Ah, the hell with it," I said, and I got up and I took my gun and my camera and my chair and my light back to the house. I never killed any pumpkin munchers that year, and it cost me in that I never got any pumpkins, either.

To date, I've never harvested any pumpkins from that pen, though every year I plant a pretty nice crop of them, and they always do well. They always end up being eaten by something that can't be seen with the naked eye, and I'm okay with that. I figure our 'live and let live' policy here on our property has morphed into 'live and let live and only let die once and no need to kill it again,' or something like that. Even if they are kinda creepy looking little things.

But hey, I just view it as if it's all part of the magic of Halloween.

The End

October 24

Natural Selection

Frank sat in his van, his completely souped-up, wheelchair accessible vehicle that might look like a regular Dodge Caravan from the outside, but which had the most state of the art devices for the handicap that money could buy, because Frank had it. Money. Lots of it. He was rich. And he was selfmade. It didn't come from Government handouts, and he hadn't inherited a dime. He'd been born into the working poor, and he'd worked his ass off his entire life, the last fifty years of it, from a wheelchair, to enter the upper class. He was not elite, but his net worth was in the millions, so he, and everyone who knew him, felt he'd done just fine.

The rally for a mask free America was being held around the corner, across the railroad tracks, and a block up. In the park on the corner. The same park that used to have a Robert E. Lee statue in it until the protesters took it down. Which protesters? Take your pick. Frank couldn't remember. This was Charlottesville, Virginia. They were always protesting something in Charlottesville on any given day of the week. And if you didn't like the protest going on down on the downtown mall, you could always just go up to the university. Those silly kids that thought life was supposed to be fair were always having protests of some sort up there, too.

But today, it was the anti-maskers, and that son of a whore, Damien Little, was leading the protest. The same Damien Little that had been setting up these protests all over the east coast. He'd finally honed in on Charlottesville, alleged capital of ANTIFA- declared so by a former city Mayor who had his ass handed to him in the next election cycle due to making that declaration- but hey, the man had been on CNN for a minute and a half that day because of it, so it had been worth it all for him.

Frank had driven to Richmond five months before, when it was being recommended that people wear face masks when out in public to help 'flatten the curve' as they called it. Not *stop* the spread of the virus, but to slow it down, so that the healthcare industry wouldn't get overwhelmed and could therefore keep up with the rate of new infections and help the people who caught it.

Frank had gone to Damien's first rally, a small one with less than fifty people, to try to talk some sense into the kid. Frank thought of Damien as a kid, because Frank was sixty five and Damien only twenty five. A bulletproof millennial.

"Look," Frank had pleaded from the crowd, and from his wheelchair. "You're young. You're fit. We get that. But not all of us are. It's not about you. It's about those of us over fifty and people who have underlying health issues that make us more susceptible to catching this thing and dying from it if we do."

"It's called natural selection," Damien had shouted back from his soapbox without even hesitating, paying no mind to the fact that Frank was in a wheelchair. Heartless, Frank thought. "For too many years now, when Americans get sick, they take a pill," Damien continued. "When they get depressed, they take a pill. When they get fat, instead of exercising to lower their blood pressure and stave off diabetes, they take a pill. Well," Damien said, pausing for effect, and looking around the small crowd to make sure he had their attention, and he did. "Now it's time to pay the piper. Mother nature is coming around and taking out those of you old, unhealthy fucks who've been hanging on to life by a pill and sucking the shit out of the healthcare system, and forcing those of us who *are* healthy into paying outrageous health insurance premiums we can't afford for coverage we'll never need, anyway, because we fucking take care of ourselves! Without pills!"

"You can't always control everything," Frank had shouted back. "Look at me. I was a nine year old kid, sleeping in the backseat of my parent's car when we were hit by a drunk driver. My parents were killed, and I was raised by an aunt and uncle. I haven't walked in more than fifty years. I have underlying health issues due to my injuries, and my age, and I can't just go out and run eight miles every morning to stay fit and trim. I'm pleading with you. Stop this movement before it picks up momentum. It's not about *you*, and all the other bulletproof millennials, and people in good health. It's about those of us who will die if we catch this thing. All you've got to do is wear a mask, man."

The small crowd in attendance were now considering Frank's point. Damien saw this, and he didn't like it. Not one bit. This whole pandemic thing presented his opportunity to become internet famous!

"Bullshit!" Damien screamed, and the crowd turned to face him. "This man is a fraud," Damien said, pointing to Frank. "We received emails, warning us about him before the rally."

Damien could see the crowd was listening, and he liked that, but he didn't like the fact that he wasn't quite sure what to say next, because he was winging it. Making it all up as he went along. He was completely full of shit.

"We know exactly who you are, old man!" Damien screamed, now directly at Frank. "You were involved in a single car accident years ago, because you were drinking and driving, and you put *yourself* in that wheelchair."

The crowd oohed at this, and Damien was pleased.

"Bullshit!" Frank yelled, and he was livid. "I've never drank in my life, because of what happened to me. I put myself through college and got a masters, and then a doctorate, and I was a biochemist for forty years before retiring a self made millionaire. You are full of shit, and no matter how much granola you eat and how many hours a day you spend in the gym, there are things outside of your control, and you're asking people to throw caution to the wind by not wearing masks, and you are going to get some good people who'd had bad things happen to them, like me, killed!"

"This guy's good," Damien said, drawing the crowd's attention back to himself. "But he's a fraud. We knew he was coming. And we're not going to give him any more attention. What we are going to give attention to at this time is the fact that this is still America, home of the free because of the brave, and men and women died in Iraq and Afghanistan and Vietnam and all kinds of other third world shitholes so we could have the freedom not to wear masks in public if we aren't sickly and haven't become dependent on meds to make it through our day. America! Fuck yeah!"

And with that, the crowd followed in unison. "America! Fuck yeah!"

It was October now, and the United States was seeing over eighty thousand new cases of the virus each day. People were dying in record numbers. The state of Virginia, like most states, mandated that one had to wear a mask if entering a public building or business, and here was Damien now, with his five thousand followers, in Charlottesville, east coast capital city of protests, protesting the forced mask initiative.

"America! Fuck yeah!" Damien and his supporters yelled, and Frank could hear them even though he was two blocks away and around the corner and he had the windows of his van up.

"I'm gonna fuck yeah, you," he said. "Just wait."

Frank had contracted the virus. He'd not gone to the doctor yet and he'd not been officially told, but he knew. He'd followed the news of the pandemic closely, and he was aware of the symptoms, and he knew he had them. He'd been issued his death sentence by mother nature. This natural selection as Damien called it.

But he was going to go out in a bang!

Charlottesville's mayors were notorious for giving the police stand down orders during the protests. Yes, this made the environment much more dangerous, and it usually led to someone getting killed, but the socialist politicians of the city could then blame everything on non-college educated white males, so there was something in it for them in making sure they didn't provide a safe environment for protesters, and they figured those killed likely fantasized about the idea of becoming martyrs, anyway.

Frank was more than a college educated white male. He was a white male with multiple degrees, and he didn't come anywhere close to fitting the profile the socialist were always trying to demonize, but he figured this would all work in his favor. Allow for a greater likelihood of pulling off his plan.

And now was the time!

The protesters were beginning their march up Water Street, on the Downtown Mall, and Frank could hear Damien in front, leading the way. "America! Fuck yeah! America! Fuck yeah!"

Frank started the engine of his van and put the transmission in drive. He slowly pulled onto the street and made the turn. He could see Damien standing in the middle of the street, two blocks away, bullhorn in hand, facing in the opposite direction, his back to Frank, inciting his followers to follow him on his march. Their grandfathers and great grandfathers had stormed the beaches of Normandy, afterall, Damien was telling the crowd, so that the generations of Americans who were to come after them would never have to wear a facemask in public during great times of plague. "America! Fuck yeah!"

Damien began walking backward, shouting their chant through the bullhorn, his followers shouting back. No one in the crowd was wearing a mask. They all appeared to be in their twenties and early thirties, and they all looked like they lived in the gym. Beautiful people, physically, but, as Frank thought, a bunch of self-centered, self-absorbed bitches and pricks.

Frank viewed it all as a better opportunity than he'd hoped for. He could punch the gas right now, by pushing on the gas lever with his right hand, as it where, in his handicap situated van, and not just take *Damien* out, but if he could gain enough speed over the distance of a block and a half, he might be able to take out some of the other protestors, as well, showing these perfectly healthy millennials that they're not quite as bulletproof as they think, and proving to Damien, though he'd never live to get it, that like Frank had told him in Richmond, you can't control everything, and sometimes bad shit just happens.

Frank pushed on the gas lever, and his van actually squealed it's tires looking for traction. When they found it, the van began racing forward like a cougar leaping and reaching full speed in two strides.

Frank quickly closed the distance on his young nemesis to three fourths of a block. Damien turned to see what everyone in the crowd he faced were looking at. He could tell by their wide eyes that it must be something important. "Fuck!" he shouted when he saw the van, and there was no 'yeah' behind it, and there had been no America before it. Just 'fuck!'

"The son of a whore recognizes me," Frank said to himself, and he did feel pleased, knowing that this self-centered little bitch prick knew exactly who was about to take him from this earth, and…

…the 3:15 Amtrak was running right on schedule, and Frank had paid no never mind to the lowering of the guard posts over the train tracks, and he'd paid no attention to the flashing of the warning light, because Frank had been suffering from tunnel vision, the only thing on his mind being taking out the little bitch prick who'd led a nationwide protest against masks, leading to Frank's very death sentence, as Frank saw it, and when the 3:15 Amtrak slammed into the driver's side of Frank's van, Frank was killed instantly, and he would not have to suffer, dying alone from the virus, and his insurance company would not have to pay out the nose, passing those costs, of course, on to the general population, later, when the pandemic was over, and the protestors who saw the shit go down stopped instantly in their tracks.

"Fuck," Damien said again. Always quick to think on his feet, he simply started walking in the opposite direction of the crash to lead his followers through a different part of town. "America! Fuck yeah!" he shouted through the bullhorn.

"America! Fuck yeah!" they responded.

The End

October 25

Curse of El Chupacabra

Soccer. The sport that's been ruining boys in America for the last twenty years!

When I was a kid, we played baseball, football, basketball, or all three. Well, unless you couldn't throw a ball, hit a ball, kick a ball or shoot a ball into a netted hoop. Which was the case for me. So in my case, I ran track. But still.

Soccer sucks!

But my boy? He loves soccer, and since I love my boy more than I love life, I keep my views to myself, and I get out in the field with him and play soccer every chance I get, which is most days, and I make sure to take him to his practices and games, and buy snacks for the team when it's my turn and all the rest that goes along with being a soccer dad.

Besides, he plays football, too, so it's okay. Real, American football!

There's a kid on my son's team named Miguel. My son and Miguel have been on the same team for the past couple of years, and they've been in the same class together at school for the same time period. Miguel's family lives right down the road from us, so there's been times we've taken Miguel to practice and brought him home when his parents were tied up and vice versa.

And this is where our story starts.

I was already nearing forty by the time my son was born, so in comparison to many of his friends' parents, like Miguel's parents, I'm considerably older. Fifteen years on average, it seems.

Miguel's family migrated to the U.S. from Puerto Rico, much like my wife, and my son, came here from the Philippines. I didn't migrate here, of course, being born and raised here, but after six years as an expat in the Philippines, I decided it was time to come home, and of course I brought my family with me. It was my son, actually, and his education and entire future that motivated the move. I could not, in good conscience, allow him to be raised and educated in a third world country, limiting his future opportunities, when I could suck it up and pay taxes and shovel snow for fifteen more years by coming back and allowing him to grow up and be educated here. If you think that's politically incorrect or culturally insensitive, go have kids in a third world country and then let's see what choice you make in regard to their lifestyle, future and education.

That's what I thought!

Once my son's grown, my wife and I fully intend to spend half the year back in the Philippines and half on our beautiful Virginia homestead, nestled in the Blue Ridge Mountains just outside of Charlottesville, and my son? He'll have choices. Options. He can go to college, the military, straight into the workforce, or join us as we bounce back and forth from the U.S. and Southeast Asia. But had we stayed there, his only option would have been getting a job that could never feed him and his own family, should he decide to have one, and he would be at a great disadvantage compared to his Western counterparts as far as qualifications of other jobs in other countries go. We're making sure he's not going to go through the real world with one hand tied behind his back. And to be honest, more like both.

Now, what's this have to do with Miguel? Or El Chupcacabra?

Well, I need to tell you about Miguel's mother. Then you'll get it.

Miguel's father, a wonderful, friendly and pleasant man of about thirty five years old works very hard in the landscaping industry. He came to America when he was about my son's age. He went to work in the landscaping business right out of high school, and now he has his own business and employs many other people. Miguel's father and his family did not come to America to suck off the welfare tit, like so many immigrants are accused of doing by people who don't know other people's stories, yet think they do enough to judge them. Miguel's father, whose name is also Miguel, we'll call him Big Miguel, came to America to live the American dream, and he and his family have been doing just that. And as a successful business owner, Big Miguel is paying tons of taxes to support many of the low-life welfare recipients who were born and raised in America and feel they have a right to judge, and who should be completely ashamed of themselves, not just for judging, but for sitting on their lardasses and not taking advantages of the opportunities we have in the U.S. that most of the rest of the world does not, like Big Miguel is doing.

And he's done that!

Miguel's mother? Maria?

Hm, different story.

Basically, for two years, there *was* no story. All I know is that though we'd met Big and Little Miguel, and Miguel's two older brothers, we'd never met Maria. We'd never even *seen* her.

She never attended any school functions, and when I'd go to their house to pick Miguel up for practice, I'd usually knock on the door, and when one of the kid's would answer, I'd ask if their mother was home- I could tell when their dad wasn't because his work truck was gone- and whichever kid had answered the door would look off to their left, my right, as if taking a cue from someone, and their answer was always the same. No, Maria was not home, and it was beyond obvious that they were lying.

And things were even weirder when we'd take Miguel home, which was usually after dark. One of the other kids, or Big Miguel if he were home, would be waiting for us outside, with the door close, and the porch light on and a flashlight in hand. Never Maria. And after Little Miguel got out of our truck and went to the door, it's as if whoever was there to get him, and Miguel as well, would look around to see if anyone was watching, and then they'd duck inside the house and slam and lock the door as quickly as they could.

Finally, after two years, and just a couple of weeks ago, actually, the first week of October, Maria surfaced, and man, what a coming out it was!

Okay, you know Salma Hayek? The beautiful Mexican actress? Remember how smoking hot she was when she was about thirty years old? (Even though in her fifties she's still just as smoking hot?) Well, that's the best way to describe Maria's physical appearance! She could have passed for thirty year old Salma Hayek's twin sister!

We arrived one Saturday morning for our kid's soccer game. We were happy it was at ten o'clock, because UVA was playing Florida State at home in Charlottesville that day, at two o'clock in the afternoon, so we'd still be able to make the college game. We rushed out to the field, and I noticed that every healthy male above the age of fifteen, and half the women, were staring at the same spot. I looked down the sideline, and I swear for just a minute that I saw a thirty year old Salma Hayak standing there, scrolling on her i-phone, but as it turns out, it was Miguel's mother, Maria.

I'd actually formulated the theory that this woman stayed hidden because she was ugly. I know that sounds terrible, but I grew up in Appalachia, and this is not a lie, there were people there when I was a kid who actually got checks from the welfare department because they were too ugly to work. Seriously! No one would hire them, because they were so ugly, so they lived off of welfare, and they never left their houses. I thought this might be the case for Maria.

I was wrong.

"Do you like what you see?" my wife, the most beautiful woman in the world, in all honesty, asked me as she obviously caught me staring.

"Is that Salma Hayak?" I said.

"Obviously, it's Miguel's mom," my wife said. "Can't you see she's with her family?"

During halftime, or whatever the hell they call it in soccer, Big Miguel brought Maria over and introduced her to us. She spoke good English, though still broken, and she thanked us for all the times we'd helped out with Little Miguel. We said she was welcome, and she began speaking to my wife in Spanish. It happens all the time. My wife is what's called

"Miztizzo," which means she is a Filipina who has a lot of Spanish blood in her ancestral heritage, going back to the time when Spain occupied the Philippines. They did for four hundred and thirty three years. And many people of South America, be it Mexico, Ecuador, etc. have mistaken my wife for being Mexican.

My wife explained she was Filipina, and Maria apologized, unnecessarily, as such a mistake would only offend an American who would view it as a great opportunity to accuse the one mistaken as being racist, rather than simply mistaken. No one else from anywhere else in the world would be offended by such a thing. The two women enjoying speaking to each other in broken English for the rest of the game.

So, to speed things up (I know, too late), we ended up being invited to Miguel and Maria's house the following weekend for lunch. Why not dinner? Well, that's part of the story.

Miguel had known I was a writer, but he never knew what I wrote about. That day, over tacos and refried beans and Spanish rice, I told him. I write about the paranormal, a little horror, cryptozoology, and well, just whatever comes to mind. I told him I'd even written a romance novel once, a book called 'The Box,' and when he laughed I said that was the general response I got from everyone, and even though it is the lowest selling novel I'd ever written, I believe it is, by far, my best.

"El chupacabra," Maria said while we were laughing at my joke about 'The Box,' which I don't really think Big Miguel understood, but he felt like he should laugh since I was.

"What?" I said, turning to face Maria, and hoping my wife wasn't going to get jealous because I was looking a little too long into the face of thirty year old Salma Hayak's doppelganger.

"My wife," Big Miguel said. "She has a story about chupacabra."

"Chupacabra?" I said. "The Mexican goat blood sucker?"

Maria said something in Spanish, and I didn't understand it, but it sounded like she might have been cussing me out.

"Chupacabra is not Mexican," Miguel said. "The first sightings actually came from Puerto Rico."

"Oh," I said. "I had no idea. Are you sure?"

"We are very sure," Maria said. "Because we are the ones who saw them!"

By 'we,' Maria had meant her siblings and her parents. Maria was just a young girl, maybe five years old. They'd had a small farm in rural Puerto Rico, and one year, the first year for which Maria had many memories, perhaps because they were horrendous memories, the family began losing all of their livestock.

"It started with the goats," Miguel said. "But they also killed the pigs and the chickens."

"We thought vampire," Maria said. "But no one in our village was missing. No people were harmed. Just the animals. And then my sister and me, we see it. This dog looking thing, sucking blood from goat.

"We throw rocks," Maria said, going through the motion with her right arm. "It look up. Eyes red. Fangs life vampire. No dog."

"What did you do?" my wife asked, believing every word of Maria's story, as was I. My wife and I saw some really weird shit in the Philippines. Want to read all about it? Go read my book 'Isle of Kapre.' That shit would blow your mind, and from my time spent in the Philippines and other third world countries, I can tell you that one of their strengths versus we superiorly educated westerners, is that they haven't written off all their supernatural activity with logic. Most people in these countries still believe in things that cannot be explained through logic, and I will testify now and forever that I have seen plenty of it myself. I had no reason to doubt Maria's story.

"This goes on for many months," Maria says. "And then we find their nest."

"Their nest?" I said.

"Yes," Maria said, and did I mention she looked like a thirty year old Salma Hayak?

"They nest underground," she said. "We find their nest. They not like normal animal. Have babies in spring. They are evil. They give birth on Halloween."

We were all enthralled by Maria's story. Everyone in the room was mesmerized, hanging on her every word. Even her family, who I was sure had heard the story a million times were as well.

"On Halloween, when I am little girl," she continued, "we kill hive. We dump gasoline, my father and uncles, they dump gasoline into hive. Big hole in field. Then they light it on fire."

"Wow," I said.

"We hear howling and screaming coming from hole," Maria said. "But we make big mistake."

"What mistake?" my wife asked.

"We look over to ridgeline," Maria said. "Where there is full moon. And we see silhouette of chupacabra. We not get them all. We see one on ridgeline, and her belly is fat with kits."

"Did the killings of the livestock continue after that?" I asked.

"They spread," Big Miguel said. "This is why you hear of chupacabra in Mexico, and now in U.S."

"I don't get it," I said.

"I have one uncle move to Mexico," Maria said. "He said it was curse of el chupacabra. They would hunt us. So he flee. He is dead a year later."

"Really," my wife said.

"Yes," Maria said. "My family and two other uncles, we come to U.S. My uncles stay in Texas, many sightings in Texas of el chupacabra. My uncles both die.

"My family comes east," Maria continued. "My parents dead. I meet Miguel, who is from Puerto Rico and move here as child, too. We meet in high school. People assume we knew each other before, in old country, but we did not."

The things you can learn about people if you listen to them, rather than judging them upon sight will never cease to amaze me.

"Miguel keep me safe," Maria said, reaching over and grabbing her husband's hand. "He keep us all safe," she said, looking around and making eye contact with all three of her sons.

I now understood why Maria, who was not ugly enough to get a social security disability check for her looks, but who probably could have gotten roles in film due to her looks, stayed hidden. She feared for her life.

"Do you think these chupacabra would even remember you all these years later?" I asked. "Would they recognize you? I mean, you were a little girl. You're a very grown woman now."

"We take one percaution," Miguel said.

"What's that?" I asked.

"We will not be raising goats."

We all laughed our asses off at that one and kept eating even though we were full. The food was *that* damn good. We laughed and talked more of other things, and around the time the sun started to set on that early October evening, moving the time closer toward a dark, chilly October night, Maria told us to leave immediately as the house must always be fortified by dark, *especially* in October.

We honored her wishes and without judgement, for, when we'd spoken more throughout the afternoon we'd shared with our friends some of the things we'd witnessed in the Philippines, and they took us at our word just like we'd taken them at theirs. My wife, my son and myself left their house, our bellies full, and got in our truck, backed out of the driveway and started heading for home.

"Watch out!" my wife screamed, grabbing the dash once we'd only gone about fifty yards down the road. I saw what she was talking about, and I'd been able to hit the brakes in time, making sure not to hit the animal that had run across the road in front of us, just as it was turning dark.

"What was that?" I asked.

"It looked like a dog," my wife said.

I glanced over into the field where the animal had run, and I could not see it, because it was now dark. But what I was able to see were the eyes.

The glowing red eyes.

The End

October 26

The Writer's Wife

This story is true. It has nothing to do with Halloween, perhaps other than the fact that if it hadn't happened, you wouldn't be reading this collection of Halloween flavored short stories right now. Plus, ironically, it *does* begin in October.

October, 2011. I'd gone back and forth from the Philippines to the U.S. a few times, all in ill attempts to grab and retain virtually any form of gainful employment in the U.S. which would allow me to bring my beautiful bride, Dearly, and our then only months old son, Daniel, to the U.S. with me and give them the best possible life I could give them. The long and short of it is that it didn't work out. I had several strikes going against me. One; it was during the great recession. Two; I'd previously been a securities dealer, and my series 7 securities license had lapsed while I was away fighting a war in Iraq (and no, that carried no leverage when trying to get on with any of the firms I called on after I got back). Three; I was strung out on more dope by way of the Army hospital and Veterans Administration after sustaining several injuries in Iraq, which led to me taking anything I could get my hands on, all of which made me not quite the guy at the top of anyone's hiring list.

Out of options, I wasn't about to stay in the U.S. alone and send money back to take care of my family and hope everything worked out. You see, my wife and son were living in Mindanao, the southernmost island in the Philippines, an island riddled with multiple terrorist networks who specialize in kidnappings for ransom, and since my son was half white, he had a *huge* target on his head at all times. It was very common in Mindanao for people to keep their eyes on children whose fathers were from the West, and even taxi drivers who were not part of any terrorist network would kidnap these kids once the fathers left the country, viewing it as easy money. Nannies and housekeepers did it all the time.

I went back to Mindanao to be with my family. At least if I were there, someone would have to go through me to get to my son, and let me tell you, that translates to someone would have to kill me to get to my son, and, just as the terrorists in Iraq had found out, I don't die easily.

When I got back to Mindanao, we left Davao City, where I'd always stayed with Dearly before, and we went back to her province, which I'll not name here, so as not to put any targets on any of her relatives' heads. We figured her large family would be a big help with our baby, and we were right, as family is still important in Philippines culture, much like it used to be here in the U.S.

It didn't take long before I sunk into a pretty deep depression. I was living in the jungle with no electricity or running water. We had a nine month old baby we were feeding off of roots and other wild edibles we could dig up in the jungle, and an ever constant supply of fish and squid I would get from the fishermen whom I helped carry boats in from sea in the mornings when they returned from night fishing. Anyone who shows up to help pull in the boats is given a handful of fish or squid by the fishermen they help. At first, no one would give me any fish or squid, because they assumed that since I was an American, I had to be rich, and I didn't need the food. They couldn't understand why I even worked. In their minds, Americans don't need to work, because they're all already rich. They believe our Government just sends us all a check every week. However, once these fishermen saw me day after day, they began giving me free fish and squid, and to their character, they gave me more than the locals. "You big American," they would say. "Need eat more food."

One night, while drunk on tuba- a wine made out of the sap from a coconut tree and that tastes like table vinegar- and crying about how I hated my life, Dearly asked me what we could do to get to America.

"The economy's in the shitter," I told her. "I've burned every bridge I ever had. The only way we could get there, and raise our kid there, and have good lives is if I were to make it as a writer."

"Then make it as writer," she said.

"That's crazy," I told her. "Do you know how many writers actually make enough money to live off of their writing?"

"No," she said.

"Neither do I," I said, after stopping to think about it for a minute, "but I'm sure it's just a few."

"Then become one of the few," she said.

What struck me about this whole conversation was how easily she thought I could do it. Did she really believe in me this much? Or was this one of those 'ignorance is bliss' moments? I'm certainly not disrespecting my wife by saying this, but here she was, a third world poor twenty three year old girl who'd grown up in a small fishing village in the jungle, who'd probably never used the internet until she went to Davao City to attend college for the few years that she could afford to do so, by way of a not so poor grandmother, who, by the way, quit paying her tuition (roughly $250 per semester in U.S. dollars), and kicked her out when she found out she was dating an American. Why should she help support her? She had a rich American boyfriend? And no, Dearly never was able to go back and finish college, because no, her rich American boyfriend wasn't so rich after all.

Anyway, the next morning, while trying to sleep off a tuba hangover, which let me tell you, is worse than a Schlitz malt liquor hangover, by far, I got my answer.

She believed in me.

"Wake up!" she said. I opened my eyes and looked up and I saw my beautiful bride standing in the doorway. She had a notebook in one hand and three ink pens in the other. She threw it all on the bed and said, "write!"

We had no computer. We had no internet. We had nothing. But Dearly had scrounged what few pesos we had, walked half a mile down the hill to the road, paid half of what we had to a tricycle driver who took her two miles into the closest thing resembling a town and back, and used the other half of what we had to buy me a notebook and three ink pens so I could write.

And with those pens, I wrote until my hands cramped. And in that notebook, I hand wrote a novel called "Off Switch." I would spend months going to an internet cafe, renting a computer for fifteen pesos an hour (roughly forty cents) when we had the money, to type it into a word document, and these months were interspersed with weeks when we didn't have the money for me to rent computer time. And the whole time I was in those internet cafes I was harassed by the locals because my nose was so long, my arms were so hairy, and my skin was so white.

But I persevered, because my wife wouldn't let me quit.

It was a long, hard climb, but we made it. Eventually, and after being taken advantage of by a lot of douchebags in the mainstream media and the internet blogging world who would publish my work without paying me- Joe The Plumber who's not really a plumber and who's name isn't even Joe and Alex Jones, who's a fucking nut case, are two, just to name two- I finally started getting paid for my writing from afar, and in time, I was earning enough money, from writing, to come back to America, get an apartment, a car, furniture, and begin the Visa process to bring my wife to America. She and our son stayed back for six months, without me, while I was in the U.S. doing this. I moved them across town, once, in Mindanao, when we had confirmed a kidnapping plot on my son, and when we got word of another, I moved them to Manila, where they lived for three months, alone, until I returned to be with them for another six months before we came to the U.S. to live happily ever after, which is exactly what we've been doing.

The reason I'm writing this story, and including it in this anthology, is because my wife, Dearly, and our son, Daniel, deserve to have this story told, and they deserve to have it preserved. The only reason I'm alive right now- the only reason I didn't drink and drug myself to death, or like far too many other veterans with P.T.S.D., like myself, the only reason I didn't comit suicide, is because of Dearly and Daniel. These two people, my wife and our son, literally loved me back to life.

Off Switch was never meant to be a novel. It was meant to be a suicide note. When I sat in that little bamboo shack, alone, because Dearly would take the baby to her mother's, allowing me time to write without interruption, I fully intended to use that notebook and those ink pens to leave my note. The one they'd find and cry about and ask themselves why they hadn't done more, etc.

But it became a book. It became a book that allowed me to let it all out. It became a book that allowed me to begin healing. And Dearly's belief in me was the seed that grew into a mighty oak's worth of healing.

Nearly ten years, as of this writing, has passed since that day in October when I moved into the deep dark jungles of the Philippines, with a hungry baby and a hungry woman and a hungry belly, convinced I would never see the U.S. again.

Today, we own a piece of property nestled in the beautiful Blue Ridge Mountains, just outside of Charlottesville, Virginia, that is bigger than the entire neighborhood in which I grew up. We live in a house on our property that is far too big for the three of us and a far cry from that little bamboo hut in Mindanao. We have a pond full of catfish, bass and sunfish. We have gardens and we have fruit orchards that we planted ourselves. Hell, a couple of months ago we went out and bought ourselves a brand new pickup truck. Oh, and yes. We have running water and electricity now, too.

Today, our needs are met and we want for nothing. Our cups runneth over. And all credit, aside from being given to God, is also to be given to one person and one person only, and no, it is not me, the writer.

It is the writer's wife.

The End

October 27

Lost Soldier

Well, here I was, so darned close to finishing up my Halloween anthology I could taste it. Back in the Army, we'd say this was so close you could finish standing on your head. Short timer. Don't even bother trying to open your chute, because you're too close to the ground.

And I was stuck.

Writer's block.

One of the things I love to do when I need inspiration is go out in the woods and sit. Listen. Listen to nature. The spirits. All part of being an empath. And I did this, for a good while, but nothing was coming. So I decided to do something else I'll often do when the words just aren't coming, and that's splitting firewood.

You see, when you have a creative mind, one of the biggest obstacles to get in your way is that creative mind. Sometimes it just thinks and thinks and thinks, and it thinks too much and all the noise is blocking out anything good. But when I chop wood, the madness stops. It has to stop.

Or I'm liable to cut off a toe.

I'd taken to splitting my wood, as of late, on a completely different part of our property. It's an odd location, as it's simply in the middle of a field and next to a treeline that marks the boundary of mine and my neighbor's property on the other side. But you see, the thing about this location is that just inside the treeline, there is an overgrown cemetery. Nothing big. Just people who'd lived in our house and on this land in the past. I know of three little girls buried there. The ones that died during the Spanish flu pandemic of 1918. But there are a couple more graves in there, as well, and I have no idea who's buried in them, nor do any of my neighbors. These graves go back further than 1918, though not by much, as the house was built in 1903.

My point of splitting wood here is that maybe, just maybe, I'd be out here some day, my mind clear of the noise, since I'd be focussing on the task at hand, and someone, or some*thing*, would communicate with me. Tell me a story. Tell me *their* story.

These were my thoughts as I began splitting wood on a day too hot to be out there doing it, when I heard someone say, "Excuse me, Sir?" from behind me. I turned around, thinking that son of a gun Jim Brown was back, because he still owed me that story, but it wasn't him. Wasn't him at all. It appeared to be someone out performing in one of the civil war reenactments which are quite common throughout Virginia in the summer. He looked about twenty years old, and he was wearing a gray wool uniform. It looked just like the kind the confederates wore during the civil war.

"Man, you must be hot," I said, after turning and seeing him. He was walking up from the road. "I'd at least take that jacket off. Too hot out here to be wearing wool."

"I wouldn't want to be caught out of uniform," he said as he continued making his way toward me, repeatedly wiping sweat from his brow as he did. He'd take his cap off, wipe his brow, then put the cap on just long enough to take a step or two and then repeat the process.

"Y'all having a reenactment out this way?" I asked. They usually have them down the mountain a way further in a huge field that's closer to the highway, because they draw a lot of tourists, but I'd noticed they move them around sometimes. There's actually a lot of wealthy people who live in my area, just outside of Charlottesville, Virginia, and some of them are history buffs, and hell, actual historians, and I figured one of them might be putting on a reenactment for the weekend just for the fun of it.

"Sir," the young man said, "I'm just trying to get home, and I think I am, but it don't look like it did when I left. And I ain't been gone but a month or so."

"Ah," I said. "I get it." And I did. I'd been to a couple of those reenactments and I've visited a lot of the historic spots around Virginia, like Mount Vernon, the home of George Washington, and Monticello, the home of Thomas Jefferson. We love going down to colonial Williamsburg. And you see, the thing about these places is that when you go there, and you see the people working there who are dressed in costumes, period costumes, meaning the outfits the people of the times they're portraying actually wore, they are in character. And if you talk to them, you have to speak to them as if you're in the period they're portraying as well, and if you don't, they'll completely ignore you. I figured I'd play along.

"Where have you come from, private?" I asked, seeing his rank on his lapel.

"Charlottesville," he said. "We was camped out on the Rivanna River. Just below Rio Hill." He finally closed the distance on me and was standing right beside me. Something seemed strange about him. He had the same sickly complexion to him that that old rascal Jim Brown had.

"Have a seat," I said, motioning to an unsplit stove length about a foot and a half in diameter that was sitting on its end.

"Thank you," he said.

"Tell me all about your troubles," I said. "And of this home you cannot find. Perhaps I can help."

"Everything was fine," the young man said. "We weren't expecting no trouble. But that blasted 'ol Custer came in and got us by surprise and had us tuckin' our tales and runnin' for the hills in seconds."

"*The* Custer?" I said. "As in General *George A.* Custer?"

"That's the one," he said. He took his hat off and lay it on his knee and continued wiping sweat from his brow. "Thing of it was," he then said, and he laughed afterward. "Is 'ol Custer's men got theirs even after we run off."

"How so?" I asked.

"They set fire to our camp," he said, "and one of our caissions exploded, and they thought we's shootin' artillery at 'em, and in the confusion they started shooting each other."

This guy was good. Or at least he'd read the history marker at Rio Hill shopping center down in Charlottesville and memorized it, the same as me. The battle of Rio Hill took place in Charlottesville on February 28, 1864. General George A. Custer had taken fifteen hundred Union troops and surprised a very small regiment of Confederate soldiers camped out on the banks of the Rivanna River. The rebels knew they were outnumbered, so they fled, just like this guy was saying in his story. But the thing was, I knew it was a story. Nothing more, nothing less, and most locals know it, because it happened locally.

"Well," I said, now laughing myself. "At least that bastard got his at Little Bighorn out in Montanna a dozen years later."

"Huh?" the kid said, and he looked up at me, and the look in his eyes made me take a step back. This was no act. He didn't know what in the name of all things holy I was talking about.

"He wouldn't know anything about that," a voice said from behind me. I turned quickly, and son of a gun there was that old rascal Jim Brown. He was walking through the treeline, from the cemetery, making his way to us. "That hasn't happened yet in his time."

"Why, Jim Brown, you son of a gun," I said. "You owe me a story."

"I know I do," he said. "It's why I came. But it looks like I've got more pressing matters here at hand." After he said this, he looked over at the young man in the Confederate uniform sitting on the stove length. "I'm here to take you home," he said.

"I think I *am* home," the kid said. "It just don't look the same."

"Come with me," Jim Brown said, offering the kid his hand. The kid took it, and Jim Brown helped him up. "I'll be back for you," Jim Brown then said to me.

"I ain't holding hands and going nowhere with you, Jim Brown," I told him, and I was starting to maybe figure this guy out. He wasn't a thief, like I'd originally thought. I was getting the impression that he's one of those guys who are into other guys, if you know what I mean.

"I'm talking about the story," Jim Brown said. "The one I owe you."

"Oh," I said.

"I'll come back on Halloween," he said.

"That'll be too late, Jim Brown!" I said, and I was angry. Something about this guy just ticked me off. Everytime he came around and I got close to him I began to feel enraged. "You know I gotta have all these stories ready well before then."

"I'll be back in four days," Jim Brown said. "But where we're going, it'll be Halloween."

"What does that even mean, Jim Brown?" I said as Jim Brown and the guy out for the reenactment began walking toward the treeline. The very treeline with the overgrown cemetery inside. The very treeline Jim Brown had just stepped out of.

I heard a car horn and I turned to see my wife and one of her friends coming up the driveway. They'd been out shopping and eating and having a good old time. I turned to the treeline to tell Jim Brown to hang around long enough to finally meet my beautiful bride, but just like that, he and the reenactment player were gone.

How convenient.

The End

October 28

Papa Smurf

Everyone's hometown has it's town drunk. But there were a few differences between my hometown's town drunk and the town drunks from most other towns. First of all, the man, whose real name was Stanley, wasn't a drunk. He never drank. And no one told their kids to stay away from him, like most parents tell their children in regard to the town drunk in other towns, rather, they always told us to make sure we were nice to him.

We called Stanley Papa Smurf, because he *looked* like Papa Smurf, the cartoon character. Well, that's if Papa Smurf would have been about six and a half feet tall and white, instead of blue. Papa Smurf, *our* Papa Smurf, not the television show's Papa Smurf, always wore a long trench coat, whether it was winter or summer, and he had snow white hair and a full beard that jutted out at the jaw, just like the cartoon character for whom he was nicknamed. Hey, it was the 1980's, so anyone walking around with white hair and a beard like that was bound to be called Papa Smurf eventually.

Though Papa Smurf didn't drink, he did smoke, and he smoked incessantly. You never saw the man without a cigarette, and the man never ran into you without asking for one. He'd always say, "excuse me boys (because my friends and I were about ten years old back then and we were always together), do you have any of those good cigarettes?"

What Papa Smurf meant by 'good cigarettes' were cigarettes that hadn't already been smoked. Sadly, Papa Smurf found most of his cigarettes on the ground. Yes, he smoked other people's butts.

Stanley had fought his way across Europe with the United States Army back in World War Two. He came home and found that his wife had left him while he'd been deployed, and she'd taken his children with her. The man never saw his family again, and I guess that's what drove him nuts. Not so much the war and what he saw there. I remember hearing this story as a child, and I didn't really understand the full weight of it until I came home from Iraq and went through a very near similar situation. I have three adult children, somewhere, that I haven't seen in a decade, and I doubt I ever will see them again, and I guess I've gone crazy in my own way, but I've learned how to live with it, and better yet, how to profit from it. Write books, perform silly shenanigans on monetized social media platforms, etc. It's entertaining and it pays the bills, but I know what they mean about the clown always crying on the inside.

And I have a new wife and a son who've loved me back to life, and with whom I'm perfectly happy, so at the end of the day, it's all good.

But I *do* know Stanley's pain.

I remember one time, while downtown as a child, seeing Stanley bending over and picking up cigarette butts that were being pointed out to him by two older boys. These boys were widely known in our small community as the local bullies. They were probably sixteen years old at the time.

"There's one, Papa Smurf," one of the boys, Todd, would say. "Pick it up and stick it in your mouth." Papa Smurf did as he was told, and he pulled a lighter out of his overcoat pocket, and he lit the butt. He pulled a few puffs off of it, and then it was done.

"Here's one, Papa Smurf," the other bully, Scott, said, pointing to the ground. Once again, Stanley bent over, picked up the butt, lit it and smoked it. Todd and Scott laughed and laughed, and they did this for ten minutes or so before deciding to go on and do other things, leaving Stanley there, alone, searching for cigarette butts in the grocery store parking lot.

My friend that was with me and I walked over to Stanley. "Papa Smurf," I said. He turned to face us. "My mom smokes. Do you like Winstons?"

"I smoke 'em all, boys," Stanley said. "But I don't wanna get you in trouble. Don't be stealing your momma's cigarettes on my account."

"I won't," I said. "I'll ask her first."

"Well," Stanley said. "Long as you ask."

"We'll be right back!" I said, and my friend and I took off running for home. Our town was small, and even at ten years old I could run from one side of it to the other in a matter of minutes, and it was only a matter of minutes before my buddy and I returned with an entire pack of Winstons for Papa Smurf. We hadn't asked. When we got to my house, my mother was taking a nap, and we stole a pack from one of her cartons. But we never told Stanley this.

For the next couple of years, anytime I was going downtown, I'd make sure to lift a handful of cigarettes from my mom in case I saw Stanely, which I usually did. He was always thankful, and I think my mom eventually figured out she was missing some sticks, but she never mentioned it to me. But I'm sure she knew exactly where they were going. I know that she knew I wasn't smoking them. And I think she knew I was giving them to Stanley, because as they say, a mother always knows.

And then, one day, Papa Smurf disappeared.

Now, for the record, he would disappear off and on throughout the year. The story was that he was actually from the next county over from us, originally, and that he had a sister over there who would allow him to stay with her. He had a cousin in our town, and supposedly another relative a county over the other way. He basically did a tri-county loop, though he was mostly in our town.

But there was something different about Stanley's absence this time. It was prolonged. Usually, he'd only be gone for a week or two. But he took off this time in the middle of September, and we didn't see him for more than an entire month.

Not until Halloween night!

"Hey, ya little shits," we heard a voice say from behind us. My buddy and I were on our way home from trick-or-treating. Our pillow cases were full, and we were excited about trading candy. And we knew the voice that had come from behind us. It was Todd. "Give us your fucking candy," Scott said next.

"Run!" my friend said, and we started to, but the teenagers were on us instantly. They grabbed us by the shirt collars and damn near choked us out with the force they used to pull us to a stop.

"You're not going anywhere," Todd said.

"Come on, honey. Let's get out of here," I heard a woman say. I looked over after hearing the voice and saw my old second grade teacher. She'd seen everything that was going down, and as someone who had once held authority over pretty much every child in our town, she could have stepped in and scolded Todd and Scott and saved my buddy's and my ass, but she didn't do that. She did not do the right thing, like she'd always talked about in her second grade classroom. She left me and my friend to get pummeled by two boys nearly twice our age and definitely twice our size. To this day, she has no idea who the two little boys wearing those Halloween masks that night were- the two little boys she abandoned for a beating- but I can tell you this, those two little boys, to this day, thirty five years later, as of this writing, remember her.

"Excuse me, boys," another voice said from the darkness after our old teacher had hightailed it. "But do you have any of those good cigarettes?"

"Get the fuck out of here, old man," Scott said, letting go of my shirt collar and turning around to face Stanley, who was approaching us slowly through the darkness. He was wearing his signature overcoat, and man, can I tell you, me and my buddy were happy to see him. "This is of no concern to you."

"Why," Papa Smurf said. "What are you big boys a'fixin' to do to these smaller boys?"

"We're a'fixin' to take their candy and kick their asses," Todd said.

"Ya'll ought not do that," Stanly said.

"If you don't turn around and leave right now," Scott said, "we're gonna kick your ass, too."

"Well now," Stanley said. "My Papa raised me right. And he told me that if I was ever gonna be in a fight, and I knew there was no way out of it, that I should hit first and hit hard."

Todd and Scott looked at each other, trying to look brave in each other's eyes, but even as a ten year old little boy I could recognize fear when I saw it, and that's exactly what I saw in their eyes, not bravery.

"But seeing how you boys ain't eighteen yet, I guess I can't really throw the first punch without having to worry about going to jail."

"That's right, old man," Todd said. "We're gonna kick your ass and say you tried to molest us, you old mother fucker!"

"Well," Papa Smurf said. "I fought my way across Europe. I reckon I can fight my way through you two little prison bound pieces of shit."

"What?" Scott said.

"What I'm trying to say," Papa Smurf said, "and I apologize for my language. But what I'm trying to say is, go ahead and hit me first. Hit me hard enough to knock me down. But you'd better hope that I don't get back up, because if I do, you're gonna feel the full fury of fifty years of anger coming through my fists and into your faces."

Neither Todd or Scott had a comeback for this. They looked at each other again, and they didn't even *try* to hide their true feelings this time. The looks on their faces said, "are you thinking what I'm thinking?" and the answer must have been 'yes,' because they both took off sprinting! They didn't want any of what Papa Smurf had to give them.

I reached into my pants pocket inside my Incredible Hulk Halloween costume. You know, the cheapos you buy at the department store which are always ripped to shreds before you're even halfway through the night? I grabbed the five or six cigarettes I'd lifted from my mom's purse before heading out for the night. I knew we hadn't seen Papa Smurf in more than a month, but I had my hopes up. "Here," I said, as I handed them to him. "Here's some of those good cigarettes."

"Thank you, boys," Papa Smurf said to my buddy and me. He pulled his old lighter out of the pocket of his trench coat, lit a Winston, and then he turned around and headed on his way.

"Thank you, Papa Smurf," my buddy and I said in unison. He'd just saved us from getting our asses handed to us. His prediction was right, too. Todd and Scott are both in and out of prison on a pretty regular basis, all these years later, and despite some of the hardships I've been through, I would not want to trade lives with them for a minute.

My buddy and I made it back to my house without further incident. We were sitting on the floor in the living room, trading candy, when my mom came in and shut and locked the door and turned off the porch light for the night. Trick-or-treat was officially over for Halloween.

"Wow," she said. "You boys got a lot of candy."

"Yup," I said, hoping she wasn't going to mention anything about any missing cigarettes. Like I said, she never did, but my paranoia stretches way back.

"By the way," she said as I handed my buddy a Kit Kat in exchange for a Snickers, to this day my favorite candybar. "I got some bad news tonight."

"What?" I said, looking at my buddy's pile of candy, hoping to see another Snickers.

"Papa Smurf's dead," my mom said.

My buddy and I looked each other in the eyes and said, "what?"

"Yeah," my mom said. "Cindy, from the next street over told me about it when she brought her kids by trick-or-treating. He'd gotten sick, so he went to his sisters'. She took him to the hospital and they put him in hospice. He had pneumonia, but what was bad was that his lungs were eaten up with cancer. They kept him sedated on morphine, so he didn't suffer, but he finally passed away."

"When?" I said, and my buddy and I had not dropped our eye contact with each other the entire time my mom had been speaking.

"Last night," she said. "What a shame. A day before Halloween."

My mom walked the bowl of remaining candy she had into the kitchen. My buddy said, "I'm going home," and got up and walked out of the house and he didn't even take his candy with him. I did the right thing and made sure he got it the next day, and to this day, we've never discussed what happened that Halloween night.

They say that Halloween, or All Hallow's Eve is the night that the dead return to walk the earth for three days before returning to their graves on November second, or All Souls' Day. It looked like Stanley wanted to return and say thank you to a couple of kids who'd looked out for him and perhaps hex a couple who hadn't. My mom, who stopped smoking entirely, by the way, a short time later, thought it was a shame that Stanley had passed away only one night before Halloween. My buddy and I, though sad to see Stanley go, as were all of us in our home town, thought that if he had to go, anyway, his timing had been pretty good. He only had to wait one night to come back and walk the earth and do the right thing, and in so doing, his death very well may have prevented ours.

The End

October 29

The Veil Is Thinning

As an empath- one with the eyes to see and the ears to hear what most others cannot- I must warn you. The veil is already thin, and it's getting thinner. But don't just take my word for it. I can assure you that I've been in contact with many other empaths and they've confirmed the same. But even more than that, let me teach you how to see beyond the veil, and then you can go out there at dusk, or into the fog on a dreary morning, or walk along the beach and see for yourself. You can peel back another layer of the ever thinning veil, you can see into the spiritual realm in a way others who consider this entire topic to be poppycock can't, and you can begin to become enlightened.

Many people believe we are physical beings, and that after death, we experience a spiritual afterlife. This, my friends, is the poppycock, because, you see, we are spiritual beings having a physical experience. Every single one of us, though few of us understand such things. Albert Einstein, himself, said that the physical realm is merely an illusion, but that it just happens to be a very persistent illusion because of the solidity of matter.

The veil, as best as it can be described, understandably, is the thin layer that separates the physical from the spiritual. Many others have described it as the place where one dimension may overlap another. Those of us who have eyes through which we can see, and more than just objects in the physical realm, but *really* see, as in, *through* the veil, can see the other side. Those of us who have ears that can do the same, hear what's on the other side of the veil, have had amazing experiences. I'll share some of mine with you, and then I'll tell you how best you might be able to develop this ability.

I grew up in a small timber town, and I spent most of my time in the woods hunting, hiking or running, or along the riverbanks fishing. Almost all the hollows heading up between each mountain where I grew up, at one point or another, had had railroad tracks, as back when people had originally logged the area, more than a century before, the way they got the logs to the mill in the town below the mountains was by train.

I remember the first time I heard the whistle blow. The train whistle. The train whistle from a train that wasn't even there. Even the track had been taken up more than fifty years before I heard the whistle and one would be hard pressed to even make out where the old track had lay, as the forest had grown up so much where the track had once been, but if you looked closely, you could still tell.

I'd been sitting in my old tree stand, from which I would bow hunt but never kill any deer (not for a lack of trying, I just never had success from that stand), and I heard the train whistle. It was coming around the bend, about two hundred yards behind me. It blew twice, and it sounded much louder the second time, as it was making its way closer.

I can remember thinking this was odd, because I knew this part of the forest like the back of my hand. I'd hunted it for years. I knew there were no train tracks in it, and I knew there hadn't been in my lifetime.

I got out of my tree stand, and it was time to go, anyway, because night was falling. It was the time of the zenith. The point between day and night. And it wouldn't be until more than a quarter of a century later that I would learn that this is one of the best times of the day that the veil becomes thinnest, and that if you're an empath, something I wouldn't learn I was as well for more than a quarter century later, you could see and hear things others could not.

I remember sharing this experience with an old man who lived very close to this location some years later. It was October, and the air was filled with the feeling of all things Halloweenish, and I'd shared my story with him, of hearing the train whistle just a ways up from his house, in the woods, and I remember he smiled from ear to ear. "I hear it every now and then, too," he said. "But be careful who you tell. They'll say you're crazy."

You see, this is the type of story that most people view as poppycock. But my old friend, dead these past fifteen years, now, was an empath, so he knew. He knew how to look, he knew how to listen, and therefore, he could hear and he could see what others could not.

Another place where one can look behind the veil, if one knows how, and the main key is simply a willingness to see and hear things that most would say is not there, is where land meets water, like on a beach, and not just the beaches of the world's oceans, but lakes work as well. Between midnight and dawn is a good time. One can travel to the top of a mountain where earth meets sky to visit a thin spot in the veil, and even treelines, where field meets forest can be powerful places.

There is another place where the veil is thin and this is where life meets death. Graveyards are the safest bet for this exposure, but, and not that I'd recommend it, combat zones are very good places to see beyond the veil as well. I have more stories from my own experiences in Iraq and the Philippines that I could share here, but what I'll tell you is that I was visited by angry ancestor spirits in Iraq, one of whom harassed me repeatedly with an influx of nightmares, because I'd made the mistake of acknowledging him, and I *did* see the ghosts of Japanese soldiers chasing the ghosts of young, Filipina maidens down the beaches of Mindanao, Philippines, with ill intentions. Oh, how thin the veil was in so many places in Mindanao. Ocean meeting land. Day meeting night at twilight. Past wars against imperialists leaving many angry spirits and the current war against radical Islamic Jihadists doing the same. The place is a supernatural hotbed.

Speaking of which, it was a very distant, yet related event which transpired recently which brought about this story in the first place. It happened not in the Middle East, or in the islands of the South Pacific, islands fiercely being attempted to be taken over by radicals, but it *did* involve a very thinning of the veil where the history of similar energies are concerned, and it happened in the beautiful Blue Ridge Mountains of Virginia.

Once upon a time I was an avid distance runner. However, after many years of running, jumping out of perfectly good airplanes, ruck marching many, many miles with too much weight in a rucksack on my back, and fighting in war, this older man's back simply can't take the pounding it used to be able to take, so this older man has switched to cycling.

One day this past summer, I was cycling in very familiar territory on a very familiar route. However, on this particular morning, I noticed something very different. There is a point on this route, about the halfway point, four miles into an eight mile loop, where there is a huge field, hundreds of acres in size that can be seen, and I'm sure far more than that that cannot be seen, as the terrain slopes over the mountainside, and I usually stop here for a quick water break and to pay the water bill (that means take a leak), if needed.

On the day I'm describing, the major difference that I saw had to do with goats. What appeared to be thousands of them. Usually, if I saw any animals in this field, it was horses, and occasionally cows. I'd run past this field for years, and I'd been cycling past it all summer, and this was the first time I ever saw goats. And it would be the last, so far, as well.

The following week I would bike the same route, and like clockwork, I stopped at my watering hole, and only to drink, which was good, because there was an older man working on some of the fencing this time as I stopped.

"How many goats do you guys have?" I asked him as I got off my bike.

"Ain't got no goats," he said. "We run cattle and horses."

"You leasing your land to goat farmers?" I asked, taking a swig from my water battle.

"Boy," the man said, "they ain't been goats on this land in near a century."

"Huh," I said. "I was by here last week and I could have sworn I saw a thousand goats out there. Must have been the cows, but really far away."

The old man looked at me, as if he was trying to figure out if I was pulling his chain or not, and I guess I passed mustard, because he then said, "that's interesting that you say that."

"Why's that?" I asked.

"My daddy bought this land off of some people who'd come here from the Middle East after World War One, and they actually raised goats."

"Really?" I said, but there wasn't any hint of surprise in my voice, because I wasn't surprised. My only thought was, well, it's happened again.

"Yeah," the old man said. "They fled what's now Iraq. Used to be part of the Ottoman Empire, until Western nations carved the place up after the war, knowing it would keep all the different religious factions over there fighting forever. These people were Kurds, and they knew the Muslims would kill 'em, so they made it over here. Several families at first. Pooled their resources, bought the land, raised goats, got rich, and by the third generation were spoiled, and sold the land to cash out, and that's how my daddy got it."

"That's interesting," I said, and he'd lain out exactly how so much self made wealth in America works. The first generation works to earn it, the second generation is pretty good at keeping it, because they remember, as children, Mom and Pop working so hard to obtain it, and then, the third generation is soft, spoiled, and possesses little if any work ethic, because everything has been given to them. They are pretty much raised with entitlement mentalities. Self made wealth in America rarely makes it to the fourth generation before being dissipated.

"You know what else is interesting?" the old man said.

"What's that?" I asked.

"You ain't the first person to tell me they seen goats in this field."

"That is interesting," I said, and I got back on my bike and I pedalled away before things could go further. No need for this old man to be considering what I might say next, this thing about the thinning of the veil, to be poppycock. Best to let him remain convinced we're physical beings who may some day, after death, have a spiritual experience, rather than the truth, that we are spiritual beings having a physical experience. Most people don't want to hear the truth when their minds are already made up.

So, how can you learn to look beyond the veil? Well, there are the ways I've described already. Open your mind. Unlearn everything you think you know. Go outside at twilight, especially where forest meets field or water meets land, or land meets sky, up on top of a beautiful mountain.

Or you could just wait a couple more days. You could wait for Samhain, which is probably the most powerful time of year when the veil grows thinnest. Perhaps you know this time, Samhain, by a different name. Perhaps you've heard it referred to as All Hallows' Eve. And if not that, perhaps you know it by its most common name of all.

Halloween!

It's coming.

Soon.

And the veil is thinning!

The End

October 30

The Spider Lady

The first time I noticed that girls were different than boys, I was nine years old. But this girl was no girl. She was a woman in her mid-twenties, and she was more than just that. She was one of those rare human beings who truly possess angelic beauty.

I was at my buddy Jay's house, and we were upstairs in his bedroom playing Pac Man on his new Atari 2600. We were amazed by this technology, and we were convinced technology had reached its limit in progression, because there was no way possible, as we saw, two nine year old kids back in 1982, that video game graphics could *ever* advance past this amazing point. A freaking dude shaped like a circle, making his way through mazes, eating dots, all while either running from or chasing ghosts to eat them too, if he'd eaten the *big* dots in the corners first, and it was so lifelike. The ghosts looked real. It was an amazing time to be alive. Before this, all we'd ever played were the handheld football games that simply displayed little red dots, and you had to try to remember which dot you were. The time to close the patent office had arrived.

Just after having been eaten by a ghost, because my big dot power had run out, and while handing the controller back to Jay, I heard a car pulling up in the driveway of the house beside Jay's. I walked to his window, massaging the middle of the palm of my left hand as I did, as those Atari 2600 remote controls were killer on this part of the hand, to look out and see who it was.

That's when I saw her. She was driving a blue Chrysler K car that looked to be brand new. And as shiny and attractive as the car was, it held nothing on her. She wore a fuzzy white sweater that hugged her breasts nicely, and a matching, and very short, fuzzy white skirt.

"Jay," I said.

"What?" he said, staring intently at the thirteen inch black and white television screen, making sure the ghosts didn't catch his round guy.

"Who's that?" I said, watching this angelic beauty as she opened the back door of her car and pulled out a backpack and slung it over her right shoulder.

"Oh, my God," Jay said. He'd stopped playing and had come to the window to have a look outside, but I was so enthralled with the woman outside and below that I hadn't even noticed.

"Who is that?" I asked again.

"I don't know," he said, and for a full three minutes after this beautiful young woman had gone inside the house beside Jay's, we stood, still staring, hoping she'd come back out. She did not, so we resumed our play.

The next day, while playing Pac Man at Jay's, we heard the car pulling up the driveway that went to the back of the neighbor's house, and we didn't even say a word. I was playing this time, and I dropped the controller and jumped to my feet and raced to the window. Jay had beaten me there. We stared out the window and below to the neighbors driveway behind the house and watched, as this time, our angel, dressed in an even tighter sweeter, but pink this time, and wearing really tight, white, butt hugging shorts got out of her car, grabbed her backpack from the backseat, and then went into the house by way of the back door. Again, we stood for a full three minutes, hoping she might have forgotten something in the car for which she'd come back out to get, but she did not, so we resumed our play.

This was our routine. At least Monday through Friday. We'd get home from school, I'd race to Jay's, and we'd hang out playing Pac Man, listening intently for the car next door.

"Well," we heard Jay's mother, Kate, say from behind us during our third week of voyeurism. "You boys like what you see, I take it?"

"Who is that?" I asked Kate, as Jay raced back to the video game, trying to make it appear as if he hadn't been gawking. I wasn't trying to hide anything.

"That's Fonda Hays," Kate said. "She's moved back in with her mother next door."

"Why?" I asked. It was the first question that came to mind.

"Oh," Kate said. "It's sad, really. Her husband died a few weeks ago."

"How?" I asked.

"Old age," Kate said.

"Old age?" I said. "She looks young, herself."

"*She* is," Kate said. "I think she's twenty five."

"How old was her husband?" Jay asked after having gotten eaten by a ghost.

"I think eighty," Kate said.

"Why on earth would a beautiful girl like that marry an eighty year old man?" I asked.

"Word is he was rich," Kate said. "But you boys didn't hear it from *me*. And you also didn't hear it from me that she got *every penny* of what the old man had. His adult children, who are old enough to be her parents, are suing her. But you heard *none* of this from me."

Jay and I stared at each other and said nothing.

"She's absolutely gorgeous," Kate said. "And when two boys not even ten years old yet take note, that's proof enough. You boys shouldn't even be *noticing* girls and women for a few more years."

"Are we in trouble?" I asked. Jay's mom laughed so hard she almost fell down, and said no, and then she asked us if we wanted to go next door and meet her.

"You're kidding," we both said at the same time.

"Jay," Kate said. "You would never remember, but when she was home for the summers from college, and you were barely out of diapers, she used to babysit you. "She'd *love* to see how big you are now."

We didn't need to be coerced. I wanted to see this girl up close, so we said yes, and two minutes later, we were sitting in the living room of the house next door, right across from the most beautiful creature Jay and I had ever seen up until that point in our lives. And to this day, nearly forty years later, she still ranks *way* up there.

"What grade are you boys in?" Fonda asked. She was even more beautiful up close than she was from a distance. And on this day, she was wearing one of those little skirts that barely came down past her panties, and even though I was so young, it was hell trying to keep my eyes in contact with hers and not look lower.

"Third," Jay and I said in unison. If I were a betting man, I'd bet that Jay was fighting hard to control where his eyes went as well.

"Well, I'll have you eventually," Fonda said, and she grinned, real naughty like, after saying it.

"Huh?" I said, hopeful, completely not aware of what was really involved with what I thought that might mean, having us someday, but completely willing to learn from Fonda.

"In class, silly," Fonda said, and then she laughed. "I teach middle school science. You'll end up having me as your teacher in about five years."

Five years, I remember thinking. That was half a lifetime for me. I couldn't wait that long for this beautiful creature to have me, even if it was only as a student.

Fonda, who we began calling Mrs. Hays that day was cordial with us for a few more minutes and then she politely sent us on our way. I remember, when leaving, looking back for one last glimpse of this beautiful young woman before walking out the door, and she was already looking at me, smiling, and I was completely in love.

Our routine changed a bit after that day. We'd get home from school, I'd race to Jay's, but instead of going inside and playing Pac Man, we'd pass Nerf football in his backyard. This way, we'd be outside when Mrs. Hays got home, and everyday when she did, we would always say hello and ask her how her day had gone. She would always spend a few minutes with us, and teasingly smile as she did, knowing we were trying to maintain eye contact as best we could, fighting to keep our eyes from straying southward, and then she would go inside, always looking back to flash us one last smile just before shutting the backdoor to her mother's house.

This routine went on for a couple of weeks before it changed again, and when it did, it did so because we'd been invited to join our angel.

"You boys want to do something fun?" we heard Mrs. Hays say. She'd come out the backdoor of her mother's house while we were passing football, and we hadn't heard her. She was wearing really tight jeans and hiking boots. She had on a flannel shirt, tied just above her belly button, like Daisy Duke, and she was wearing a green hat with a big M on it. Marshall; her alma mater.

"Yeah," we said, letting Jay's last pass to me go incomplete and not caring at all. We had no idea what she had in mind, but we would have done *anything* with this woman, fun or not.

"Go ask your parents if you can ride up the road with me to that big field just outside of town. I need to catch grasshoppers for my spiders, and you boys can help me."

"Okay," we said, and we both took off at a dead sprint for our respective houses.

I never even thought about spiders. I didn't care. I was going to go hangout with the most beautiful woman I'd ever seen, and let me tell you, I'd already been having thoughts about marrying her the minute I turned eighteen. If she married a guy nearly sixty years older than her, maybe she wouldn't mind marrying a guy only fifteen years younger than her, once, of course, that guy turned eighteen, and especially, and just maybe, if that guy was me.

Our parents gave us permission to go with Mrs. Hays, and in pretty short order, we were at the huge field right outside of town catching grasshoppers. Jay and I had caught grasshoppers before, and it wasn't hard, but what *was* hard was trying to squeeze them into the empty ice cream box Mrs.

Hays was using to keep them in without allowing all of the ones already in the box to jump out.

"Here," Mrs. Hays said, sauntering over with her painted-on jeans. "You have to do this."
She grabbed the grasshopper that was in my hand and that I was about to put into the box and she ripped both of its back legs off. "They can't jump *anywhere* if you do this." As she opened the box to put the now back legless hopper in, another jumped out, and she caught it with catlike speed, and she ripped its back legs off, too, and put it back in the box. She smiled at me, and winked, and then she sauntered back into the field to catch more grasshoppers.

Even at the young age of nine, my gut told me that though this woman was beautiful on the outside, she might be something entirely different on the inside. But still, she was the most beautiful creature I'd ever seen, and when I grew up, I was still going to marry her.

When we got back to Mrs. Hays' house, she asked if we'd like to go into her spider room and feed her tarantulas. Of course we said yes, and we did, following her upstairs, our eyes focused not on the stairs as we climbed them, but on her backside, swinging back and forth like a pendulum in front of us, as she climbed the stairs ahead of us.

"Welcome to my bedroom, boys," Mrs. Hays said, leading us into her bedroom. Her bed looked comfortable, warm, and as if it would be perfect for sharing with her. I had no idea what married people did while sharing a bed at the time, but I was determined to find out when I turned eighteen and Mrs. Hays showed me.

"Here are all my lovers," she said, drawing our attention away from her bed and to the other side of the room. The entire wall had been shelved, and there were aquariums filled with various types of spiders on each shelf. "Who wants to go first?" she asked, looking at Jay and me.

"I will," Jay said. Mrs. Hays took the lid off of the ice cream box and extended it out toward Jay. He took one of the back legless hoppers out of the box and she opened the lid on an aquarium containing a tarantula. Jay dropped the poor insect to its doom, and the spider was on it instantly.

"Your turn," Mrs. Hays said to me, smiling.

"I'll pass," I said.

"Squeamish?" she asked.

"No," I said, lying. "I just want to look at your other spiders."

"Knock yourself out," she said, and then she extended the box to Jay again, and again he took out a prey and fed it to another of her predators.

"Stay away from that one!" Mrs. Hays yelled, coming over and grabbing me by the back of the shirt and pulling me away so forcefully that I was flung across the room. I landed on her bed. Oh, the fantasies I had. I just couldn't see any details, because I knew not what those details involved back then. "I'm sorry," she said, coming over and helping me up. "But that's a brown recluse. Don't even get *close* to that aquarium."

"What's a brown recluse?" I asked. Jay and I made our way to the aquarium, though we stood a good six feet back from it.

We were social distancing back before social distancing was cool.

"It's one of the most poisonous spiders in this part of the world," Mrs. Hays said. She bent at the knees and peered into the aquarium at the potentially deadly poisonous spider. "I actually have five more of them in there somewhere," she said.

What she did next blew our young minds. She opened the top of the aquarium and she stuck her hand in. One of the brown recluses that had been in hiding came out of hiding and walked up her index finger and onto the back of her hand.

"If this spider were to bite you," she began, "you'd probably need medical attention. Since you're young and healthy, though, you probably wouldn't die. But if you were old, or if you had underlying health conditions, like a bad heart, its bite would probably kill you."

"Why isn't it biting you?" Jay asked.

"Because he loves me," she said, and then she giggled. "Further," she continued, pulling her hand up to her face so she could look the potentially deadly creature in the eyes. "The toxin which kills you is almost impossible to trace. If you're over seventy, and you die from a bite from one of these, the coroner, more than likely, would simply write your death off to natural causes."

"How do you know that?" I asked.

"Trust me," she said, now diverting her eyes away from the spider and to my eyes. "I'm a science teacher. Remember?"

And I guess she was right.

Jay and I told Jay's mother about what Mrs. Hays had done to the grasshoppers after we went back over to his house. How she'd ripped their hind legs off like it was nothing. About how she fed them to the spiders like it was nothing. And the creepy things she told us about the brown recluse.

"Well," Kate said. "She *is* a science teacher," and then she went back to making their family's dinner.

And I guess she was right.

***

The years would pass, and I did, indeed, end up having Mrs. Hays as my science teacher once I reached middle school. However, she was no longer Mrs. Hays. She was now Mrs. Myrtle.

And I was pissed!

I'd been heartbroken the year before when I'd heard Fonda, as we'll now call her throughout this story, had gotten remarried. Why hadn't she waited for me? I only had four years to go and I would be of legal age. But no. She hadn't waited, and not only that, but her new husband, Mr. Myrtle was in his freaking eighties! He'd owned a coal mine in the next county over for more than half a century, he was worth billions, and Fonda was his *fifth* wife. And at thirty years old now, she was actually the oldest woman he'd ever married. Story was, all of his previous wives stayed with him just a few years each before leaving him, and he'd always been more than happy to give them five million dollars to sign off on a no fault divorce just to see them go.

The worst part of it all, though, was that I didn't even have Jay to lament my broken heart to. His parents had gotten divorced just two years before this, because Jay's father was a good looking man-whore who was screwing half the women in the neighborhood, and Jay's mother had taken Jay and his little sister with her to live with her parents several counties away.

"Remember when we used to go catch grasshoppers to feed my spiders when you were a little kid?" Fonda said to me on the first day of class while she was calling out the roster and she'd gotten to my name. I said, "yeah," and for that entire year, it was the only individual attention she gave me, and boy, did that piss me off. I gave her quite a bit of trouble in that class that year, and she sent me to the principal's office a couple of times, and eventually to the guidance counselor, but all I was doing was trying to get her attention, and I knew she was intentionally withholding it from me. She was a tease. She was evil, and she was making me suffer just like she'd made those grasshoppers suffer by ripping off their back legs.

Halfway through that school year, Fonda's husband died. They said it was from natural causes, and I guess since he was in his eighties, it made sense, but I couldn't help remembering back to the day that Fonda, who I was by then referring to as the spider lady in my angry, rebellious, pubescent mind, told me what she'd told me about brown recluses. Call it a bitter rage, jealousy, or anything else you will, but I was convinced there was more to the spider lady's story than anyone ever knew. Beautiful beyond comparison? And widowed twice now by the age of thirty, by men old enough to have been her grandfather? And she conveniently inherited all of their wealth?

Poppycock!

My jealousy and bitterness eventually led me to the police, where I made my claim that the spider lady had killed her husbands, by way of allowing one of her brown recluses to bite them, more than likely while they slept. Boy, that didn't go over well. All I did was bring embarrassment to myself and my family when the cops, just because they *had* to, went and talked to Fonda that evening at her home. My old man gave me one hell of an ass whooping, even though I was fourteen by then, and scolded the hell out of me for bringing such allegations against that poor, grieving young woman who'd just lost her second husband.

And the next week, Fonda moved.

She left the state.

***

Call me crazy. Others have. But I always felt that Fonda left the state because the heat was on. Sure, at the beginning it was just some love struck fourteen year old kid who'd had a crush on her making accusations because at fourteen, he finally understood a lot more about the grownup world than he had in years past, and he desperately wanted to spend some of his grownup years doing grownup things with the woman upon whom he'd had his first crush and upon whom he'd held that crush for so long.

But might there be more?

It was a small town. People talked. A week after Fonda had left town, many other people started scratching their heads, wondering if there might actually be something to the accusations that some fourteen year old kid had made. News spread. Everyone knew what I'd done.

And some of the town's people thought I might just be right.

***

Many more years would pass. Decades, actually. And I'd get back in touch with Jay, off and on, by this amazing thing called Facebook. Turns out we'd been wrong back when we were convinced technology would never surpass Pac Man on Atari 2600. We'd been *way* wrong.

Out of curiosity, shortly after I'd gotten back in touch with Jay, and this was shortly after Facebook had come out, I searched and searched for the spider lady.

And I found her!

I felt my heartbreak again. I felt my jealousy and rage return. For you see, once again she was married, but this time, she was married to a guy that was fifteen years younger than her. She was married to a guy my age! Why had she not waited for me? But I guess I burned that bridge when I'd gone to the cops and accused her of murder.

I lurked on Fonda's Facebook page for a month or so. I saw that she and her younger husband, who, by the way, I'll admit, was as good looking as any male model I'd ever seen, were living the high life. But hey? Why not? She'd inherited *millions* from those old codgers that I always thought she'd killed, and man, was she still beautiful, even well into her fifties. But I finally came to my senses, I got in a healthy relationship of my own (ironically with a woman I'm now married to and who happens to be fifteen years younger than me), and I stopped lurking on Fonda's page.

Until two weeks ago, the beginning of October.

I tried to find Fonda on Facebook, just for kicks and giggles, and because I was curious to see if she was still drop dead gorgeous, now that she would be in her sixties.

She wasn't.

She had dropped dead.

Her Facebook account was gone, so I Googled her after finally remembering her last last name, and I found her obituary. It stated that, sadly, one of the woman's brown recluse spiders had bitten her while she'd been feeding it, and she had died pretty quickly afterward. Her much younger husband inherited all the wealth she'd inherited, and about three months after her death, he went on to marry a really gorgeous woman, about fifteen years younger than *him*, and who, as it turned out, actually *was* a model.

I can't help but think now, though I'll not be going to any authorities to make any accusations, that what had been good for the goose ended up being good for the gander.

The End

October 31

(Happy Halloween!)

The Ballad of Jim Brown

It was late August. It was hot as hell. And I was in the shower.

I'd just mown the portion of the yard that my wife usually mows, because she was out with friends, and I wanted her to be surprised when she got home. She'd planned on mowing it that evening, but I didn't want her out there in the heat doing it, so I did it for her. I mow roughly two acres of our property, the part riddled with trees, bushes, shrubs and other natural obstacles, and she mows the one acre field right in front of our house which has no obstacles. She does it because she knows I have a bad back, and she doesn't want me bouncing around on that riding lawn tractor anymore than I need to, which does, at times, make my back pain worse. She's truly a sweetheart, and sweethearts deserve surprises, like their husband's doing their part of the chores for them while they're gone, and so I did.

I pulled the shower curtain open to grab the towel after I'd turned off the water, and egads, and gad's be, there was that old spook of spooks, Jim freaking Brown, standing right in the middle of my bathroom. "What the hell are you doing, Jim Brown?" I screamed at him.

"I came to give you that story I promised I'd give you," he said.

"Can't you give a man some privacy, Jim Brown?" I said, making sure to hold the shower curtain in front of me.

"Take my hand," Jim Brown said, extending his hand. "Come with me."

"Now you listen, you old rascal," I said, feeling very vulnerable as I did. "I done got you figured out! At first I thought you was tryin' to rob me, but now I'm convinced you're trying to get involved with me in such a way that I ain't comfortable with. Now look. I ain't got no problems with men who lay with other men, but I ain't one of 'em."

"Take my hand," he said again, and when I didn't, Jim Brown stepped forward and he grabbed my left hand, with which I'd been holding the shower curtain, and just as I was about to open my mouth and tell him to let me go, there was a bright flash of light, and then…

…we were no longer in my bathroom.

We were in the living room, but things were different.

"What the hell's going on here, Jim Brown?" I asked, and I couldn't help but notice that I was dressed. I was wearing the exact same clothes I was wearing when I'd mown the lawn, but they were now clean and dry.

"Just watch," Jim Brown said.

I looked, and saw before me, three men, laying, sleeping on the floor. There was a dim glow coming from the woodstove, but so much was different. Sure, we have a woodstove in the living room, but this was not our stove. And all the furniture was gone. Just three guys sleeping in what looked like wool blankets on the hardwood floor, and even *that* was different. It was different boards. Just oak slabs.

"What's going on here, Jim Brown?" I said. "Where are we?"

"We're at Halloween," he said. "The year 1904."

I couldn't believe my eyes, so I just watched, and as I did, an old dog, which looked to be about an hour away from death came walking into the room from behind us. Our backs were facing what is now our master bedroom, which is downstairs, and as I looked down, noticing the movement from the dog, I also noticed snoring coming from the master bedroom as well. I peeked in there, and I saw four men laying on the floor, and I saw a dim light coming from a wood stove inside the room. We do not have a wood stove in that room, though there is a flew from where one used to be.

"Goddamn, you, mutt!" I heard a gruff voice say in the living room. I turned my head just in time to see some big, burly and quite filthy looking son of a bitch kick the old dog that had meandered into the living room. The dog let out a yelp, and the big, burly, dirty man rose to his feet and walked out the back door. And that was odd, too. This room leads to a dining room, but during this event, it led only to the back door. It was then that I remembered that the kitchen and dining room both were not added onto the house as extensions until the 1950's.

The man went out the original back door and into the dim light of pre-dawn.

"What's going on here, Jim Brown?" I said again, unable to think of anything else to say.

"This is your story," Jim Brown said, now looking over at me and taking off that creepy looking black hat. "This is how I died. This is your interview with a ghost."

"What?" I said.

At that moment, one of the men who'd been sleeping where our master bedroom is came running out of it. "Goddamn you, Jessop!" he screamed, and then he ran out the back door.

"That looked like you," I said to Jim Brown.

"That *was* me," Jim Brown said.

Jim Brown and I walked out the back door, and Jim Brown from 1904 was beating the ever loving shit out of 'ol Jessop.

"I told you if you kicked 'ol Pup again I'd wear you out, you inbred son of a devil!" Jim Brown from 1904 said, and then he smacked 'ol Jessop one good, hard, and last time, right upside the head with a hard right, and 'ol Jessop went back to sleep, but it hadn't been by choice. Jim Brown from 1904 went back into the house for a minute or two, and then he came back out with a carpet bag hanging over his shoulder and that old dog that had been kicked by 'ol Jessop inside the house by his side.

Modern day Jim Brown, my guide, began following his doppleganger from more than a century before, and instinctively, I followed with him. We made it halfway across the field to where a mighty oak stood. This, too, was different, because today, this mighty oak stands at the edge of the treeline that separates our back meadow from what is now a forest. But on this adventure, there were no forests within sight. It was nothing but fields that I saw while I looked around, now able to see in the dawn's early light.

"You wait right there, you quaker ass son of a dickens!" a voice came from behind us. We turned and saw that 'ol Jessop had come to. He was tracking 1904 Jim Brown down. "I ain't done with you, boy!"

"Now you listen, Jessop," 1904 Jim Brown said. "I done warned ya. If you ever hurt 'ol Pup again I's gonna whoop ya! You went and kicked him again, and I went and whooped ya. We're even."

"Where you think you're going?" Jessop said, drawing face to face with 1904 Jim Brown and coming to a stop. Jessop was easily a head taller than his foe, and he had to have outweighed him by fifty pounds. And he was a mean, evil looking son of a bitch.

"I'm a movin' on," 1904 Jim Brown said. "I'll just head back up Pennsylvania way. Plenty of work for me between here and there. Someone'll take me on. It's just best me and you part ways."

I could tell that 1904 Jim Brown was terrified. He'd obviously whipped 'ol Jessop out of pure rage and adrenaline, but that rage and adrenaline were now gone, and I think 1904 Jim Brown realized that 'ol Jessop was about to hand him his ass.

"Think you're gonna whoop me like that and just walk away?" Jessop said.

"Look, Jessop," 1904 Jim Brown said, a pleading tone in his voice. "All the other fellers were in the house sleepin'. No one knows about it. I won't come back. Promise. Just let me and 'ol Pup go."

"Hm," 'ol Jessop said, and then he looked down. He crossed his arms and placed one hand on his chin. "Tell ya what," he said. "You can go, but 'ol Pup stays with me."

"What do you want 'ol Pup for?" 1904 Jim Brown asked. "You hate him."

"I know," Jessop said. "I aim ta kill 'im."

"You ain't killin' 'ol Pup, you son of a slug," 1904 Jim Brown said, and all of a sudden he was pissed off again. "Not without killin' me first."

"If you say so," 'ol Jessop said, and he hauled off and hit 1904 Jim Brown so hard that I heard his neck crack. 1904 Jim Brown was lifted a foot off his feet, and he landed flat on his back, and he never moved.

Again.

"Ah, nah," 'ol Jessop said, realizing what he'd done. He turned quickly, looking back at the house, making sure no one had seen what he'd done. They had not.

"You dumb son of a woman beater," Jessop said, grabbing 1904 Jim Brown by the shirt colar and dragging him back behind that mighty oak. "You went and made me do it. This is your fault. Not mine."

Modern day Jim Brown and I watched as 'ol Jessop buried the body of 1904 Jim Brown under the freshly fallen leaves of October. He made his way back to the house, and the story he gave the other guys was that 1904 Jim Brown had woken early that morning and told him he was heading home to Pennsylvania. No one questioned him, because they'd all had their asses beaten by 'ol Jessop at least once, and no one wanted seconds. The men spoke in hushed tones from time to time of the rumor they'd all heard that 'ol Jessop had actually shot and killed both of his parents as well as a local lawman several years before back in his part of Virginia.

"What did he do with your body?" I asked modern day Jim Brown while we stood at the base of that oak tree. I noticed, though large, it wasn't *nearly* as large as it is now.

"I fully believe he intended to bury it," modern day Jim Brown said. "But it wasn't there when he came back later in the day to do it so. After the other men had hit the fields."

"Where was it?" I asked.

"I don't know," modern day Jim Brown said, and I immediately thought of the Legend of Sleepy Hollow. You know, the horseman who came back on Halloween looking for his head? Was Jim Brown coming back all the time looking for his entire body?

"No," modern day Jim Brown said, with a chuckle, when I ran this idea by him. "Something dragged it off. I know that. I just don't know what."

"What do you mean, what?" I asked.

"If I knew, I'd tell you," he said, and he looked at me. "It looked like an animal, but it was no animal like I'd ever seen."

"It didn't happen to walk on two legs, did it?" I asked.

Modern day Jim Brown looked down, concentrating hard on pulling up a memory. "I've had visions," he said, "of what took my body. But they're never clear. They're fuzzy. Like, not quite in focus. But yes," he said. "I do believe this animal walked on two legs.

"But what happens next is what I believe will interest you the most," he said. He then snapped his fingers, and it was almost dark. Twilight.

"Where are we now, Jim Brown?" I asked.

"We're still here," he said. "Halloween 1904. But we need to walk across the way, there." He pointed across the road from my house, and there appeared to be quite a ruckus going on over there. Today, there's an old farmhouse standing there that was built a few years after our house was built in 1903, but on this trip that that old rascal Jim Brown had taken me on, there *was* no house. Just more field and another mighty oak. There were half a dozen men or so beneath the tree, and it looked like they were having a scuffle.

"This property used to be part of a two thousand acre plantation," Jim Brown began explaining to me as we were making our way to the scuffle. "When I worked here, as a sharecropper, it was down to five hundred acres. The family that owned it had to continuously sell land to maintain their lavish lifestyle since they no longer had free labour by way of enslaved people."

"So you were one of the original sharecroppers to live in my house?" I asked him.

"One of the first to live here," he said, "and definitely the first to die here. Or *be* killed, I should say. But 'ol Jessop, there. He was number two."

Jim Brown raised his hand and pointed. We'd made our way to the other side of the field, and all six of the other guys who had lived with Jim Brown and Jessop were teaming up on 'ol Jessop and whoopin' him something awful. It looked like it was taking all six of them to do the job, because no matter how many times 'ol Jessop got knocked down, he just kept gettin' back up and comin' at 'em.

That's until one of the men who'd readied a noose threw it around 'ol Jessop's neck and then slung the other end of the rope around the bottom limb of the old oak tree. Together, like men playing tug of war, they pulled 'ol Jessop up off the ground, and once his feet were a good two feet off of it, they held their position until all the life was taken out of him.

"Damn," I said.

"They didn't believe his story," Jim Brown said. "The one he'd told them about me leaving. They knew we hated each other, and they'd assumed, correctly, of course, that he'd killed me. They figured any one of them could be next, so they took matters into their own hands."

We watched as the men let 'ol Jessop's corpse drop to the ground. After it had, they dragged him back across the road- which, by the way, was made of Virginia red clay, not asphalt, like today- and up into a small patch of woods behind my house. There is a graveyard there with at least five graves in it that I can tell. I know three of the graves belong to three little girls who would live in this house about fourteen years after the murders Jim Brown had just shown me and who would succumb to the Spanish Flu of 1918. I now knew that one of the graves belonged to 'ol Jessop, because I watched his killers bury him. To this day, I have no idea who the last grave belongs to, but I also now know it wasn't there in 1904, because it wasn't there while they were burying Jessop.

"Why are you showing me these God awful things, Jim Brown?" I asked my guide.

"Because you can see me," he said. "And you've acknowledged that you can see me."

I stood in silence, knowing not what to say.

"You know that old cuss you used to have problems with? The guy whose parents live across the street, right where you saw Jessop killed? The guy who used to take the hay off your land and then became a total prick once you stopped letting him have it?"

"Yeah," I said.

"It's not all his fault," Jim Brown said. "I'm not the only one who walks this land on a regular basis. 'Ol Jessop has walked this land for years, and he got in that man's head when he was just a boy. Jessop's angry, and he's made that man angry.

"And are you aware of what happened to the man who lived in your house just before you?" he asked. And I did, and I told him that I did.

The man who'd lived in my house before me, only thirty two years old at the time, had committed suicide. His wife and he had been sitting in their car in the driveway arguing, so that their children in the house who were sleeping wouldn't hear them, and the man, during the argument, pulled a loaded handgun out of his console and said, 'this is all your fault,' and then he blew his brains out right there in the driveway, and right in front of his wife. No one told us of this before we bought our house, and when we found out from a guy we hired to clean our chimney three months after we'd closed, we understood why the house had sat on the market for two straight years even though it had been priced far below market value. Further, we understood that all our neighbors who'd come over to introduce themselves, and who stated they miss whatever dude's name was, but never told us what had happened to whatever dude's name was, were fake and plastic as shit. We have nothing to do with them. And the annoying neighbor who used to take the hay, and who came by to harass us until I ran him off with a crayon never mentioned it, either, but we already knew he was an asshole.

"Jessop had gotten in his head," Jim Brown told me. "The guy who killed himself."

"That brings up a good point," I said. "There's been times you've come around, like *all* the times you've come around, when I've gotten angry for no reason whatsoever. There's been a couple times I thought you and me was gonna get in a fight, because I just felt so angry."

"I'm sorry about that," Jim Brown said. "I guess I'm still angry. I died a violent death. To my knowledge, I wasn't given a proper burial. No one knew where I'd gone, and to be honest with you, there wasn't anyone in my life who cared enough to come looking for me."

"No need to apologize," I said. "I've been through some shit, too."

We stood in silence as we watched the men who'd killed 'ol Jessop throw the final shovel of dirt over his grave.

"And I have to let you know," Jim Brown said. "There's more than just me and 'ol Jessop roaming around here. This land has known pain, anger and death for longer than you could imagine."

"I know there were Native American Indians living here fourteen thousand years ago," I said, trying to impress Jim Brown with my knowledge. "I researched it."

"Hah!" he said, throwing his head back in laughter. "That doesn't even scratch the surface."

"How do you mean, Jim Brown?" I said.

"Tens of thousands of years before that there were people here," he said. "And they were doing the cruelest of things to each other that you could imagine. And their spirits are still here. Many of them. And those Indians you talk about. Same thing. And the enslaved people who were worked until they dropped dead and then were buried all over these fields in unmarked graves. And all the murders that have gone on in the past century that no one knows anything about. Bodies buried all over these old farmlands scattered throughout this county, throughout these mountains, and throughout this country."

"Hold on, Jim Brown," I said. "You're scaring me."

"Then stop looking," he said. "Or you'll see it. You'll see it all. You're going to see exactly what you're looking for, and all the others, all the other empaths and people you've taught to do what you can do, they will see, and they will hear, and unless they're prepared for a lifetime of nightmares, they have got to stop looking.

"Further," Jim Brown continued, "and most dangerously. If you acknowledge them, and they see that you acknowledge them, you'll never get rid of them. Just like that annoying farmer across the road and the guy that killed himself in your driveway have never been able to get rid of 'ol Jessop. What I will tell you, is never go to bed angry. That man and his wife should have fixed things. But they didn't. And it gave 'ol Jessop and in, and he fixed things for them in the worst kind of way."

Jim Brown stopped. He had to catch his breath. He'd really gotten worked up while saying all he'd said.

"The veil is thin, and it's getting thinner," he said. "As time goes on. But always remember one thing and never forget it."

"What's that, Jim Brown?" I asked.

"The veil is always thinnest on Halloween."

With that, Jim Brown reached out and grabbed my hand. He said, "just one more thing?"

"Sure, Jim Brown," I said. "Anything."

"Take care of 'ol Pup."

With that, he grabbed my hand, and again there was a bright flash of light, and when it was gone, I was in my bathroom, naked and wet, holding the shower curtain in front of myself, as if shielding myself from someone's view.

"What are you doing, honey?"

It was my wife. She'd just walked in the door.

"Taking a shower," I said. "I just mowed the field for you."

"I saw that, honey," she said. "Thank you." Then she walked into the kitchen to put the grocery bags she had in her hands on the counter.

"You didn't see a guy riding down the road on a bike while you were coming in, did you?" I asked.

My wife paused, looked to the right and down a bit, and then she said, "actually I did." She waited a moment, and I held my breath, and then she said, "he looked like that creepy kid from that movie Children of the Corn we always watch in October, close to Halloween."

I dried off and got dressed and never said a word to my wife about Jim Brown. I was happy that she'd finally seen him, though she had no idea who it was she'd seen.

That night, as we lay in bed sleeping, with my psychotic cat sleeping on our dresser, I was awakened by what felt like something jumping up on the foot of our bed. I looked up and saw the cat, still on the dresser, back hunched up, hair standing, and she let out a light hiss.

"Come here, 'ol Pup," I said, patting the bedcovers beside me. "I won't hurt ya."

Tiny feet that could not be seen made tiny imprints in the comforter. A large indentation appeared on the comforter beside my chest. I put my arm around something I could not see and that I could not feel and I went back to sleep, and I slept soundly for the rest of the night.

The End

Maybe…

***If you enjoyed this work, please consider reading other works by author Kevin E Lake, available on Amazon in both print and e-version.

Printed in Great Britain
by Amazon